THE RIGHT MR. WRONG

"I'm going to take my time and I'm going to savor every second I have. Don't plan on sleeping any tonight."

Oh.

He didn't take his eyes off her and she couldn't drag hers away, not when his eyes were deepening so quickly—and inviting. "Is that a problem?"

She shook her head, unable to make a sound.

His hands loosened on her wrists. One finger ran up her arm while with his other hand he cupped her jaw. "Why have you changed your mind?"

"I think I was wrong and you were right," she whispered. "This is...passion." She chose her word carefully. "And I think it needs to be dealt with."

"You think you can deal with me?"

That old arrogance brought back her smile. "I think for one night. Yes. I can deal with you." She had to.

DEAR READER,

I'm so thrilled you have this book, my first Harlequin KISS novel, in your hands! I'm super excited to be part of Harlequin's newest series. I love fun, sassy stories with style, spark and a whole lot of emotion! I hope you do, too.

In this book I was very intrigued by the idea of "what if"—especially in relation to those in-the-blink-of-an-eye decisions that go on to have a profound impact on the rest of our lives. What if you had said yes to that invitation, or in this case that proposal? What if you had said no? When I think back to how my own romance played out, I realize there were definite "turning point" decisions.

So what if we made the "wrong" decision—might fate offer the chance to try again? In this book I decided to explore exactly that. But although fate might offer us a second chance, I think it is still the decisions we make as individuals that determine whether or not something is going to go the distance.

So what decision does my heroine Victoria make in this book? How does Liam react? I hope you'll read on to find out!

I loved writing Victoria and Liam's story and playing at fate, and I really hope you enjoy reading it as much as I've loved writing it for you.

With very best wishes,

Natalie

THE RIGHT MR. WRONG

NATALIE ANDERSON

Recycling programs
for this product may
not exist in your area.

ISBN-13: 978-0-373-20716-9

THE RIGHT MR. WRONG
Copyright © 2013 by Natalie Anderson

THE WEDDING DRESS DIARIES
(Prequel to The Wedding Season continuity)
Copyright © 2013 by Aimee Carson

This edition published by arrangement with Harlequin Books S.A.

For questions and comments about the quality of this book, please contact us at CustomerService@Harlequin.com.

® and TM are trademarks of Harlequin Enterprises Limited or its corporate affiliates. Trademarks indicated with ® are registered in the United States Patent and Trademark Office, the Canadian Trade Marks Office and in other countries.

Printed in U.S.A.

www.Harlequin.com

ABOUT NATALIE ANDERSON

———————

Natalie adores a happy ending, which is why she always reads the back of a book first. Just to be sure. So you can be sure you have a happy ending in your hands right now—because she promises nothing less. Along with happy endings, she loves peppermint-filled dark chocolate, pineapple juice and extremely long showers. Not to mention spending hours teasing her imaginary friends with dating dilemmas. She tends to torment them before eventually relenting and offering—you guessed it—a happy ending. She lives in Christchurch, New Zealand, with her gorgeous husband and four fabulous children.

If, like her, you love a happy ending, be sure to come and say hi on Facebook/authornataliea and on Twitter @authornataliea, or her website/blog, www.natalie-anderson.com.

This and other titles by Natalie Anderson are available in ebook format—check out Harlequin.com.

For Dave. Always.

CONTENTS

THE RIGHT
MR. WRONG

PROLOGUE

Christmas Day, five years earlier.

They were almost all there. Her parents. Oliver's family. Oliver's friends. The only one missing was Stella, her rebel sister, whose name hadn't been mentioned once in the four years since she'd left.

Victoria Rutherford looked at the pile of presents under the tree. There wouldn't be one for Stella, of course, but she hoped there was at least one for Oliver's friend. She stepped closer, scanning the tags for his name.

Liam.

She really shouldn't worry about it. He was Oliver's friend, Oliver's guest. Of course his parents would be polite enough to have something for the guy who'd only arrived in England this week.

'You're not going to start shaking the boxes, are you?' a low voice murmured behind her.

She started, a smile irresistibly springing to her lips. It shouldn't. It really shouldn't. But he made her laugh with his comments—even just the wry expression he could shoot from his way-too-warm eyes. She'd had to stifle shivers when he'd looked at her in a way he shouldn't. Not that he did now.

Unfortunately he'd looked at her that way the first moment they'd met—when he'd not known who she was. She was still trying to get over the embarrassment of him coming across her in the guest bathroom wrapped in nothing but a towel. He'd had clothes on but that hadn't stopped her from noticing things she really had no business noticing.

'Your streamers look awesome, by the way,' Liam added.

'Thanks.' She'd stayed up way too late the other night to finish them. With a not-so-little helper.

She swallowed, suppressing the memory of the moment just before she'd taken herself to her small guest bedroom super quick. *Nothing* had happened. She had nothing to feel guilty about. And yet.

He was her boyfriend's best friend. A guest in her boyfriend's home for Christmas. The *last* person she should look at.

As everyone gathered around for the present sharing there were the usual joke gifts, a tradition in Oliver's family, as well as the 'proper' gifts. And the gifts for guests—including Liam.

And then there was only one little box left. She figured it was one for Oliver's mum. In the lull and under the cover of various conversations, she couldn't help a quick glance at Liam. Massive mistake because he gave her a quick flick of his eyebrows from over his new ugly knitted Christmas jersey.

She turned away, biting back her giggle.

'I think this might be for you.'

Victoria jumped as Oliver suddenly appeared in front of her.

'You've already given me a present.' Victoria blinked, taking a minute to pull back from the dangerous place her mind had wandered to.

Then she saw Oliver was on his knee in front of her. Why was he on his knee? His blue eyes were dancing and everyone around them had fallen silent.

'Victoria, you know how much I love you.'

She smiled, but inside she was stunned. Was this—? No way was Oliver about to—

'Will you marry me?'

Victoria stared at him. Somehow she kept the smile on her lips.

Oliver, her first boyfriend, who she knew and trusted. And here, in front of her parents, his parents and—

'Victoria?' Liam interrupted.

OMG. Don't look at him. Don't.

She couldn't resist.

His eyes were fixed on her. His too-warm, gold-flecked intense eyes staring right through her as if he could read her every thought. Every doubt.

Every desire.

'Do you mind?' Oliver sounded more stunned at the interruption than annoyed. 'I'm asking her a question.'

But Victoria's eyes were locked on Liam. She should look away, but she couldn't. She sensed restlessness ripple through the people surrounding them. *Her parents*. Any second now someone else would speak. Would question.

Oliver cleared his throat. Oliver, the one perfect for her, who had their future mapped out. She couldn't hurt him, embarrass him. Him or any of them.

'Victoria?' Oliver said. Now he sounded slightly annoyed.

Victoria immediately, mutely, looked back to Oliver, the

guy right before her. She smiled—automatically soothing because that was what she did. And she wanted to because she loved Oliver, right? She wanted everything that he wanted—what they all wanted and expected—didn't she?

Oliver smiled back. And as she sat flushed, yet frozen, he repeated the question.

'Will you marry me?'

ONE

————

'Yes, of course,' Victoria answered brightly, ignoring the burning muscles in her hand. 'Absolutely.'

She'd do whatever it took. That was what entrepreneurs did, right? Made sacrifices. Worked all night. She'd read *You Too Can Be a Billionaire* months ago, so she knew. Not that she wanted to be a billionaire or even a millionaire. She'd settle for solvent—no more of that screaming red ink on her bank statement, thanks.

Anyway, writing another five place cards in flourished copperplate was nothing on the number she'd already done. So long as those passed their impending inspection. They'd better. So much depended on this.

Victoria watched her client, Aurelie Broussard, cross the ornately furnished room to the large writing desk where she nervously waited. Like everyone else who'd ever been in Aurelie's presence, Victoria couldn't help staring. The 'in-another-realm' woman glowed in a long white summer dress and navy shrug. Her hair fell to the middle of her back in long, loose curls. Its colour matched her eyes, as glossy and dark and sensual as hot fudge sauce. Athlete, model, businesswoman. And about seven months pregnant judging by the graceful swell of her belly. Victoria hadn't known about the baby, but then she didn't know much about the former world-champion surf star other than that she was getting hitched in five days' time. Victoria deliberately didn't take an interest in water sports—they flowed too close to deep-buried, sharp-edged memories.

She'd never met a more beautiful woman. Or anyone with the power to improve her business so drastically— or destroy it. If Aurelie liked her work, she'd be set. If she didn't, Victoria was screwed. And brides were notoriously picky—especially brides with squadrons of celebrity friends and a 'super wow factor' wedding to pull off in less than a week.

Victoria slowed her movements to hide her nerves, carefully laying out some of the completed cards on the antique wood. Aurelie silently studied them. They'd taken Victoria more hours than she could count, working under bright lights all through the night to get them finished. She'd been contracted at the last minute—not ideal for a calligrapher whose craft required light, space, time and serenity to get it right.

'They are beautiful.' Aurelie finally gave her verdict. 'Exactly what I wanted.'

Victoria rapidly blinked back burning tears of relief. Two hundred and thirty-four painstakingly calligraphed cards—so many in such a short time she *was* in pain. But she wanted to be sure all were perfect.

'I've done them exactly as they were written on your list but someone will double check them?' she asked. She didn't want some A-lister offended by having her name incorrectly spelt.

Aurelie nodded. 'My assistant. Perhaps you can do the extra five while you're here?' She slid open the top drawer of the desk and drew out a sheet of paper with a list of names typed on it.

'Of course I can...' She'd brought her pen and ink and spare card with her, but the implication of five more guests suddenly hit and caused tunnel vision. 'Umm...with the extra guests...' Victoria's innards shrivelled. 'Does that mean you've changed the seating plan?'

That plan had taken so very, very long already. One large board with all those two hundred and thirty-four names written yet again in flourished copperplate, plus titles for the table—surf beaches. The thought of redoing the entire thing sent Victoria's brain spinning. The nerves in her hand shrieked.

'Yes.' Aurelie turned her beautiful face towards her, and drew up to her full height—almost a head taller than Victoria. 'Will that be a problem?'

'Not at all.' Victoria somehow stretched her mouth into a smile and lied. She'd stitch back her eyelids and work round the clock for the next five days and nights to get this done—and she was going to need every one of those hours to do it.

She remembered being a bride, wanting everything to be perfect. She'd work as hard as she could to help Aurelie have everything the way she wanted. But while Victoria's own ceremony had been fairy-tale pretty, her marriage to Oliver hadn't been perfect. It had been a slow-imploding mess.

Working on Aurelie's wedding would help her recovery, financially at any rate. There were so many privileged people coming, with her best work on show, she might get more commissions.

The irony of having a career where she helped people create their perfect weddings wasn't lost on her, given her own spectacular matrimonial failure. But she wasn't cynical. For the right couple, a wedding was a wonderful beginning.

Hopefully Aurelie's fiancé was a decent guy. Victoria knew even less about him than she did about Aurelie. She hadn't looked up any Internet info—the turnaround time was so tight she'd had to get straight on with writing. But she'd recognised the names of some of their guests—elite sports people, celebrities, models.

'I'm sure I can count on you.' Aurelie smiled.

It was one of those smiles with an 'I'll kill you if you screw up' edge. Well, while Aurelie was counting on her, Victoria would be counting on coffee—dump trucks of it.

'I can do the cards here and now if you'd like, but I'll need to redo the table plan at home. I don't have the supplies here.'

Aurelie nodded. 'I'll get my assistant to email you the changes for that.'

'And I'll bring it here as soon as it's done.'

'And when will that be?' The ice cool question, the smile. No pressure at all.

Victoria hesitated, desperate to please but not wanting to over-promise. 'Well in time for the wedding.' Victoria clung to her smile as Aurelie looked at her for what felt like hours.

Finally Aurelie smiled back. 'Thank you.'

Great. Victoria put her bag on the chair and took out her pen case and ink bottle. Five cards shouldn't take that long and she'd please her client. Then she'd rest up on the train and study the seating changes at home. And call by the shop on the way to load up on stay-awake supplies.

'Do you like the candles?' Aurelie suddenly asked.

Victoria turned. Aurelie had opened the lid of a big box stacked beside the desk. It was filled with tissue-wrapped cylinders neatly packed end to end. Aurelie lifted one out and unwound the delicate covering and revealed a candle in a gorgeous soft white.

'They're surfboard wax scented.' Aurelie giggled. 'My favourite.'

Victoria grinned at the quirkiness. To be married in a French chateau by candlelight with handwritten calligraphy and lace and silk everywhere? Not to mention fireworks and orchestra and fountains? Aurelie might be doing some things slightly out of order, but there was a lot that was traditional in her plans—and fun. She was having it all. Good for her.

'They're beautiful. This whole place is beautiful. It is going to be enchanting.' Victoria meant it, she really did.

Aurelie put the candle back. 'It is going to be *parfait*!'

'It is.' Victoria drew in a breath for courage. 'Now, the menu hasn't changed, has it?' she asked, mentally crossing every crossable part of her body as she waited for the answer.

'No.' Aurelie laughed—a peal of infectious amusement that had Victoria smiling again. 'I see why you were recommended,' Aurelie said. 'You don't get flustered. You just say yes.'

Victoria maintained her smile despite the tweak on her nerves. In two minutes Aurelie had nailed her. Victoria had been so good at saying yes. To her parents, to Oliver. To the people she'd been desperate to please more than anything—more than herself. And then what Aurelie had said registered.

'I was recommended?' Who'd have done that? She'd

only been in Paris seven months—most of her income was derived from the secretarial work she got from an agency. She'd only recently relaunched her online calligraphy and personal stationery design business. Perhaps it was a contact from when her company had been flying high in London? Either way she was grateful—despite the last minute panic that Aurelie had just dumped on her.

But Aurelie didn't answer, she'd swiftly crossed to the window. Now Victoria too heard the crunch of the gravel outside. A car.

'Oh, no,' Aurelie gasped. 'He's here. He can't see any of this. If he comes in here, hide it. *Everything.*' With superior athletic grace, even with that burgeoning belly, Aurelie ran from the room.

Victoria blinked at the suddenly empty atmosphere. Presumably *he* was the groom. Curious to see what kind of guy had landed the incomparable Aurelie, she walked over to the window and peered down the two levels to the grand entrance.

The discreet-but-gleaming black car parked right in front was empty. As she watched, one of the conservatively clad assistants strode across the courtyard towards it. No doubt he was going to park it somewhere where it wouldn't ruin the picture-postcard perfection. While it might be a 'miniature' chateau, it was still one of the grandest buildings Victoria had ever been in. Surrounded by formal gardens with long avenues and hidden nooks and a selection of trick fountains, it was gorgeous.

She went back to the desk, picked up the completed cards and dropped them back in their protective box. She didn't want any damaged; she had too much to redo already. She took out several blank cards from the other box she'd brought in case, frowning as she arranged them.

The desk was beautiful, but it wasn't angled like her one at home. It'd be better if she could do these there, but she wasn't about to say 'no' to Aurelie.

She prepared her pen, drawing up ink, and worked on a practice card—warming up her fingers and getting the ink to flow smoothly.

'Aurelie, you in here?'

Victoria froze, her pen digging into the card. Shock curdled her blood. Ink spilled but she hardly noticed. Because she knew that voice. That warm, laid-back, confident call.

She turned her head as he walked into the room. Her heart paused for a painfully long time between beats. She held her breath even longer.

Liam?

Utterly gorgeous, absolutely unattainable Liam?

Her eyes were so wide they wanted to water. But that wasn't happening. Not in the presence of this particular guy. Never ever.

He paused, barely noticeably, before walking towards her. But, as always, Victoria noticed *every* tiny thing about him, so she saw that slight hesitation. She also saw his height—his tall, lean, muscled physique. He'd always been an athlete and more competitive than most. *Dangerously* competitive. Liam Wilson wanted to win, no matter the cost.

And he'd won the best, hadn't he?

Aurelie.

His sunflower-flecked brown eyes locked on her. Staring right back, Victoria saw the trademark easy-going stubble covering that sharp-edged jaw. She saw the dark brown hair, cropped closer than it had been the last time she saw him. Only vaguely did she take in the jeans and white tee because she was fully mesmerised by his expression—that intense, purposeful focus.

OM freaking G.

Liam Wilson. She couldn't believe it. Completely thrown, she looked down for a sec to collect her scrambled thoughts. How could he have grown even more attractive? How could she take one look and *want* all over again?

Pulling the plug on the visual didn't work. Because now she *remembered* so much of a time that had been so short. Now she wanted to hide. No one had ever exposed her the way Liam once had—with just one look.

'Victoria.'

She fixedly stared at the ink-splodged mess she'd made on the card, aware he'd stopped a few feet from her chair.

He cleared his throat. 'Long time, no see.'

She heard the smile. He'd always spoken with that easy-as smile. That innate confidence had been part of what had drawn her to him. The kind of confidence she'd never had. She'd been jealous of his 'I-don't-give-a-damn-what-you-all-think' attitude too, because she'd *never* had that.

Focused, hungry, *fascinating*. Liam had an edge Victoria hadn't encountered before or since. Tall, strong, determined to do what he wanted, he'd sliced through any opposition.

Until Oliver. And her.

Unable to resist, she chanced a glance back at him. That element of danger? It was still there—now lethal. Because, despite that smile, his eyes weren't just focused and relentless, they were hard.

There was no point clearing her throat. It wasn't going to work. *Nothing* in her body—especially not her brain—was working this second. Or the next.

'How've you been?' he asked.

Oh, he had to be kidding. Five years since she'd last seen him, five years since he'd interrupted her own wedding proposal and here he was five days from *his* wedding and he was greeting her like some old schoolmate?

Then again, how else to handle it?

She looked at the blank cards on the desk, glad she'd packed the others away. Aurelie hadn't wanted him to see them.

Aurelie. Liam.

Aurelie Broussard was marrying Liam Wilson.

Liam was the father of Aurelie's baby.

Liam was getting married.

Why was it so hard to compute?

She'd once had the chance to say yes to Liam. Not to marriage but to *something*. She hadn't. She'd said yes to someone else and life had moved on for all of them. And she was okay with that, wasn't she?

Yes.

She straightened, ignoring the churning riot of recollections and emotions inside. She was *happy*. And she'd act like it.

'Fine, thanks.' *Score*. Her voice sounded almost normal. 'How are you?'

'Stunned to see you.'

Hardly stunned. He was still standing, tall and fit in those blue jeans and soft leather boatshoes and an eyewateringly bright white tee with seams that had to cling hard to contain his broad shoulders. It ought to be impossible, but the guy was *more* gorgeous than he'd been back then. But what really stunned her was the glint in his eyes. He blatantly stared—at her hair, over her face, seeming to take in each feature—lingering on her mouth and then dropping below, taking in her figure. Was he sizing her up as he had that very first time they'd met? Back then it had been excusable—he'd not known who she was. But now?

Victoria tensed beneath his inspection, willing her body not to let the remnants of that old attraction show. Because that was all it was, like muscle memory—an imprint of an old infatuation. Not real. Certainly not *worse*. It couldn't be.

'It's been a long time,' he said. 'And, as impossible as I'd have thought it, you're even more beautiful now.'

Her breath quickened as her body absorbed his words—words that mirrored her thoughts of him. Her system responded *so* inappropriately. Heat shot everywhere—most of all deep and low in her belly.

Her brain clicked more slowly, taking too long to realise that it was meaningless, just his usual flirt talk. That was all it had ever been. *Talk*. But he had no right to tease her. Not that she could put him in his place the way she wanted to. Not when it was his fiancée she was working for. No, she was going to remain calm and professional and brush him off politely.

'You're looking good too,' she said crisply. She even smiled. She could handle this unfortunate coincidence and she could handle him. Of course she could.

He leaned against the table right next to where she sat. Her feet tingled, her legs itched. But she wasn't running, not showing how badly he got to her. She knew he was playing. He'd played with her before. She remembered that exact roguish expression from the first night she'd met him in the guest bathroom at Oliver's parents' place. Then, as now, Liam looked like a wicked cat who'd just spied a juicy mouse and he was going to have fun devouring it ever so slowly.

Victoria Rutherford was never going to be a mouse again.

'Thank you,' he drawled.

Her eyes narrowed as anger seeped through her polite armour. He really was the same game player? After all this time? Even now he was about to get married?

'Victoria,' he murmured softly, as he'd once murmured her name before. Now, as she had then, she steeled her heart.

How could she be this affected again by his mere presence?

Victoria froze as he moved, leaning across her—far, far too close. She held her breath but it was futile. He still smelt of ocean spray, sunshine and freedom. A heady, intoxicating mix that had once made her almost crazy high. The ultimate, *forbidden* temptation. Her boyfriend's best friend.

As her client's fiancé, he was even more forbidden now. So her suddenly over-excited hormones could just go back into dormant mode. Liam Wilson—even if he was single—would *never* be hers.

'What are you doing?' she squeaked—totally mouse—as he came closer still.

His gaze didn't leave hers; his mouth curved as he moved into her space. She was transfixed by that intense, challenging look. And he was so close now, she could see the individual, unfairly long lashes that framed his dangerously warm eyes.

'Mind if I take this?' He pulled the pen out of her clenched fingers with a sharp tug. 'It's looking a little like a weapon there. You stabbed me in the heart once. I'm not chancing it again.'

She gaped. As if she'd hurt him? Quite the reverse. He'd hurt her. And Oliver. He'd thrown a spanner between them—damaging the bond that was never fixed quite right after. But he didn't need to know how much he'd mattered.

'I hurt *you*?' She pulled herself together and faked a light laugh. 'No woman has ever hurt you.'

A single eyebrow lifted. 'You think?' He shook his head. 'Aren't I as vulnerable as anyone else?'

'No,' Victoria said bluntly.

'Come on,' he drawled. 'You know exactly how human I am,' he purred.

'Are you hitting on me?' she whispered—utterly amazed—and aghast. 'Seriously?'

When his seven-months-pregnant fiancée was in the building and he was getting married in less than a week?

Screw the prospects this job might bring. As far as Victoria was concerned, Aurelie didn't need flourishes. She needed a new fiancé.

'Liam!' There was a squeal and a vision in white darted across the room. Aurelie really was too swift for a heavily pregnant woman, not to mention perfectly chic and elegant even in her third trimester.

'Hey.' Liam wrapped his arms around Aurelie for a tight hug before pushing her back to arm's length and gazing at her adoringly. 'You. Look. Amazing.'

'I look huge but I don't care.' Aurelie laughed and leaned closer, smiling openly up at him. 'And I'm so glad you're here.'

Victoria's stomach twisted. Because he was a flirt cheat—not that she was jealous. There was nothing to be jealous of. She was happily divorced. Happily single. The last thing she wanted to do was revisit past mistakes and Liam Wilson had been an almighty mistake.

A mistake that *Aurelie* was about to make. Aurelie, whose features appeared brighter—her lips shinier. She'd disappeared for those few moments to touch up her make-up? Someone had to warn her about him. Only Victoria couldn't—she could never go there. Instead she loudly scraped together the blank cards on the table.

'Don't worry, Aurelie,' Victoria interrupted the scene, not wanting to watch them indulge in more PDA. 'He's not seen anything.'

Aurelie and Liam turned, the spell between them broken.

'All the surprises are safely hidden,' Victoria continued with determined firmness. Why were they looking at her as if she were speaking Martian?

'I've put everything away...' she faltered.

Something had flashed in Liam's face—a frown? A flicker of anger? It had passed so quickly Victoria couldn't decide. And now came the smile—the one that charmed everyone.

'Yes, don't worry, I left the groom downstairs.' Liam jerked his head to the door. 'But he'll be up here in a second if you don't hurry to see him.'

But Aurelie didn't hurry. She gazed up at Liam, her palm flat on his chest. 'It is so good to see you. I wasn't sure you'd come.'

'I didn't want to miss it.'

'Yes, you did.' She laughed again and patted his chest a couple of times. 'But I am glad you're not. Thank you.'

'Anything for you.' He winked and gently brushed the back of his hand along the edge of her fine-boned jaw.

'Now you'd better go stop him from coming up and spoiling any of your surprises.'

As Aurelie left the room Victoria sat in a swelter of confusion and defiance and embarrassment.

'You thought I was Aurelie's fiancé?' Liam walked back towards her, his smile had widened yet he managed to look less friendly.

Could he blame her when Aurelie had said 'he'd' arrived and then Liam had walked in as if he owned the place?

'You thought I was marrying her?' He stepped closer, suddenly very tall and a lot like a roadblock. 'And playing you?'

Victoria tried to glance behind him but it was impossible. He was fully in her face and expecting an answer with his eagle eyes. The only thing to do was play it cool. *Frigidly* cool. 'Do you blame me for thinking that?' She arched her brows as if that could make her taller. 'You have form.'

His eyes narrowed. 'I could spend some time arguing that, but why bother?' He stayed in place, right in her space. 'Just as I was five years ago, Victoria, I'm here as a guest.'

A *guest*. He truly wasn't Aurelie's fiancé.

For a second relief flooded her. But then mortification screamed back. Her cheeks burned under his mocking scrutiny.

Of course she'd thought he was the groom. In the rare moments she'd ever let herself think of him in the last five years, he'd *always* been the groom. The guy she'd never said yes to and refused to ever regret.

'Your name wasn't on the guest cards,' she said defensively.

'I didn't think I was going to be able to make the wedding,' he explained. 'That's why I'm one of the late additions.' He pointed to the sheet of paper Aurelie had put on the desk.

He hadn't made it to Victoria's wedding. She wasn't sure he'd even been invited. Not after what had happened. It was the only time she'd seen Oliver uncontrollably angry. She'd gone upstairs and the rest of the family had retired to change for lunch. Oliver and Liam had gone outside. Victoria had pressed close to her bedroom wall, secretly peering out of the window.

Liam had taken the blow without putting up any physical defence. The spot on his jaw had reddened, but all the while he'd quietly insisted to Oliver that nothing had happened. That she'd done nothing. That his interruption wasn't her fault. It had been his mistake alone.

He'd been facing the house. He'd glanced up, seen her. Their eyes connected for one split second.

Withdrawing. Apologising. Leaving.

He'd never looked at her again. Until today.

But had she done nothing? Really? Who had made the bigger mistake? Whose fault was it really? She'd been scared. She'd never had the strength to stand up to any of them—her parents, Oliver. Even Liam. She'd always done as they bid because she'd needed their approval. And all of them had steamrollered over her. But she'd let them—she'd *helped* them. That wasn't happening again. Only now she did look at the list Aurelie had handed to her. The third name down?

Liam Wilson.

'Oh.' She faked a bright smile. 'I thought—'

'I know what you thought,' he said, easing back into position against the desk. 'You never thought much of me, did you?'

That wasn't true but she couldn't reveal what she'd

thought of him all those years ago. She couldn't admit it then, she couldn't now.

There were five names on that list: three men, two women—one of whom had the same surname as another of the guests. The other woman's name was written last, beneath another man's name. Liam's name stood alone in the middle there. Was he coming to the wedding without a partner?

She didn't need to know. She really didn't. Because it didn't matter.

That didn't stop her glancing at his hands—his fisted fingers. Bare knuckles didn't mean anything for men. Many guys didn't wear wedding rings or, if they did, only when convenient. And even if they did wear them?

Victoria knew all too well how a wedding ring wasn't necessarily an obstacle as far as another woman was concerned. Or for a husband who was no longer satisfied in his marriage. Liam's lack of ring meant nothing. Nor did his lack of date.

But still that unwanted excitement heated her blood and anticipation zinged through her veins. What was she, some teen girl going to meet her fave ever boyband?

But he might be free. And now? So was she. There was nothing to stop them from finally exploring this *thing*...

Only the ten tonnes of baggage she was constantly pushing in front of her. And the baggage he'd worked into some kind of bullet-proof vest that he wore beneath that easy-come, easy-go attitude.

'I'm sorry.' She looked up at him. For today, for all those years ago. For what could never have been and never could be. She'd moved on; she didn't want to go back to the doormat she'd been. She had *plans* and they didn't involve anyone else. Not him. Not any man.

Liam looked right back at her, his mouth curved in that slight, sexy smile. Time shifted—five years disappeared in that unspoken communication. She was drawn right back into those feelings that should have been forgotten—warmth, want, desire.

And she had to get out of there before she did something really dumb.

He wrapped his fingers right round her wrist—halting her just as she moved. 'I'm not anyone's fiancé.' His grip was sure and warm. 'That means I'm free to flirt with whoever I want,' he added.

'Not with me,' she said huskily, swallowing to ease the dryness in her throat. She didn't want to flirt with anyone.

'Yes, you.' His smile was oddly gentle. 'You're not anyone's fiancée either, or wife.'

So he knew her marriage had ended.

'I can't believe you still blush like this—'

'I'm not here to flirt,' she interrupted him quickly. 'I'm here to *work*.' The emphasis was for herself as much as for him. She couldn't afford to be distracted by this quirk of fate.

His gaze rested on her for a long moment, as if he were weighing the truth of her words. His grip remained firm—could he feel her pulse accelerating?

He let her go. 'Then let's see you in action.' He handed back her pen.

As if.

'I can't do this with you watching.' Her palms were damp; she'd already smudged ink everywhere just from hearing his voice. She'd be less competent than a two-year-old with a pack of finger-paints right now.

'You always had a problem with me watching.'

She tensed, hoping to stop him from seeing her all-over tremble. She *had* always been aware of the way he watched her. 'It's not you,' she lied sassily. 'I don't like anyone watching me work.'

'In case you make a mistake?'

'Not at all.' She lied yet again. 'I'm not afraid to make mistakes. I've made many.' Too, too many.

'Then you're fine to write in front of me. Write my name.'

She shook her head. She wasn't going to make *more* mistakes. She had to focus now.

'You're still a chicken,' he jeered.

'You're confusing cowardice with being sensible.' She had always tried to do the sensible thing. No shame in that, right? 'And with these smudges?' She held up her fingers. 'Why would I waste my time and resources?'

He glanced at the table. 'You're really into all this?'

'I want Aurelie to have what she wants.'

'So you've not been put off weddings and all that's wonderful about them?'

'Of course not,' she mocked. He was the cynical one, not she. 'You think because my marriage didn't work out, I'd go all bitter and anti?'

His lips twitched. 'No. I just…wouldn't have expected you to be so into weddings, I guess.'

'I'm into *other* people's weddings,' she said smoothly, putting her pen back into its case. 'And you're still not into weddings at all.'

His shoulders lifted. 'And yet here I am. Happy to enjoy someone else's wedding.'

'That's an improvement on the last time I saw you. You didn't seem to want anyone to marry then.'

'And I was right, wasn't I?' He casually picked up a candle and breathed in the scent.

She took that hit. 'You couldn't have foreseen what was going to happen.'

'Couldn't I?'

No. She rejected the idea totally.

'You and I both knew it wasn't right,' he said softly, lowering the candle and coolly looking at her. 'Even Oliver knew it wasn't right.'

'I think it's best if I go home and work on these in my studio,' Victoria said through gritted teeth.

'Where are you staying? Paris?' Liam asked, his lips curving in that suspiciously sinful way. 'I can give you a lift.'

'You're not staying here?'

He shook his head and straightened, looking all man-of-action. 'I have some things in town I need to do.'

She couldn't possibly get a lift with him. Never. The train was the only option.

Victoria looked up to meet his gaze and saw the mockery written all over him. But as she was about to answer he laid a finger over her lips.

'What are you so worried about?' he taunted slyly. 'You'll be stuck with me for less than an hour. What harm can come?'

To be stuck in a car with the guy who'd once tempted her so completely? She'd be mad to contemplate it. She had to think of some excuse.

'With you driving?' she tried to tease archly. 'You always travelled too fast, Liam. So I'd say all kinds of harm could come.'

'Oh, well.' His answer came lazy and insolent. 'If it's speed you're afraid of, why don't you drive?'

TWO

———

Liam tried not to hold his breath as he waited for her answer. Victoria Rutherford—the only woman he'd wanted, but had never had. The one who'd got away. It was such a cliché, but face to face with her for the first time in five years?

He still wanted.

She was even more beautiful now. Until today he wouldn't have thought that was possible.

'Sure.' Her very pretty chin tilted upwards as she finally gave him an answer.

Liam had to suppress more than a sigh of satisfaction—there was a burn in his blood and in his gut as well. Last time he'd asked her something it had been a denial she'd issued. Not today. And, as crazy as it was, Liam had more to ask of her. Much more. He wanted to hear 'yes' from her mouth many times over.

Maybe then his mind would be freed from all those memories.

Victoria willed confidence. Of course she could drive that big black car. It might have power but it'd also have every safety feature ever invented. And no doubt it had a fancy sat-nav system and automatic clutch. It'd be a cinch. 'I'd love to drive.'

Yeah, she just oozed faux confidence—refusing to show how flustered she was.

She carefully packed her gear into her bag. Shame she didn't have some light leather driving gloves to don with chic aplomb. Gloves would hide the almost permanent ink stains. 'Let's get going. I've got a lot of work to do.'

But the car that an assistant brought to the front entrance of the chateau wasn't the big black machine she'd seen from the window. It was a tiny two-seater.

Victoria eyed the sleek gleaming silver with its explicit promise of speed and seduction and turned to Liam. 'Who do you think you are—James Bond?'

Even she, no car fiend, recognised a vintage Aston Martin when she saw it. No automatic clutch, no sat-nav, no airbags. No roof even. And no chance she was driving it.

He held open the driver's door for her. 'You don't think it's gorgeous?'

That wasn't the point. 'Is it yours?'

Of course he had some zippy racing thing. The guy only knew one speed—supersonic.

He shook his head. 'It's a rental. But I figure that's no reason to be boring.'

As if he could ever be boring. Still, the ownership gave her an out from the nightmare. 'Then insurance won't cover me. I'm not taking the chance of damaging a rental car.'

'But you wouldn't mind damaging mine?'

Her gaze clashed with his. He didn't look away. Nor did she. Like swords crossed to the hilt, their eyes were locked. Neither would disengage.

'You're driving,' she spoke through lips that barely moved.

'See, you are a coward,' he answered equally softly.

'I choose not to take unnecessary risks.' She broke the fierce challenge by walking round to the passenger side, yanking open the door and sliding into the seat. She really couldn't afford a bill if she pranged. And given how shaky her hands were right now, a prang seemed inevitable.

After a minute that felt like an hour, she glanced over to where he still stood by the open driver's door. He was smiling as he stared at her.

'If you're not willing to drive either, please let me know so I can catch a train,' she said impatiently. 'I need to get home to get on with my work.'

'Of course,' he answered ever so politely.

Frankly, she didn't see how a guy with legs as long as his could actually fit into a tiny roadster like this. But he did with a way-too-sensual ease, pulling sunglasses from a small compartment and putting them on. That was when she registered the next problem. The two-seater was a close fit. It wasn't big enough for her to be able to slink into the far corner. Instead his shoulder was merely inches from hers.

Too intimate.

Swallowing, she glared out of the window. She'd focus on the external view, not the Greek-god-gorgeous guy sitting so close.

He revved the engine and cruised down the gravel driveway. Victoria breathed again, inhaling the fresh summer air. They'd be on the motorway and he'd put his foot down and they'd be back in Paris in no time and this would all be over. As they reached the end of the drive she braced herself for the acceleration. But when they hit the road, Liam didn't quit the leisurely pace.

'What's with the speed, Grandpa?' she finally asked. She wanted away from him as soon as possible. 'Are we anywhere *near* the speed limit?'

'If I drive too fast, I won't be able to hear you.'

Hear her what? Breathe? She wasn't about to have any kind of deep and meaningful conversation with the man. As far as she was concerned, the less they talked, the better. Her overly sensitive nerves didn't need to hear more of the laughter that was always audible in his voice. So she sat silent, keeping her eyeballs glued to the window. After five minutes they were still going at that ridiculous pace.

'You'll get pulled over for holding up the traffic,' she finally muttered.

'There aren't any cars behind me and, if there were, there's a lane for them to overtake me.'

See, there it was. That latent lazy humour. As if everything was warm and easy with him. Well, if he was going to insist on the snail's pace—and he clearly was—then she might as well quench some of the curiosity burning out her brain. 'Why are you at the chateau so far ahead of the wedding? Isn't your life so busy you could only fly in the day before?'

'I'm on holiday. Thought I'd help her out with some arrangements.'

As he'd helped prepare for that Christmas years ago? He'd worked alongside her—helping out in all kinds of ways. As if he, like she, couldn't cope with sitting around idly all day. She'd always wanted to feel needed. But she didn't think he craved other people's approval in the same way she did. 'You don't want to laze on the beach?'

He shook his head. 'I'd want to be on the water.'

'You're not good at having a holiday.' He'd always sought out something to do.

'I prefer to keep busy.'

'Why's that? You can't relax?'

She glanced at him. His eyes were hidden by the sunglasses, but his mouth curved into that wicked grin.

'I can relax,' he said softly.

'By 'getting busy', right?' she asked sarcastically, knowing that was exactly what he was thinking of. 'But you can't cope with quiet? You scared of being alone with your thoughts?'

'I'm a professional sportsman, right? Therefore I don't *have* thoughts.'

Oh, he was no brainless jock type. He was smart, successful—you didn't need to note the expensive watch and discreet-but-mega-expensive clothing labels to know that.

'So what have you been keeping busy with these last five years?' Once more she gave into her urges and asked.

'You don't know?'

She sent him a cool look. 'No. You left on Christmas Day and that was that.'

His brows waggled above his sunglasses. 'You mean you didn't Google me?'

'No.' Laughter bubbled out at his irrepressible arrogance. 'I'm sorry to deflate your ego, but I haven't spent the last few years cyber-stalking you.' Which wasn't to say she hadn't ever thought about him. But she'd resisted curiosity then and pushed him from her mind. Now his answer made her wonder. 'Did you ever Google me?'

He smiled at the road ahead, his fingers rhythmically tapping the steering wheel.

Oh, my. 'You *did*.' She twisted in her seat and stared at him. '*When* did you Google me?' It would have been easy to find her. She hadn't changed her name—something that had really bothered Oliver. She had a website—it even had her picture on it. And she was on Facebook like anyone. She frowned, drew her lip between her teeth. What had Liam found out about her online? What info was out there that she didn't know about?

'When I heard you and Oliver had broken up,' he said.

All that time later? A lone butterfly fluttered in her stomach. 'How did you hear about that?'

'I'm still in touch with some people in London.'

But not Oliver? 'You know he's gone to Canada.'

He nodded.

So he probably also knew Oliver hadn't gone to Canada alone. What else did he know?

Suddenly cold, Victoria didn't want to find out. She didn't want to think what some of her old acquaintances might have said about how it all fell apart.

'How do you know Aurelie?' She turned back to stare out of the windscreen, folding her arms across her tummy.

There was a pause. 'I'm one of her ex-boyfriends.'

Victoria clenched her fingers into fists, glad they were hidden under her arms. She kept her eyes firmly on the window. So he had wanted Aurelie. He'd *had* Aurelie. Then she remembered the expression that had briefly flared in his eyes when she'd interrupted him hugging Aurelie. Was he hurt because his former love was marrying someone else?

Victoria released the breath she'd held too long. 'You're still friends?'

'We're close.' He inclined his head and briefly glanced at her. 'Is that hard to believe?'

Frankly yes. What woman could be 'just friends' with Liam Wilson? He was too intensely attractive.

And what surprised her more was that he chose to remain in touch with Aurelie. He'd been the burning bridges type a few years ago.

'Is she the one who got away?' She tried to joke but it sounded flat to her. 'Do you still hold a torch?'

'I care very much about Aurelie, but—'

'You care about yourself more?' She couldn't help interrupting rudely—she regretted asking anything now. She didn't want to know.

He chuckled. 'What is it about me that threatens you so much?'

'Nothing. You don't. I'm not bothered by you.' Lord, could she sound any more flustered?

She tilted her head back and hoped the breeze would cool her cheeks.

'No? I bothered you once. I made you want something you thought you shouldn't.' His smile was still there but all sense of joking was dead.

'As arrogant as ever, I see.' And a game player. He'd considered her sport. He'd done it because he couldn't help himself—consumed by that driving need to win. Even over his best friend. Oliver had told her about the new sailor who'd come into the team—that he was driven like no one else.

He was driven to win in everything.

But even though she knew that to be the truth, her heart puckered. Surely it hadn't entirely been a game? That attraction had been intensely fierce. Surely there was no way it had only been her feeling it for real?

And the night they'd first met, Liam hadn't known she was Oliver's girlfriend. Not until that heated look and those soft, searing words had already been exchanged.

'You'd be disappointed if I wasn't.'

She rolled her eyes but she couldn't help those urges again. 'So you and Aurelie?'

The wry smile on his lips told her he was amused by her curiosity. She lifted her chin and ploughed on anyway. Because, damn it, they'd shared something. They weren't mere acquaintances. A moment of connection had forged a thread between them. Incredibly, she almost felt a *right* to know. He'd once interfered in her personal life—didn't that give her certain leeway in return? 'How long were you together?'

'On and off, almost three years.'

She snapped her mouth shut, almost as shocked as when she'd first seen him walk into that room at the chateau. He'd been with Aurelie longer than she'd been married to Oliver? He must have loved her.

Liam chuckled. 'I've surprised you.'

'Yes.' She drew a breath and nodded. 'You have. But in a good way.'

'Why good?'

'You committed that long.'

'You didn't think I could commit?' His brows shot high, an odd note sounding in his voice.

'It doesn't fit with your image.'

There was a pause. 'What's my image?'

Victoria swivelled in her seat again to look directly at him, determined to play it up and ease them back into that slightly wary, almost joking mood. 'Untamable. Challenging. Arrogant.'

There were so many more adjectives she could add to his definition. But she wasn't going to feed his ego any more.

'And that makes me seem like I wouldn't commit?'

'Well, you're such a flirt,' she said bluntly.

He laughed and his hands tightened on the wheel. 'Only with you.'

'Yeah, right.' That was a prime example of his flirt talk just there. And it totally wasn't true. He'd had them all eating out of his hand all those years ago. She'd seen how the other girls there had watched him. They'd looked at him the same way Victoria had covertly looked at him. With dazzled hunger.

She couldn't believe he'd been with Aurelie three years. What had happened to break them up? Why was she marrying someone else? Victoria thought she already knew. Liam wasn't the marrying kind. Not even to a total dream-girl like Aurelie. He'd never be pinned down by any woman—not for life. No doubt there were too many other challenges—races, trophies, women.

'Are you in a new relationship now?' That curiosity got her once more.

'No,' he answered with a soft drawl. 'I have commitment issues.'

She couldn't help it. She laughed. Even though she knew it was the truest thing he'd said all day.

'What about you?' he asked. 'Are you with someone new?'

She shook her head. 'I have commitment issues too.'

Now his laughter rolled.

'Well, you can't blame me for being wary now.' She smiled wryly.

He stopped laughing immediately. 'No.' He turned his attention to the road ahead. 'I'm sorry it didn't work out.'

'I thought you were all 'I told you so'?'

He shook his head. 'He was an idiot.' There was a silence. 'We were all idiots.'

Victoria shrank in her seat. She'd been the biggest idiot.

She'd been unable to stand up for herself and say what she'd really wanted. And in some ways, what she'd really wanted had been neither of them. She'd needed freedom and independence and she'd been too afraid to reach for it. But she had it now and she wasn't giving it up.

'The calligraphy's going well for you?' He changed the subject.

'Yes,' she said proudly. It mightn't be world famous but it was doing okay.

'It's an interesting way to make a living. Doing the purely decorative.'

'It's nice to make things beautiful for people. Life shouldn't just be functional,' she declared, knowing he was deliberately provoking her and responding regardless. 'Anyway, it's no less meaningless than sailing from point A to point B as fast as possible. You're hardly securing world peace with that career.' She tucked a stray strand of hair behind her ear with an affected gesture. 'At least what I do makes a difference to a few people—it makes them smile.

'I make people smile too, you know,' he said slyly. 'I make people cheer. And scream.'

She bet he made many women scream. 'Is that why you do it?' She couldn't resist a little provoking either—asking him in terribly polite tones, 'You need the adulation?'

His resulting chuckle made her smile inside. 'I just like to win.'

He hadn't won with her. He still wouldn't.

She looked at him. 'Not everyone can win all of the time. Not even you.'

'That's not going to stop me trying.'

No. Hadn't he made a play for her even when he knew

she was with someone else—someone who was supposed to be his best friend?

But once more her conscience niggled because he could argue he hadn't made a play. He'd not said or done anything out of line once he knew who she was. Then again the man was so devastating he hadn't *needed* to do or say. He'd only needed to *look*. And when he had finally spoken? In front of everyone? She sighed. He was the one who'd got away.

'This the street you meant?'

Despite his determined effort to fly well under the speed limit for the entire journey, they were indeed finally in her neighbourhood.

'Yes.' She directed him to her apartment and he pulled up outside.

Her heart thundered. Her silly hands were actually sweating as she unclipped her seat belt. She was going to say goodbye to him again. For ever. Good, right?

He turned in his seat and faced her. She should get out of the car. She should open the door and walk away. But she couldn't; somehow she needed to see him—see his eyes. See if that look was there.

And he knew it. He took off his sunglasses, meeting her eyes. His were serious, but there was that glint of laughter and of something else.

Determination. Desire. *Challenge*.

She recognised them all. But she couldn't let this happen. Even if she was *dying* of curiosity inside. She'd resisted him once, she could again, right? She had a new man-free plan and she was sticking to it.

'Victoria—'

'No.' She pre-empted him. She was not inviting him in. She was not touching him. She was not letting him—

He smiled. Reaching out, he touched her burning cheek with just the tips of his fingers.

She clamped her jaw together.

'Even now you want to resist it?' he murmured.

'You can't just pick up with five years in between when we last saw each other.' Did she have to sound so breathy?

'Why not?'

'Because...' So much had gone down between then and now.

'I'm single.' He glanced at her hands in her lap. 'You're no longer attached.'

'And you're pleased about that,' she said tartly.

He clamped his hand over hers, a quick frown pulling his brows. 'Of course I'm not. Believe it or not I wanted you to be happy. I wanted you both to be happy.'

She swallowed, conscious of the strength of his hand pushing on hers. The heat of it. 'We were,' she said hoarsely, but honestly. 'For a while.'

'I'm sorry it didn't work out. But it not working out was nothing to do with me.'

'I never said it was.' And she wouldn't. But the edges of her heart shrivelled because, while Oliver had been the one who'd cheated, she'd been the one who'd withheld part of herself. She'd not been honest with him. Or herself. Or anyone.

Liam leaned closer. 'Don't make me pay the price of him hurting you.'

'I'm sorry?' She narrowed her eyes. 'What is it you want to do?'

'What I've always wanted to do.' His shoulders lifted. 'From the second I first saw you in nothing but a towel and steam. At least I'm honest enough to admit it.'

She felt the steam now as heat surged through her body.

'This thing between us?' He shook his head. 'Still the same, even after all this time. You can't deny it.'

Of course she'd deny it. Self-preservation was a basic instinct. 'I can.' Because she knew all that was important to know about Liam, yet he knew nothing of what was important about her. Like the fact she wasn't about to let herself get distracted. 'You don't know me now, Liam. You don't know what I want.'

'So you're going to take the easy option and avoid it? You're good at that.'

She shook her head. 'You thought you were so clever. That you saw it all. But you saw nothing of what was really going on with me. You didn't know me.'

'I knew enough,' he argued. 'I still do.'

'And what do you think you know? That I was sexually attracted to you?' She kept her head high despite another flare of heat in her cheeks. 'You intrigued me then, yes, I admit it. But I'm not interested now.'

'Then prove it.' His gaze locked on hers. 'Come closer without blushing.'

'Oh, please.' She covered up with a laugh. 'I don't need to prove anything to you.'

'What about to yourself?' he challenged right back, his expression wicked and tempting. 'Isn't that part of what you're doing now? Isn't your move to Paris all about proving things to yourself?'

'You still think you're so smart.'

'No, but I know when I'm right.' He brushed that strand of hair behind her ear for her. 'You're out here on your own. Proving you can do it. You can handle it.'

'And I can,' she whispered.

He smiled. 'Yet you won't even try to handle me.'

THREE

———

'You do not have to see me to my door.'

'Yes, I do.' Liam wasn't letting Victoria walk out of his life again. At least, not yet. Not when there was this much unfinished between them. He was going to get *something* from her today. Even just an admission. He wanted to hear her say it only the once, a whisper even. She reckoned she didn't want him? She reckoned wrong. He knew that as well as she.

'I have to work.'

He knew that too. 'I'm not asking to stay the night.' Though he would if she offered. One night was all he'd need. Why she could do this to him, he didn't know, but from the first second he'd seen her it had been there. That hot response in every cell of his body.

Want.

But he wasn't the kid he'd once been. He wasn't going to lose it as he had back then—he was in control of everything now, right?

He'd experienced lust plenty of times. Course he had. Had acted on it too. But it had never been as extreme as it had that night he'd first met Victoria. When she'd opened her mouth and answered him back? When she'd been as enthralled as he had?

She still was. He'd seen it flash in her eyes when he'd walked into that room, before she'd had a second to school her face. He saw it now in the way she went out of her way to avoid touching, or even looking at, him.

But he looked at her. And he wanted to touch. In fact he wanted to provoke—that would only be fair. Because that rampant lust was back as bad as it had ever been.

He followed her up the stairs, trying hard not to stare at her sweet curves. Instead he glanced around, checking out her digs. The distraction was not good.

The stairwell was poorly lit but he could still see the grimy, peeling paintwork and he could smell something horrendous—like several stale dinners mixed with the stench of wet wool. How many tiny apartments were squished into this ugly building? They passed a million doors as they marched on. No wonder she was looking fit given all these stairs she had to climb.

'So you're doing the garret-in-Paris thing?' He ground the feeble joke out. This place was hardly the Left Bank and giving her a nice view of the river.

'I'm not starving. I'm doing very well,' she said as they finally got to the top floor. She unlocked her door and paused. 'And calligraphy is a craft as much as it is an art. I'm happy.'

'Good for you.' He ignored the 'goodbye' in her tone and walked right past her, into the shoebox of an apartment— a child's shoebox at that. 'But there are better garrets. With better views.' He frowned, learning all there was to know in a swift glance. One room with a cupboard for a kitchen and another for a bathroom. The place sucked.

'I don't need a better view. I only need good light.'

She'd set up a small workspace in the room. The biggest bit of furniture was her desk. Angled and pushed against the window to maximise use of the natural light. On a flat desk beside it was her computer. Against the far wall—as if it were an afterthought—was the smallest single bed he'd ever seen.

The place wasn't miniature doll's-house cute, it was cramped.

'How can you work in here?' He looked away from the itty, bitty bed. 'It's hardly a 'studio' is it?' It wasn't big enough for anyone to be comfortable in. Not even petite blondes with leaf-green eyes.

'That's exactly what it is.' Her chin lifted high, as if she was just waiting for the criticism.

Confronted with that expression, much as he wanted to criticise, he found he wasn't going to. She was trying—independent and alone. Far more than she'd been five years ago. Good for her, right? Except for some reason it annoyed him more. Why should it matter? Couldn't he, of all people, understand the need to succeed?

'Why don't you come to my hotel and work there? I have a suite—it's three times the size of this place.' He knew before he'd finished saying it that it was a mistake. He knew how she'd react—call him worse than a flirt. Thing was, he meant it. Grudgingly. It wasn't a line.

'Oh, please, that was so unsubtle.'

Yep, she boxed him right back into flirt mode.

'But we wouldn't have to share a bathroom this time.' He walked up to her, giving into her expectations—and his own need to provoke. And stand closer. 'Unless you wanted to.' He smiled and lifted a hand to her jaw, unable to resist touching her again. 'Now, that was unsubtle.'

He'd never forget the time he'd walked in on her in the

bathroom. It had been his first night there that Christmas break. To his relief she hadn't screamed the place down. She'd been mortified. In truth so had he. He'd covered up by joking, of course. But he'd soon got derailed. The towel had covered her most private parts—parts he'd ached to see. But there'd been so much damp skin on show and with the steam and the sweet scent of her soap? Of course he'd made a play. A huge one.

It wasn't until the next morning that he'd learned she was Oliver's girlfriend—the one he'd been with for a couple of years. Who Oliver's family loved and expected him to marry. The good girl who slept in her own room when she stayed—not Oliver's. It was all so *perfect*.

But it was already too late. Liam had been young and dumb and so callow. He'd mistaken insta-lust for love at first sight. He'd been unsubtle in his attention. Unable to stay away.

'That wasn't just unsubtle.' Victoria lifted her chin sharply, so his fingers slipped from her skin. 'That was sledgehammer.'

'This is a dodgy neighbourhood,' he said, wishing he could see her out of here.

'Don't try to get me there under the pretext of caring for my welfare.' She looked amused.

There was no shifting her. And—albeit reluctantly— he respected that. 'So where do you see it—' he waved his hand at her desk '—in a few years?'

'You want to know my business goals?'

Yep, oddly he did. 'How are you going to expand when it's so dependent on you? What happens if you sprain your wrist or something?'

'I have business insurance. In terms of expansion—is

it necessary? I only need to make enough for me to live comfortably.'

A single bed was never comfortable, no matter how slight she was. She clearly needed to make more than she currently was. 'How are you going to factor in holidays? When you own your own business, it's very easy to forget about holidays.'

'How do *you* factor in holidays?' She laughed at him.

'I love my work. Work *is* a holiday for me.' Sailing was and always would be his first, his ultimate, passion. He loved the challenge on the water. It was his home—the place he felt safest. And the most free.

She turned and looked at him. Her green eyes were very bright—he felt their power right into his bones.

'And you don't think it's possible for me to feel the same about my work?' she asked.

Frankly? No. 'Not in this environment.' This place was stifling at best. 'But maybe it doesn't matter to you. Maybe you only see what you're working on.' He walked over to the scrupulously tidy desk. 'You're very good at what you do.'

Victoria couldn't get over his nerve. He couldn't try to make it better now with flattery. Not when he hadn't even seen her work. He'd only seen that mess on the card at the chateau. She'd boxed the others away and right now her desk was completely clear. So he had no idea how good she was. Unless—

A horrible suspicion occurred to her. 'Did you recommend me to Aurelie?'

He stilled.

'You did. You Googled me. You found my website. You—' She broke off.

For once the self-assured expression was wiped from Liam's face. He looked guilty. He *was* guilty.

Victoria gritted her teeth. She couldn't back out of Aurelie's job now, but a huge part of her wanted to.

'I didn't think I was going to make it to her wedding.' Liam offered an explanation. 'And I never expected to see you even if I did. But, yes, I wanted to help.'

Help who—her or Aurelie?

It shouldn't bother her. It really shouldn't. But she didn't want to feel beholden to him. And she'd felt so stupidly proud to have gotten this commission. That she was succeeding independently and on her own merit. Oliver had implied that her early success in London had only been because of his contacts. Not the quality of her work. She'd thought this job an antidote to that bite.

'I mentioned your name when she was boring me with wedding details one day.' Liam fiddled with one of the tins she had on her desk, pulling out the pencils one by one and dropping them back in. 'She looked you up herself and decided whether or not to hire you. She likes your work.'

Victoria swallowed. She couldn't let pride ruin this. She could still get business off the back of Aurelie's wedding. Her work *would* speak for itself.

He glanced at her, his sharp eyes assessing. 'You're unhappy with me.'

'Not at all,' she lied. 'It was very nice of you to suggest me to her. I'm amazed you could even remember my name.'

'Come off it, Victoria.' He stepped closer.

She instinctively retreated. Because sometimes he saw too much—past her polite veneer to what she was really thinking. And wanting.

'You're so determinedly independent now?' he asked,

his brows lifting at her attempt to put distance between them. 'Can't accept anyone's help?' A muscle worked in his jaw. 'Least of all mine?' He let his gaze slowly lower— trailing over her body.

She stood her ground, hoping to school her response and this time truly hide her thoughts from him. But once again he seemed to know.

'What are you so afraid of?' he baited. 'You have nothing to fear from me. It would only be the once.'

Victoria smiled, keeping the rest of her expression smooth. 'Why? Isn't it going to be very good?'

His attention snapped back to her face. 'I've done the convenient relationship. It doesn't work. One-night stands do.'

The 'convenient relationship'? So he hadn't been in love with Aurelie? Or was this his way of hiding his own deep hurt?

'I'm not a one-night stand person,' she answered honestly.

'Maybe you should try it. Once.'

She held his gaze—still feeling that pull towards him, but she was older and wiser and stronger now. 'You don't like to give up, do you?'

There was a slight hesitation. 'No. I told you I like to win.'

'And that's what this is?' She gestured—fluttering her fingers towards him and then herself. 'Like an event to be won?'

'If we don't explore it, there'll always be that curiosity. Be honest,' he drawled, taking another step closer. 'You're dying of curiosity. That burning wonder of what might have been.'

'So poetic?'

'It's the Irish ancestry in me. And I'm right. We both know that.' His voice dropped. 'We also both know how good it's going to be.'

'Liam.'

His lashes lowered. 'It's always going to be like this,' he muttered. 'It's inevitable. It always has been.'

No. She'd ceded control of her life for too long—always doing what others wanted. She was in control now.

He'd stepped near enough to touch her and now he did. Reaching out to brush the tips of his fingers on her shoulder.

'Only once, you say?' she asked, letting some tease out. Determined to make him pay for this casual attitude. As if all this was was sexual curiosity that could be assuaged in one hit.

'Feel free to make me change my mind.' His mouth quirked. 'Love to see you try.'

She stepped back.

'No,' she said. 'Not happening.' She folded her arms across her chest. 'Feel free to make *me* change *my* mind,' she threw at him. 'Go on. Do your worst.'

Startled, he stepped after her. 'Victoria—'

'Was this only ever lust? You're so driven by base urges you ruined your friendship with Oliver? You almost broke up a relationship? For a quick fling?'

Or was it even less than that? She took another step from him, using the last bit of space behind her and bumping the backs of her knees against the small cot she called her bed.

'Was it just your overblown need to win?' she continued. 'You're so insanely competitive, did you need to get one over him? Was I nothing more than the trophy of the day?' She kept her smile on but it was slipping. Quickly.

'No.' He frowned.

That didn't satisfy her. 'Then don't cheapen this. Don't cheapen *me*.'

Now he looked angry. 'I didn't betray Oliver.'

No?

'I didn't seduce you,' he argued, standing so close she could feel his warmth and almost taste the salty ocean breeze that he always seemed to evoke. 'And I could have.'

'You think?'

'I can't give you everything you want. I can only—'

'You don't know what I want.'

He shrugged one shoulder. 'Marriage, babies, Labradors.'

'I tried that. It's not for me.' Maybe she just wanted acknowledgement of what could have been between them. That this had been *more* than just a sexual attraction. That somehow, unbelievable as it might have been, there had been a real connection between them that week.

'So what do you want?'

'A career. My business.' She lifted her chin. 'I was making headway before the divorce. Oliver hated that I was more successful than he was.' The banking crisis had hardly been her fault. Hundreds in the city had been laid off—Oliver had been one of them. But for whatever reason, her little enterprise had gained traction. But after his affair and the divorce she'd lost it. Now she was back at the beginning. But she believed in it. In herself. 'I want to build this up into something great. And to do that I need to finish this for Aurelie. That's what I want. To have work coming out of my ears. For people to love my work.'

He was silent, his eyes boring into her, for a long moment. Then he glanced around her small room again. The plain, utility style room with her neatly lined tins and stacks of paper and materials.

'That's all you want?' he asked.

'That's all I have time for.'

'No time for anything else?' He suddenly smiled, wicked-incarnate again. 'Not even one night?'

'Typical.' She rolled her eyes, her good humour lifting at the swift return of his. 'You just want to bang the one who got away.'

'What, and you think you're unaffected?' he teased. 'I see how you look at me.'

She averted her eyes immediately. 'Unbelievable.'

'But true nonetheless.' He nodded. 'Look, I respect your aims. And you're right, you have no time. But let's clear the air a little.'

In what way exactly? That wicked look in his eye was only growing.

'I don't think the air needs clearing,' she said firmly.

'One kiss,' he tempted. 'We never even kissed.'

That was true. She'd turned away. She still didn't know how she'd managed it. But she was repeating it now—there'd be no kissing.

He laughed at her expression. 'Don't look so worried. It might be a huge let-down.'

'I thought you were too much of a Casanova to let any woman down that way.'

'You might let me down,' he taunted.

'You're questioning my abilities?' She winced at the high pitch of her attempted comeback. Not exactly sizzling.

His smile came so quick, so lethal it shot heat into her abdomen. 'Well, how good are you?'

'Better than you.' She snapped the obvious answer

straight back—smart all the way and unwilling to concede a thing.

His smiled broadened.

But hers faltered. She thought about what she'd said. Fact was she was more fizzle than sizzle. The fantasy was shattered. She wasn't good at all. She'd had one lover in her life—Oliver. And he'd gone and found greater warmth with another woman.

'Victoria?'

Liam's smile had died. Was it concern that he was looking at her with? She looked away again. She didn't want that. She didn't want a pity kiss, she didn't want to be a disappointment.

'It's not going to be good.' She cleared her throat and then glued on a smile so he'd think she was feeling it as an easy joke. 'So let's just keep it as an unfulfilled fantasy.'

He muttered something, she didn't know what. She just wanted him to leave now. She had a headache coming on, she had so much work to do. And the emotional spin he'd put her in? It was like going through the washing machine on heavy duty. Only he wasn't washing away all those old emotions. He was hauling them out again—the stains of the past. Want and desire and silly things that she'd forgotten about.

Except she'd not forgotten. And it still wasn't the right time. It never would be.

He touched her. His hand cupping, then lifting her chin. She couldn't look at him. All that sass-talk of a few minutes ago fled, leaving her empty inside. Doubt flurried into the vacant spaces within. He might have stuck with only one girlfriend for a while, but he was still vastly more experienced than she. He'd laugh at how hopeless she was.

He stepped closer, into her space. 'Look at me.'

She swallowed, trying to suck back the stupid pity moment. She lifted her chin herself, working her stiff mouth into some kind of smile, summoning the words to brush him off and escape this embarrassment. She didn't need to be mortified. She didn't need to kiss him and be exposed. He knew too much as it was.

'Liam, I—'

He put his hands on her waist. Firmly. Her gaze collided with his and was captured. Whatever she'd meant to say slipped away.

Silence. Heat. Sensation.

Light from the late summer sun streamed through the window, encasing him in a golden glow. There was no hiding from his scrutiny, or his expression. And his expression revealed desire. Naked want.

Victoria blinked but couldn't tear her focus away from the fire in his eyes. His hands slid over her firmly, shaping her hips. Her hands were useless—her fingers curled into fists. She held them pressed tight in the space just beneath her breasts. She stood as still as a small bird aware of a predator too close by.

He swept a hand to the small of her spine and then downwards. He pressed her forward, until her hips collided with his. She trembled at the searing impact—the shocking, undeniable proof of his attraction. That big bulge pressed against her—instantly scattering some of her doubt. Her dry lips parted so she could draw in a shaky breath. He stared, his focus fixed on her eyes.

They must have shown him something good, because his mouth eased, one corner lifting slightly.

He pressed her closer, then eased the pressure before pressing her against him again. He didn't break contact with her, but the rippling rhythm intensified the sensations cascading through her. Her skin felt scalded—as if she'd been plunged into a pool of boiling water. She couldn't look away from him, from the way he was watching her so intently. Lulling her. Inviting her. Making her feel as if it was all going to be okay.

It was going to be more than okay.

Breathing became difficult, as if the heat between them had burned all the oxygen. She tried to draw more air in. But breathing deeper took her chest closer to his. She lifted her hands—pushing them against his rock-hard heat. But slowly, unable to resist the urge, she stretched out her fingers to splay them over his broad chest. Through the navy cotton she could feel his skin burning, and she could feel the strong, regular drive of his heart. She pressed her lips together again—firmly, trying to ease the swollen feeling of them as her blood pulsed faster to all her most sensitive extremities.

He shifted, planting his feet wider. Both his hands were at her back now. Bending her into his heat. Saying nothing in words but everything in actions. She felt the impact right to her toes.

I've wanted to kiss you for so long.

She heard the words in her head though his mouth hadn't moved. Nor had hers. Did he say it? Did she? Or had she just dreamed it?

Her throat was tight; she couldn't have spoken if she'd tried. But she felt the most intense yearning deep within herself. And within him.

She was so hot. And that heat slid in greater waves over her skin as he teased, pulling her closer, closer, closer. Stringing out that searing tension. Tormenting her with his steel-strong body.

Until she could no longer bear it.

Until she lifted her chin.

Until her lips broke apart as she gasped in defeat.

Until in hunger she pressed her mouth to his.

He instantly moved, wrapping his arms right around her, locking her fast into his embrace. One hand held her core against him, his other swept firmly up her spine, to her neck and into her hair. Tangling there. His lips rubbed over hers, firm and warm and possessive. His tongue teased—a slide across her mouth, then a stroke inside—tasting, taking.

She quivered at the intimacy. Her nerve endings sent excitement hurtling along her veins and deep into her belly. She slid her hands over his shoulders, exploring their breadth before smoothing her palms on the back of his neck, his head. Holding him. She'd dreamt of holding him so many times—but never had she imagined she'd feel as hot as this.

Her breasts were pressed to his chest. She shivered in delight as her taut nipples rubbed against him. Her pulse sprinted. It was too quick, her heart thumping too fast, too hard. She couldn't breathe at all. She didn't want to. She didn't want to break the seal of her lips to his. The moan came from some place buried a mile within her.

Such a long time.

The kiss grew hotter, wetter. So did she.

Her body weakened, strengthened, slid. She wanted to fall to the floor and lock her legs around him. Wanted the weight of him, all of him on her, inside her. Most of all she never wanted it to stop.

He held her close, taking her weight with his large, strong hands. Kissing her the only way a woman should be kissed in France—stroking her tongue with his, nipping her lips. She felt the spasms inside, the precursors to physical ecstasy. It wasn't going to take much—but she wanted it all.

She felt flayed, so hot it felt as if her skin could be peeled from her. It was so much more than a kiss.

Nothing sounded in the room but roughened breathing and the occasional moan pulled from that locked place inside her. It threatened to burst out of her completely. He pulled her closer, crushing her against him. Her fingers tightened on him as uncontrollable desire smashed into her. She wanted him. Everything. Now.

'Liam.'

He broke away, his head snapping back with a violent jerk. His eyes went straight to her mouth. 'I've bruised you.'

He hadn't. She liked the kissed-to-full feeling. She wanted more of it. She wanted him to fill her in every way imaginable.

His eyes were wild and wide, but his face was surprisingly pale. He coughed. 'I'm leaving now.' His breath came fast and uneven.

'Okay.' Her wits were completely scattered. And it wasn't okay. She didn't want him to go.

He cleared his throat. 'You have to work.'

Work? Oh, yeah. She did. 'Okay.'

'So I need to go. Because if I don't go now...' He looked at her.

'Okay.'

'Victoria?'

'Okay.' She just sat where she was, landing on her miserable, single bed. Her legs felt wobbly, her brain fried.

He hunched down in front of her and looked into her face. 'Okay if I stay or okay if I go?'

She stared at him. Then her glance slid past, to her

table—and she remembered all the ink and pens and pretty card she had to spend hours over.

'I'm going to go,' he repeated roughly, standing.

She looked back at him—encountering his long, strong, legs. 'Okay.'

Cold descended on her. If he hadn't made that decision, if he hadn't pulled back, she'd be beneath him right now and not caring at all about the deadline hurtling towards her. Well, not 'til she'd come floating back to earth.

Then she'd feel bad.

'Your timing is so lousy,' she said softly. 'It always was.'

He whirled away, scooping up her small bag from where she'd slung it on a chair when they'd first got in.

'What are you doing?' she asked.

He'd unzipped the bag and pulled out her phone. Now he tapped the screen. 'If you don't want people playing with this, you should put a password lock on it.'

'That slows me down.'

'And you don't like to go slow?' A whisper of a chuckle. 'We're not so different, you and me.' He tapped the screen a few more times, then walked closer, stretching out his arm to hand her the phone but staying well out of touch zone.

She took it, watching his face but unable to determine a thing.

He looked back at her. With a small sigh he took one step closer and ran a finger along her lower lip. 'I'll be in touch.'

'Okay.' Victoria tossed the phone onto the bed before she dropped it from her trembling fingers. How was she supposed to work now? How could she possibly hold her pen with a steady hand? She clenched her fists.

He'd gone already. The door banged, she could vaguely

hear the thuds as he headed down the kazillion steps. And what was she doing sitting here like a lemming?

All she'd been able to say was okay. Okay, okay, okay.

She punched the jelly feeling from her legs and stood. She was as pathetic as she'd been all those years before. So meekly acquiescent. All her progress had been obliterated in less than a minute. From what—some kissing? To just swoon in his arms and say *okay*? It was beyond pathetic.

Why hadn't she shoved him away and said enough? Or, given she'd really wanted it, why not haul him close and have him completely? What was with the passivity? Why had she let him make the decision for her?

She *wasn't* the malleable, eager-to-please girl she'd once been. She couldn't revert to that type. She had more focus and strength than that now. But that weak part of her whimpered—*so good*. It had been *so good*.

Fantasy, she told herself. Just fantasy. Even though she'd blocked him from the forefront of her brain, she'd built him up. Finally being in his arms, it was sensory overload. Anyway, it had been so long since she kissed a man. Over a year. Maybe it wasn't *him*; maybe it was hormones? Her body saying she needed to get out more, score herself something of a social life?

Or just score.

She closed her eyes and pulled on some strength. She'd work. She'd fake it. That was what she did these days. She'd get this work done. Then she'd find a love life.

And she'd never see Liam Wilson again.

FOUR

———

Cold showers. Many, many, cold showers. Showers to wake her up, showers to keep her awake and—most importantly—cool her down and keep her thoughts from straying into the forbidden hot zone. But that part of her feeling socially deprived needed some happy thoughts, so she mentally planned, listing the nightclubs she'd go to once the job was done. She'd head out on Saturday night when Liam was at that wedding. There'd be hotter looking guys than him at those clubs.

Liam.

Damn, she was thinking about him again. She bent closer to the huge sheet of card in front of her, narrowing her eyes as she prepared to write the next, the forty-fifth, name on the seating plan. She almost had the nib down when her phone rang.

Surprised, she lifted her pen quickly and checked. No blot or mark. Good. She scooped up her phone and put on her 'professional' voice.

'Victoria Rutherford Design.'

'How many have you done?'

She squeezed the phone hard so it wouldn't slip from

her fingers. Her heart squeezed harder. He'd always been an early riser and even over the scratchy connection she could hear his smile. 'Pardon?'

'Names on the table plan. How many?'

'A few.' Not enough.

'How many?'

'Who do you think you are?' she said, trying to recapture some smarts. 'I don't have to report to you.'

He chuckled. 'You never used to argue back. I remember you used to do everything anyone asked of you. Obedient and unquestioning. Eager to please.'

Victoria braced herself against the subtle suggestion in his last sentence. She hadn't done what he'd asked her to. But she was hardly going to remind him of that. 'Yeah, well, I've grown up a bit since then.'

She only did what others asked of her now if she wanted to. Like this work for Aurelie. Ultimately it was Victoria's choice. But she knew part of her was still eager to please. She'd been so weak in Liam's arms last night. If he'd asked she'd have done everything, and let him do anything. She'd wanted to please—and be pleased.

Not going to happen. Not with him. Not at this time.

She straightened up from bending over her desk and twisted from side to side to ease the kinks and literally strengthen her spine.

'Do some stretches,' he instructed.

She froze. 'Pardon?'

'You'll get stiff if you don't take regular breaks. Walk around the room while you're talking to me.'

She immediately bent back over her desk. 'I just told you I don't do everything anyone asks of me now.'

'But this is for your own good.' His amusement sounded louder. 'Don't take the independence thing too far. Just

because it's not you but someone else who suggests something doesn't automatically make it a bad idea.'

Victoria tried to stiffen, to resist the sound of his smile.
Him calling her like this was *not* good for her. 'You don't
need to do this, you know.'

'Do what?'

'Act like you're interested.'

'Victoria,' he chuckled. 'It's no act.'

Yeah, but it was only the one thing he was interested
in. One thing, one night. He couldn't have made it clearer.
'Well—' she gritted her teeth '—*I'm* only *interested* in finishing my job. And I need to get back to it now.'

She ended the call, afraid that if she didn't she'd say
something she shouldn't. She drew in a deep breath and
pushed it out in a sharp, frustrated sigh. She didn't want
him to phone and distract her. Yet part of her was glad
he had. That part of her wanted him to think of her. To
want her.

Because she still wanted him.

Fool.

She mocked herself. She wasn't going to act on it. Instead she looked at the board.

One letter at a time.

Three hours later her phone rang again.

'Time for another break,' he said before she'd finished
giving her name.

She pressed a fist to her chest, as if the pressure could
settle her skipping heart. 'What makes you think I haven't
been taking regular breaks already?'

'I know the lengths you'll go to, to keep someone happy.
I remember you staying up almost the whole night to
make enough streamers for Oliver's mother to hang in
the hallway.'

Oh, Lord. Victoria chuckled. She remembered that. The endless rolls of crêpe paper had nearly killed her. In the end Liam had come and helped her. He and Oliver and the others had gone down to the local pub for a few. Victoria had opted to stay and help. She'd needed some space from the stranger who made her feel so self-conscious with the way he watched her, teased her, tempted her.

The boys had got home late. Oliver had staggered straight up the stairs to his bed, drunk. Liam hadn't. He hadn't been drunk. He hadn't left.

Victoria had determinedly kept on going with the darn decorations, trying to pretend he wasn't there. But Liam hadn't let her. He'd chatted—easily maintaining a one-sided conversation for the first fifteen minutes, until she'd got over herself and actually giggled. Then it had been a fun tease.

Until she'd tried to move out of the chair. She'd not realised how stiff she'd got sitting still so long, folding ribbons of the thin paper over and over.

That was when Liam had come to help. That was when he'd rubbed her shoulders to ease the ache. That was when he'd stood too close and touched too much and that ache had become a burn.

That was when he'd turned her in his arms and looked at her—

Don't.

Victoria closed her eyes and banished the memories. 'I've learned to take care of myself better now,' she said briskly. 'I even use a timer.'

'So efficient.' The old amusement was audible.

She didn't want to hear that tease. It had always melted her, always made her smile. She should hang up—but she couldn't yet. 'How is your holiday going?'

'It's pretty frustrating.'

'Oh?' Her heart slammed against her ribcage.

'There's no water.'

'Are you drowning on dry land?'

'Pretty much.'

She laughed. 'You get itchy when you're away from the water too long.'

'Yep.'

'Why is that?'

He was silent for a moment and she knew he was actually seriously considering the question. 'It's my home.'

'You're a merman? Mr Atlantis?' she joked lamely.

'It's where I'm free. It's where I can be in control of my own destiny.'

'You can't be in control of your destiny on land like normal people?'

'On land there *are* other people. In my boat, I'm alone.'

Solo sailor. He'd gone for months at a time without seeing anyone as he'd circumnavigated the globe solo. In his team events, he was the captain. Reliant on his crew, yes, but ultimately the one in charge.

'You don't want to have to factor anyone else into your life?'

'I am that selfish, Victoria.' There was none of the tease now, none of the amusement. It was a warning—as loud and clear as a foghorn.

But she didn't know whether to truly believe him. The Liam she'd met five years ago had been fiercely competitive, fiercely determined. But he'd also been helpful. Yes, he'd been on the fringes, watching how Oliver's family—and her family—played out. But he'd helped, he'd wanted to be involved. Was it merely to have something to do?

'Why don't you ask Aurelie if there's something you can do to help her get organised?'

'Not necessary. There's a wedding planner here. She's scary.'

'Scary?' Victoria chuckled. As if Liam would ever be intimidated.

'Seriously scary. Check this out.'

A second later her phone pinged. She swiped the screen and smiled. He'd sent her a picture of the chateau. Uniform-clad minions were busy constructing a big marquee. There were white chairs everywhere. There was one ultra-efficient-looking woman in the middle of it all with clipboard in hand, wireless phone piece in her ear and her hair ruthlessly scraped back. She was very attractive in a headmistress sort of way.

'She's not scary.' Victoria cleared her throat. 'She's gorgeous. And she looks like she's fabulous at her job.'

'She's a robot,' Liam answered shortly. 'And she has everything under control. There's nothing that needs doing.'

'It looks like it's going to be amazing,' Victoria said.

'It will be.' He suddenly sighed. 'So you'd better get back to your writing.'

Victoria held onto the phone for a couple of minutes after he'd rung off. Was his abrupt switch from joke to sigh because of that in-his-face wedding scene? Because of Aurelie?

Her skipping heart ached.

A few hours later Liam couldn't help placing another call just to hear her voice. Over the phone she sounded blood-pumping breathy yet brisk at the same time. Just hearing her got him hard and he couldn't resist it any longer.

'I think you should take twenty minutes and come and

see me,' he said the second she answered. And what he really wanted was to see her *come*.

He'd been deliberately bold the other day. He'd wanted to bait her. Get a reaction from the woman who provoked him to insanity with just a glance. Get her to admit the vibe between them for once.

But he'd done more than provoke. He'd unleashed them both. He'd had to stop when he'd realised she wasn't going to say no. It had nearly killed him to pull back, but it hadn't been the right time. He didn't want either of them to have regrets. But the right time was going to have to be *very* soon.

'Twenty minutes?' Victoria answered in an unimpressed tone. 'That's all you want?'

He grinned. It'd be more like two given the state he was in. And frankly? He'd settle for anything now.

'For the first round,' he amended for form's sake. 'Then we could settle in for the rest of the night.'

'Have you been drinking?'

'You know I don't.' The way his father had drunk? Obliterating reality from his mind? He hadn't been an abusive father in a physical sense, he'd simply been negligent. Never there. Either at the wharf or at the pub, he couldn't have been less interested in his only child. Liam shook off the memory and focused on his much more appealing immediate future. 'Why try to ignore the fact that the genie is out of the bottle?'

She'd said yes the other night. Not in words, but in actions—she was all the way to yes.

'Throw another cliché my way,' she answered snappily. 'That one doesn't work for me.'

He laughed. 'When did you get so tough?'

'I told you, I finally grew up.'

Had she? She'd been so sweet back then, soft and pretty and pleasing. She'd been all things to all people. She'd had to be—her parents had demanded perfection. Liam looked out over the gardens, his eyes narrowing as he wondered about how that whole thing had played out for Victoria. 'How are your parents? Do you see them?'

There was a moment before she answered. 'I see them occasionally.'

Her answer was too diplomatic, too reserved. 'Are they unhappy about you and Oliver?' He pressed the phone closer to his ear, trying to catch the nuances.

'Very.'

Did they blame her? He bet they did.

Oliver had told him that Victoria had a sister who'd left home as a teen. A total rebel who'd fallen in with the kind of people Victoria's family would have nothing to do with. So they'd then had nothing to do with her. The sister had become persona non grata—her name never mentioned, memories of her life expunged from the family home. And then Liam had watched Victoria—seen the way she'd deferred and smiled and obeyed. Too afraid to ever rock the boat. But she'd spoken up with him that first night when she hadn't known who he was. Without fear she'd been a spitfire. In company, she'd been meek. It still annoyed the hell out of him. His annoyance grew at the thought of her parents blaming her for her marriage break-up. But he couldn't resist asking her one last question. 'Do you ever see your sister? Did you ever track her down?'

She'd wanted to. Working late on the crêpe decorations that night, she'd mentioned the sister—and that desire— so briefly after she'd asked about his background. Then they'd both changed the subject.

Now there was silence.

'Victoria?' he prompted.

'Yes, we met up a while ago.'

She spoke too cheerfully.

'Was it okay?'

'It was fine.'

'Are you still in touch?'

'We're very different people. I send her a Christmas card.' Her words came faster and lighter. 'Look, I'd better go now, I'm still behind on where I need to be.'

Two seconds later Liam pocketed his phone and looked at the almost luminous green lawn. Knots turned in his stomach as if he were land-sick. He hurt for her—she was alone and she shouldn't be. He wished it didn't bother him. But it did.

Victoria's phone rang the next morning at five-thirty. So he knew she'd be awake and working already? She answered on the first ring, an unstoppable smile leaping to her lips. 'You must be really bored.'

'I'll come and pick you up. You have to stop for a food break some time.'

'Food? You're going to take me to lunch?'

'I was thinking sooner than that. Breakfast in bed, actually. Good idea, don't you think?'

'You just can't help yourself, can you?'

'No,' he answered. 'I think of you, sex comes too. It's like peaches and cream, cheese and crackers. Victoria and sex—inextricably linked.'

She giggled but a weird disappointment pressed heavy into her chest at the same time. It would only be the once and then he'd disappear from her life again. 'So this is the only reason you're calling me three times a day?'

In the resulting silence her discomfort grew. Because

she *liked* talking to him. She liked laughing with him. But was all this merely a means to an end for him? He was putting in the spade work to get what little he actually wanted?

But she didn't want to sleep with him once and then lose him from her life for ever. She wanted more of *this*. It dawned on her that since the move to France, she'd been lonely. She wanted to laugh more—and she laughed when she talked with him.

'I want you to get this work done,' he finally answered, no smile in his voice this time.

Her work? *That* was what he cared about really? She stopped. Her work was for *Aurelie*. Victoria winced, so glad he couldn't see the mortification staining every inch of her skin red. Of course, he wanted his ex-girlfriend, the woman he'd been with almost three years, to have the wedding of her dreams. He was just passing time flirting with Victoria while keeping an eye that things were on track. A bit of fun, that was all. He didn't mean it— well, okay, he was sexually attracted. But that was all. He didn't want anything more. And his *primary* concern was for his ex. The one he'd liked enough to spend years with, not just one night.

Fair enough.

'Well,' she said, smiling brightly at the telephone so he wouldn't hear how hurt she was. 'I'd better get off and get it finished, then.'

Liam frowned as he slid his phone into the back pocket of his jeans. There was a vibe hurtling along the ether that he couldn't ignore. But she had to get her work done. He couldn't go see her—much as he wanted that breakfast in bed. He wanted Aurelie to have her nice cards and more than that he wanted Victoria to be paid and have her work noticed. He wanted what was best for Victoria.

Truth? He wanted this weekend to be over so he could go to her and finish what they'd started the other night.

She was right; his timing *was* lousy.

He paced. He only had a few days before he was due back on the water but he didn't want to leave until he'd had what he wanted.

He hated himself for that. She didn't want what he wanted. She didn't want him to cheapen whatever she thought this was. But lust *was* all this was, right? Nuclear-hot chemistry. The other night it had exploded. But he'd had to walk—to let her get her work done, to let her cool down from that kiss. Because he didn't want the regrets that a spontaneous, quick tumble would have brought.

Truthfully that insane, insatiable need had taken him by surprise. The overwhelming compulsion to bury himself inside her and stay there had been so sharp he'd run from it. Because Liam never *stayed* anywhere for long. He couldn't. Not for Victoria, not for anyone. She wanted and needed more than he had to offer. He ground his jaw, clenching his muscles—because that desire was still so incredibly strong.

And he'd seen her anxiety before he'd kissed her—the flash of self-consciousness, her admission that it wasn't going to be that good. Oliver had done that to her. He'd betrayed her by going off with another woman. Liam wanted to punch him, as Oliver had once punched him.

Oliver had let her down. Liam wanted to fix it and in that one small way he could. He could give her that relief, restore that confidence in her sensuality.

Bitterly he mocked himself. What, he thought he'd be doing her a *favour*?

He'd told her the truth. He was selfish. All he really wanted was her. Wanted to have her so bad he was almost certifiable.

He changed and went for a run to burn off the energy accruing inside, but he couldn't find his rhythm—couldn't shut his thoughts down. She'd been hurt. Not just by Oliver, but by her parents, her sister. No doubt her friends too. She didn't want to be hurt again.

He couldn't blame her for that.

All he could offer was one night. Nothing more. Was that fair to her?

No.

Calling her so often this week had been a mistake. He'd drop contact completely—go back to the stalemate of the last five years. Some things just weren't meant to be.

FIVE

———

'Good,' the Rottweiler disguised as the wedding planner said to Victoria.

Coming from her, the one word was effusive praise. Thank heavens. It was all Victoria could do not to collapse into the nearest chair and cry in relief.

She'd done it. She'd worked all through the night because she couldn't sleep for thinking about Liam anyway. Work had been a distraction. She'd focused on nothing but and she'd finished it.

He hadn't called again. No more scheduled work breaks and instructions to swing her arms around and flex her fingers to prevent cramp. He'd clocked off. He was probably busy catching up with other, *real* friends who'd arrived for the wedding now. Maybe he'd met another woman. That was fine. Of course it was. Excellent in fact. All she needed to do was get out of here as fast as possible.

'If you would like to, you're welcome to look at the set-up on your way out,' the wedding planner said. 'But, please, no pictures.'

'Of course.'

She couldn't resist a peek. There was no risk. Liam

would be out chatting up some other woman, taking his mind off Aurelie's upcoming marriage. And she needed a walk. She'd been cooped up in her apartment for the last four days.

Outside she turned away from the more formal area where the marquee was set, instead walking into the narrow alleyway that led to a small grotto.

Her heart leapt into her throat when she saw the figure ahead. She swallowed hard, but there was no denying the burst of excitement in her belly.

He walked towards her with that charismatic grace. As if everything was easy for him. She figured it actually was.

'You're helping?' she tried to ask brightly, as if his presence hadn't just sent her senses into overdrive.

He shook his head. 'Nothing for me to do. Everything is sewn up by that wedding planner from hell. She has a legion of minions and doesn't need another.'

Liam was no minion. But he was restless; she could almost see the energy sparking from him.

'I don't think you being here is a good idea,' he said roughly.

'I delivered the dinner seating plan and the last place names,' she said proudly, wanting him to know she'd done it.

'Right here, right now. You shouldn't be here,' he repeated, a frown spreading over his brow.

He didn't want to see her? He was angry with her?

With a muttered growl he took her hand and tugged, twisting her towards the other side of the path. 'They're testing the fountains—you're about to get really wet.'

Too late. As he spoke a whooshing noise all but drowned his words. Suddenly water showered in all directions.

'Oh, it's so pretty.' Victoria stared as light refracted in

the droplets, creating rainbows in the air. She turned to smile at Liam.

One look and she froze.

She'd been spared the soaking. He hadn't.

His white tee bore the brunt and was now drenched on one side. The fabric had gone transparent and clung to his chest. Victoria didn't know where to look. Actually, she did. The chateau and the grounds weren't anywhere as majestic or enthralling any more. All she could see was Liam. Her mouth dried. Her cells shrieked for his touch.

She wanted to murmur his name. It was on the tip of her tongue. The desire to call him closer, to touch him, to tumble in this long alleyway—behind the ornate pillars and symmetrical archways. She wanted to steal the moment she'd always wondered about and explore the chemistry that had always drawn her so compulsively to him. Did it matter that his heart was elsewhere? Wasn't it his body she wanted? But something pulled inside her— stretching to a dull pain.

'Victoria.' A low warning.

She snapped out of it, lifting her hand to brush her hair back and take a moment to recover her equilibrium. 'What?'

'You really ought to go.'

'Am I bothering you?'

'You know you are. And you don't want what I'm offering.'

Actually she didn't know what she wanted any more. But it *was* something more than this. She was heartsore for all they didn't have. 'Why can't we just hang out together? Why can't we just walk through this beautiful garden and catch up like old acquaintances? Why can't we be friendly?'

'Are you that naive?' He glared at her.

'You can be friends with an ex-lover, one you were with on and off for three years,' she pointed out. It hurt. It was stupid, but it hurt. 'But you can't be friends with me? A woman you've kissed once?'

She caught the flare in his eyes as he strode towards her, but she was so taken by surprise at his speed she just stood there as he captured her face between his palms and planted his lips on hers.

Hard.

His body collided with hers a split second later—his taut, fit length sweeping against her so forcefully she grabbed for something to stop herself from falling backwards. She got two fistfuls of tee. No matter that the shirt was wet and the water cold, his skin beneath burned through. It fired her blood as much as the demands of his mouth on hers were.

She pushed back to balance, opening for him at the same time. He took total advantage, his tongue plundering and tasting in total dominance—overwhelming her with the intensity of his passion. But that intensity sparked her own—she found the strength to push back again, twirling her tongue around his, across his lips, into his mouth as she sought to explore him with equal rapaciousness. She felt the low rumble in his chest and he dropped one hand from her face to wind his arm around her waist in a grip that was gargantuan in its strength. She shifted, reaching up to curl her fingers into his hair, eager to clutch him closer and hold him as tight. His wet tee dampened her dress but their skin sizzled. She widened her legs so she could feel him more intimately against her. She loved the sensation of his denim-clad, granite-hard leg between hers and rubbed against him, suddenly wanting the fabric to disintegrate so there would only be sweat and steam and skin.

But as she rocked he suddenly let her go, lifting his hands as if there were a twenty-strong SWAT team aiming their guns on him.

'Now it's twice,' he growled, stepping back to put distance between them with an insulting speed. 'Two times too many. No, we can't be friends. Not until—' He broke off.

Until they'd had sex and this tension would be broken?

Breathless, Victoria watched him. His fury surprised her. His lazy tease had disappeared altogether. All that remained was one lean, hungry, angry man. One she suddenly, instinctively, knew she could push. 'You only want what you can handle?' she taunted, putting her hands on her hips at a provocative angle. 'What's with all these boundaries? Why do you have to be so in control?'

His biceps bunched as he fisted his hands and shoved them into his back pockets. He took in a deep breath, his chest expanding. He stood with his feet wide apart on the grass. His jeans emphasised the length of his legs, the strength, the absolute raw masculinity.

But as he exhaled that mask slid down again—smoothing out the lines of need that edged his mouth. Now it was the smile that returned.

'Women like it when I'm in control,' he drawled.

And that was so not true. Not for her.

That kiss had ignited something in her. Want, yes, but also, like him, anger. Her fury rose to meet his, because this desire was so strong it was irresistible.

For her.

Now his tease—something that usually made her smile—goaded her. Could he really step back so easily?

She saw red—refusing to believe it. Anger propelled her to act like the vamp she'd never been.

'I think I'd like it best if you weren't in control at all.' Deliberately shameless, she stepped towards him, bunching a bit of her dress so more of her thigh was exposed.

The sudden flare in his eyes filled her with sexual confidence. He *did* want her. And she wanted him to want her *badly*.

His mouth compressed, his brows pulled together, his eyes were riveted on her.

'Victoria.' He spoke slowly, his voice spliced with a rough thread. 'Be careful what you wish for.'

Through his wet tee she could clearly see his nipples. Despite the summer heat they were diamond hard. She boldly looked lower to see how the front of his jeans was sitting. Stretched. Yeah, she'd felt that straining erection and she was sure it wasn't going down in a hurry.

She smiled.

He'd walked away so easily the other day. While she was grateful in some ways, she'd also been put out. How had he been able to *think*? How had he found the strength to make such a decision? She wasn't letting that happen again.

Wild excitement burned every one of her doubts to cinders. She took another fateful step forward and fearlessly pressed her pelvis against his jeans, lifting her chin defiantly as she slowly circled against him. She was so taut with need, so tired of fighting it, there was no resisting the urge. She wanted what they'd started the other night. Hot sex?

Yes, please.

His hand clamped on her butt, holding her in place hard against him. She shivered at the fierce, close contact. His eyes hadn't left hers—his were dark, the pupils like black tunnels and she wanted to go the length.

His other hand slowly slid up the back of her thigh, his palm pressing firm but at the same time his fingers massaged her muscles—as if he couldn't help but caress. Hot, tight, yet softening inside, she gazed up at him. His expression seared as he stroked higher up her thigh, stealing up under her skirt—still not high enough. She wanted absolute intimacy. His erection dug into her stomach and twisted her tighter so she leaned right against him, letting him take her weight, letting him feel how pliant and willing she was.

He cupped the curve of her butt with both hands now—one outside her skirt, one underneath. She wanted him to slide his fingers inside her underwear, wanted him to tease her, take her. She'd lie with him on the sweet-smelling grass and satisfy this elemental longing. Here, now. They'd finish it.

But she didn't move more, didn't lift her mouth up to kiss him. She didn't sweep her hands over his chest. She was spellbound, lost in the glittering intensity of his eyes and the banked ferocity within them.

There was so *much* control in him. But it was close to tearing. She wanted it torn. The other day she'd been the one to break. It was his turn and she was waiting for it, holding his fierce gaze with a defiant dare in her own. Something rippled through him—surely not a tremble? A split second later he flinched, every muscle hardening. The spasm hit his hands too—his fingers pinched and he swore.

Victoria gasped but smiled as he thrust against her. Satisfaction surged as he bent his head—a kiss, completion, was only a sigh away.

'Victoria?' A row of trees over, the wedding planner's high-pitched call pierced. 'Has anyone seen the calligrapher? Is she still here?'

Once again Liam's fingers dug into her flesh. He thrust against her in another powerful move before stepping back and releasing her completely. She only just caught her balance.

'Lucky escape,' he ground out through gritted teeth.

Not lucky at all. 'Lia—'

'You want more than this,' he whispered harshly. 'But this is all there is.'

'Victoria?' The wedding planner sounded closer.

'I'm here. Just coming,' Victoria called out.

Well, she would have been. Instead she stood watching Liam stride away from her, from the chateau, his broad hand kneading the back of his neck as he went. Anger apparent in every line of his body.

A thin thread of satisfaction pulled her mouth into a frustrated curve. Yes, he might have wanted her to get Aurelie's work done. He might still hold a torch for Aurelie. But he still wanted *her*, Victoria. And he wanted her a lot.

Who was she kidding to think it had been anything more than sex? What drew them together was fire. Rampaging lust and hormones. Where, for whatever reason, their bodies were feverishly attracted.

It *was* just sex. And wasn't that all she wanted? Just sex. She didn't want another relationship. He most certainly didn't. It didn't fit with his lifestyle. He'd been right to offer the one night. He'd been honest.

She hadn't. She'd been confused. But things couldn't be clearer now.

Did she really want to spend the rest of her life wondering? Was she going to pass up the chance to be with him—even for a short time—a second time?

This wasn't roses and rings and happy ever after. That wasn't in her plan. She wanted to build her company. And she wanted to be like any other normal woman in her twenties. She was free. If she wanted a fling, she could damn well have a fling. He was here for a few days. There'd be no anxiety about seeing him unexpectedly in the future. What better chance did she have of some fun? And of getting rid of this old 'what if' obsession.

Her blood zinged. High on the hit of sensual confidence and assertiveness, she went back into the chateau.

'Is there a problem?' She found the planner.

'Not at all, I wanted to know if you had some business cards on you. I might find them handy.'

Victoria's confidence multiplied more. 'Of course.' She gave the woman a stack, but she couldn't ignore the sizzling sensation in her blood. Not any more.

She went into the marquee, the tables already set for the wedding. She found the card that she'd had to write five times before getting it right—*Liam Wilson*—in that flourishing swirl. She flipped it over to the blank side. And in very ordinary writing, with a ballpoint pen she borrowed from one of the minions, she wrote a bald message.

SIX

————

In the foulest mood imaginable, Liam pulled on his jacket. He'd actually tried to do the right thing. He'd left Victoria to get on with it. She didn't want complication—not even for a night.

Only she'd come onto him in the alleyway of the garden and torn his resolve to bits. She wanted to spend time with him. *Really*? What a horrific joke. Sure, he could text her. Tease her. Talk to her over the phone. But get him into the same airspace as her and all he wanted to do was kiss her. He couldn't see straight for wanting her. Lust in another league from anything he'd ever experienced.

He'd enjoyed his relationship with Aurelie. But in truth most of the time they'd been a couple, they'd been apart. Him competing in one ocean, her surfing in another. It had been convenient and easy and he'd always been able to walk away.

It had nearly killed him to walk away from Victoria in the garden this morning. He didn't like it. He didn't like feeling *tied*. Even if it was only a sexual bond.

He frowned at his reflection. Today his suit gave him a social veneer, but in reality he worked in a competitive, ruthless, isolated world. He was away for weeks, months at a time. The only relationship that could possibly survive that was with one very tough chick. Victoria wasn't anywhere near tough enough. He feared he'd tangle up her emotions. He knew he'd done that to Aurelie for a while— by taking what he wanted and not giving her enough. It eased his guilt, and pleased him, that she'd gone on to find what she needed with another, better man. Love— and that security and grounding.

Liam didn't do grounding. Liam did freedom—sailing fast over the water. He didn't want to feel as trapped as he had all his childhood. All he'd ever wanted to do was sail and keep on sailing. It wasn't a family gig. It wasn't a safe gig. And he didn't want to be dependent on anyone else. He liked to be alone. Just like his father. They were not family men. He wasn't having a kid only to ignore him the way his father had ignored him. And he would, because being on the water was the most important thing to him.

Victoria had always tried to give all of herself to everyone else—doing what she thought she had to to keep their affection. She had needs he couldn't meet. She'd be unfulfilled. And more importantly, she knew what she wanted now and she was going for it and he wasn't going to get in her way.

But he still wanted. And so did she. She'd wanted him back then—he'd seen it written all over her face. There was the irony. To anyone who'd bothered to look, her emotions were obvious. It was just that Oliver hadn't looked— not hard enough. Nor had her parents.

Oliver had cared more about himself than he did about her. And as a result her confidence had been crushed. She'd got less than she deserved.

But *Liam* too was so much less than she deserved. He

couldn't give her the security he believed she still wanted. She'd been hurt already. Any kind of a relationship with him would see her hurt again.

But he could give her physical pleasure. He could show her. He ached all over wanting to give her that. He snorted at his own arrogance. So shallow. The best thing he'd done was shut it down and walk away.

Two hours later he watched Aurelie and Marcus exchange vows and wondered about Victoria's wedding. How had she looked on that day? His stomach cramped. He'd never been able to imagine it. He'd avoided all mention of it amongst his friends of the time, certainly avoided any pictures.

Now jealousy of that past wedding boiled in his gut. He really needed to sort his head out. He'd go back to the coast early and train hard.

He followed the other guests through to where the tables were set, the silverware gleaming in the candlelight. Her calligraphy marked each guest's place. It was overwhelmingly romantic. He sat and picked up the card bearing his name. Victoria's letters were pretty and polite and flourishing. He ran his thumb along the edge of the card and then flipped it over. He suddenly felt as if he'd been shot straight into the sun. What was written on the back was penned by the same hand, but the flourishing swirls were absent.

One night. Tonight. Everything. Agreed? V.

Victoria poured herself a glass of wine. So much for hitting the club scene and finding a social life. Or even a sex life. She didn't get dressed up, she stayed in her old shorts and work tee with a thin cotton robe over the top and sorted her desk. She had a new project, she'd get on with that—forget the past and take on the future. But she couldn't help wondering what Liam was thinking as he watched Aurelie say her vows to another man. Victoria's stomach twisted. How hard that must be. She shouldn't have left him that message. As if he'd want to see that at Aurelie's wedding? What had she been thinking?

And she'd not heard from him. What if someone at the table read it? They wouldn't understand it, right? Good thing she'd only left her initial, not her full name.

Mad with her idiocy and annoyingly one-track thoughts, she pulled her hair into a ponytail and gathered the materials needed for the two-day job that she had all of the next week to do. But she needed to keep busy tonight. She'd keep very, very busy.

Forcing concentration took huge effort. She took her watch off, put her phone in a drawer in the bathroom, put her favourite song on replay and wouldn't let herself move from her desk. For hours.

Eventually she settled into it. For this project she needed to be extra precise and neat. It was just what she needed.

The thud on her apartment door who-knew-how-long later killed her heart. Three seconds later it started beating back at a frenetic pace that had her breathless. She stood, glancing out of the window as she did. It was still reasonably light, not that late into the evening at all. So it wouldn't be Liam. The wedding party would only be starting.

Whoever it was pounded on her door again just as she got to it. She opened it, took one look at him and had to lean against the jamb because her legs went so weak. Tuxedos made any man look good; the effect on Liam was mind-blowing.

'It's early.' She sounded as if she hadn't spoken in years.

'You thought I'd stay there when you left me this?' He lifted his hand, flipping the place card in his fingers.

'I didn't mean for you to miss the party.'

He gazed at her, his expression dark. 'I'm not.'

'How was the wedding?' she asked, suddenly nervous about his answer.

'Beautiful.'

She bit the inside of her lip—anything could be read into the way he'd said that. And suddenly she needed to know exactly what he was feeling. 'Do you still love her?'

Liam put his hand flat against her belly and gave her a little push so she stepped backwards. He followed and then carefully closed the door behind him. Only then did he turn and face her. 'There's a part of me that will always love Aurelie.'

Victoria pressed her lips together, trying to stay strong and not let that stupid, unwonted hurt at his words show.

'She was as different from you as I could get,' he said. 'It should have been the perfect set-up. She was busy with her career, happy to let me get on with mine. We met up whenever our schedules let us. It was fun—and carefree. I thought it was all I needed and all she wanted. But she became unhappier, wanted more. Then one day she called to say she'd met Marcus. I wasn't heartbroken—in fact I was happy. We were more friends than we were lovers. And I'm happy to see her so happy. I'm not hurt.'

Victoria released the breath she'd been holding—the blockage in her throat eased. 'For what it's worth, I think she's crazy to marry someone else.'

Her words dropped between them—leaving a sudden

silence in their wake. She bit her lip, holding back from admitting more.

'I couldn't watch you marry him.' His voice was so soft it was almost a slur.

Victoria's breathing quickened as she tried to hold back the emotional storm building inside her. This wasn't supposed to go this way. They should be in a tumble already. 'Because you knew I was making a mistake.' It wasn't because her marrying Oliver had hurt Liam. Not really.

'You both were. You weren't the right woman for Oliver.' Like a statue, he remained a few feet from her. But his soft words carried as clear as the sound of a glass shattering on a stone floor. 'Why didn't it work out?'

'You know why,' she said simply. 'That I even looked at you?'

'So why did you say yes?'

'How could I say no to him? How could I humiliate him in front of everyone? And I wanted to please him, to please all of them...' She swallowed. 'They cast Stella out. She became nothing to them. I didn't think I could cope with being nothing. Having no one.'

He stepped forward, his eyes not leaving her face. 'Would that have happened?'

It had happened—almost. While she wasn't as shunned by her parents as Stella was, it wasn't far off. The relationship was icy; they disapproved of her current choices. Blamed her.

'He was supposed to have been the safe bet,' she answered in a sad whisper. But he was human. As much as she.

'I'm sorry,' Liam said.

'Don't be.' She smiled. 'I learned lots. And I like this

me better than the old me.' She had some backbone now. She had her plans.

'He was an idiot.' Liam's expression clouded. 'I'd never have done that to you. Never would.'

'No.' She actually managed a laugh. 'You'd never have married me in the first place. You'll never marry anyone.'

His lashes dropped. 'You're right.' He lifted his head and intently looked at her again. 'But I'd never cheat on you.'

She believed him. He had honour. All those years ago he had wanted, he had asked, but ultimately he had resisted. There was no real reason to resist now. She touched her tongue to her lips, her mouth dry. She wanted this conversation to be over. She wanted what she'd always wanted from him.

Touch.

He stepped closer still and she felt his magnetism pulling—urging her to move nearer too. But he still didn't reach for her.

'Why now?' he asked.

'I don't want to make the same mistake.' The mistake had been *not* saying yes to him.

'Are you sure?'

'You wouldn't be here if I wasn't.'

'I thought you didn't do one-night stands?'

'I can't fight it any more.' She lifted her shoulders. 'It's what I want.' She wanted to be released from the passion that imprisoned her—that made her think of nothing and no one else.

He looked at her—his gaze lifting to her hair and then down her body. That old smile tugged one corner of his mouth.

'What have you been doing?' He lifted a finger and pressed it against her forehead and then pulled it away and held it in front of her eyes. A sparkle of gold glinted on his finger.

She wiped her forehead herself and looked at her fingers, grimacing wryly when she saw more of the sparkles on her hand. 'I've been working on a poem for an anniversary. Using gold leaf.'

'What anniversary?'

'Fiftieth—the golden.'

'Wow.' He nodded.

'Yeah.' She smiled. 'It's a lovely poem too.'

'You're not tired from Aurelie's work?'

Of course she was.

His smile quirked. 'You're a gold-flecked angel.'

'I'm not that much of an angel.'

He traced the spots of gold on her face with his finger and then leant forward, pressing his lips to each marking. 'You're gilded.'

Victoria shivered and took a step back. She hadn't expected such tenderness and didn't know if she could handle it. She wanted fast, furious passion—care*free*, right? 'You're just feeling soppy because you've been to a wedding.' She reached for his belt buckle, her intention clear. 'Enough talking.'

'No.' He grabbed her wrists and pulled them away, locking them behind her back. It forced her chest right into his so she wasn't exactly disappointed. But why was he saying *no*?

His gold-flecked brown eyes drilled into hers. 'I've wanted this for a long time and even though we have only one night, I'm not going to have it over in five seconds. I'm not going to just strip you and screw you and walk out the door two minutes later.'

She swallowed, sure he could feel her heart pounding against him.

'I'm going to take my time and I'm going to savour every second I have. Don't plan on sleeping any tonight.'

Oh.

He didn't take his eyes off her and she couldn't drag hers away, not when his eyes were deepening so quickly—and inviting. 'Is that a problem?'

She shook her head, unable to make a sound.

He released her wrists, lifting his hand to cup her jaw. 'Why have you changed your mind?'

'I think I was wrong and you were right,' she whispered. 'This is…passion.' She chose her word carefully. 'And I think it needs to be dealt with.'

'You think you can deal with me?'

That old arrogance brought back her smile. 'I think for one night. Yes. I can deal with you.' She had to.

His eyes flicked to her hair. The way he looked at her made her so hot. She wasn't sure she was going to be able to go slow and savour; she thought she might incinerate first. She needed to cool off. And suddenly she was conscious of the ratty shorts and tee she had on—and the even rattier cotton robe she'd shrugged on as the evening cooled. 'I was going to shower.'

'Later,' he said, his voice husky.

His fingers traced over her skin—her jaw, down her neck—causing her to shiver even though she was hotter than she'd been in her life. She drew in a deep breath and shifted her feet—*so* restless.

'Slow,' he reminded her with a smile.

'I don't want slow.'

He kissed her neck, his teeth giving her a scrape before his tongue and lips soothed the sensitive spot. 'Yes, you do.'

Frankly she wasn't going to be able to do slow if he kept touching her like this. She was embarrassingly turned on already, suddenly desperate for him to be inside her. She wanted that intimacy—and that orgasm—right this second. She inhaled deeply and stepped back. 'Let me undress you.'

His eyes widened.

'I want to. I have to. Otherwise...' She trailed off.

'Okay,' he answered. 'If that's what you want.'

She wanted so many things, but doing this first might help her settle into it.

She started with his jacket, working one sleeve and then the other. He bent his head as she passed in front of him, briefly brushing a kiss on her jaw. She glanced up at him and smiled but said nothing. Slowly she undid the buttons on his shirt and opened it to reveal his chest. Sleek, hewn muscles, smooth strength. The kind of definition that was only built from daily training. And sweat.

Yeah, the guy was fit. So fine.

She hadn't realised she was holding her breath and she released it now in a harsh sigh. He was silent now too but his chest rose and fell a little faster than it had before. His belt was leather and soft and her fingers struggled to work the fastenings. But he didn't offer to help and she was glad. She wanted to do it all, discover it all.

She dropped to her haunches as she pulled his trousers down. He wore clinging black boxers beneath, fortunately made from that stretchy stuff as they were straining now. She slid her hands into the waistband. She pulled out the elastic, sweeping the boxers wide past his erection and down his muscled thighs. He stepped out of them. On

her knees she glanced back up at him—practically agog
at the magnificence of him.

'Now you're the one overdressed,' he said roughly.

She didn't care. She just wanted to put her mouth on
him.

But he drew in a hissing breath and stepped forward,
bending to haul her to her feet.

'My turn.' He didn't smile. He looked tense.

He pulled the belt of her robe right through until he'd
tugged it completely free. She glanced at the length hanging in his hand. 'What do you plan to do with that?'

'I know how to tie knots.'

'Yeah.' She knew that; he'd had her in knots for a long
time now.

But he tossed the belt to the side. 'This time, I want to
feel your hands on me.'

But another time he wanted to tie her up?

'Ditto.' She glanced at the belt. 'But just so you know,
I know how to tie some knots too.'

'I'm sure you do.' He stepped closer and took the hem
of her tee in his hands. His fingers were trembling. She
didn't think he could fake that.

In a second her shirt was over her head and had landed
somewhere on the floor. She wasn't wearing a bra—often
didn't at home. So now her painfully tight nipples were
bared and screaming out for his touch.

He'd frozen—staring at her. She put her hands to the
fastening of her shorts—that got him moving.

'No.' He put one hand over hers and pushed them out
of the way.

He undid the button and slipped her shorts down.
Then, so slowly, he slipped her thin knickers down too.

She stepped out of them both. For a fleeting moment

she was surprised she wasn't more self-conscious. But how could she be when he was on his knees looking up at her like that? He reached out, putting strong hands on her legs—one just above each knee. She stilled, her legs parted.

'You're even more beautiful than—' He stopped, suddenly pressing close, his tongue swiping over her. She cried out and bent forward to put her hands on his shoulders for balance. Instinctively she pressed her hips close to him again.

It wouldn't take much for her to orgasm. Another touch? It was crazy how close she was just from being stripped by him. But suddenly she didn't want that—to come in a nanosecond. He was right to want to take this slow—to savour it. To indulge *fully* and finally complete what had been started so long ago. But she wouldn't feel as if it was complete until—unless—he was right there with her, every step of the way.

She wanted him to feel this as strongly as she was.

'I want to come when you're inside me,' she said in a quavery voice. 'When you come too.'

His hands tightened on her legs as he lifted his chin, kissing her right there again. But then he stood, wrapping his arms around her and drawing her close.

'I'm not entering you until you've come.'

She blinked. 'What?'

'You heard.'

She snapped her spine and tilted her chin to look into his eyes. 'Well, I'm not coming until you're in me and on your way yourself.'

A smile stretched across his face. 'Gonna be a fun night, isn't it?'

She rose onto tiptoe and kissed him—openmouthed,

wet, demanding. He shifted, widening his stance so he could keep them upright as she thrust against him, pushing her weight onto him. She could feel his erection slammed against her belly. She felt the way he kissed her back—as hot, as hungry, his hands sliding over her body, touching every part of her.

She smiled. So much for slow.

He lifted his head; his own smile was wicked. He kissed her again and his hands went to her breasts. She gasped at the touch. He didn't dive straight for her nipples, instead he cupped the full weight of her breasts, gently pushing, fingers circling. She felt the tug deep inside as he kissed her again. The guy had the most incredible sense of rhythm—sweet, carnal torment.

Suddenly she couldn't stand any more. Literally. He caught her as her knees sagged and he lifted her to her hideously narrow bed. She breathed out in relief, her legs parting, holding her arms out to him as he knelt over her.

But he didn't put his weight on her, didn't line up his pelvis with hers the way she really wanted. Instead he put his mouth and hands to work in tandem again—repeatedly, rhythmically sweeping over her until she was hot and writhing and so *ready*. She arched her hips, thrusting them against him again and again.

'Liam,' she begged. *'Please.'*

He leaned back on his arms to look into her face. 'I've always wanted you,' he said, his expression strained. 'Always wanted this.'

'Me too,' she confessed shamelessly. 'Please, please, *please* get on with it.'

To her immense relief, he left her, efficiently scooping his trousers from the floor and pulling a new pack of condoms from his pocket. A minute later she heard the snap as he sheathed himself.

She lay back on the bed and spread her legs in welcome. But he wrapped a hand around her ankle and started all over again—kissing from her toes, all the way up the length of her leg. It was torture. But it was bliss.

Why had she thought this wouldn't be a good idea? This was the best idea she'd ever had. She writhed beneath him, almost in tears, almost laughing, and totally furious that he could still hold back from plunging into her. She rolled, deciding to take matters into her own hands—to mount him and initiate the ride herself.

He let her on top—but he didn't let her slide onto him. Instead he laughed and caught her hips, using his insane, superior strength to keep her in place just above him. But still he didn't penetrate.

'Tease,' she groaned.

'Not 'til you come first.'

She closed her eyes. 'Not without you inside me.'

He laughed. 'Then we're at a stalemate.' He bent his knees and slid down the bed while lifting her so she remained in place—now higher above him.

'You know how much I like to win,' he muttered, lifting his hands to palm her breasts again. 'I'll do whatever it takes to win.'

He shifted a little more so he could kiss her right where she needed him to. His tongue swept into her.

She cried out, her head falling back at the extreme intimacy. 'Liam.'

'Come on me,' he muttered. He licked again and then fastened his lips around her clitoris and sucked.

Her thighs quivered and she pressed her fists onto her knees. He reached up, filling his hands with her breasts.

She breathed hard, knowing there was no way she could beat him at this.

'If I come...' she panted.

'Yes.' He broke the rhythm of his tongue for only a split second to answer.

'If...' She couldn't get it out.

'Yes.' He manipulated her breasts more—perfectly in time to the sweeps of his lips and tongue.

'I...'

'Yes.'

'Oh—yes!' She shuddered as the orgasm hit. Unstoppable. Delightful. Her prolonged groan escaped through gritted teeth.

A satisfied sound rumbled from his throat as he kept tormenting her, so the waves of pleasure kept rippling through her in intense contractions.

She gasped, panting for breath. '*Please.*'

He released her and she slid, bumping her head on the wall as she tumbled to the side of him.

'Careful.' He pulled her into his arms, moving to slide her beneath him, but her stupid bed was too small.

They gave up on it, falling to the floor in a tight embrace. Victoria felt consumed by fire. Hooking her legs around his body. Her hands knotted in his short hair.

He looked down at her. His eyes gleamed. Wide, focused. *Desperate.*

A sense of power filled Victoria. 'Now,' she commanded.

Immediately he bore down on her, driving so deep it almost hurt. And it was so incredibly good she wanted more. She arched, urging. He pulled back and pushed into her again. Again. She grunted as she took the brunt of each powerful thrust.

'Okay?' he asked, his face creasing in agony as he paused.

'Don't stop,' she begged, grabbing his butt in her hands and squeezing to push him closer. 'More...' She groaned again. '*All*.'

He resumed his punishing, perfect rhythm. She wound her limbs round him and just hung on. She couldn't stop the feral moans as he ground into her, closer and closer with every pounding motion.

'Liam!' She screamed as she was tossed into the intense waves of pleasure. Her nails dug into his shoulders, her heels into his lower back.

He roared. His body stiffened, his hands gripping her hard and painfully tight as he shouted again as the tension mirrored in him was released just as violently.

A long moment later he lifted his head from where he was slumped over her. 'Don't go to sleep.'

In answer she tightened her grip on him so he couldn't lift away from her. She didn't think she'd ever sleep again. Every cell and nerve in her body was so wired she didn't think they'd ever calm enough for sleep to claim them. She was so hypersensitive she was afraid she might cry. She really didn't want to do that.

He lifted his head again and looked at her—nose to nose. 'I'm starving—you?'

His easy return to reality made her laugh. Relief swept through her as she relaxed. 'You didn't eat at the wedding?'

'Funnily enough I didn't feel like eating much after I got your message. Too tense. I couldn't wait to get out of there.'

His honesty kept her smile wide. 'Well, I'm sorry to disappoint you but there's nothing in the pantry.'

He rose up from the floor and walked over to the kitch-
enette area of her studio. He opened the one cupboard and
sighed. 'That's because you don't have a pantry, you have
a shelf. But—' he turned and winked at her '—you'll be
amazed what I can conjure out of nothing.'

'Really?'

He nodded. 'I've come up with some desperate options
in my time. Bet you've never had frozen-pea sandwiches
the way I make 'em.'

'Nice.' She laughed but her heart tugged at the same
time.

But he was laughing easily. 'Especially with stale bread.'

In the end he found some rice and cooked it up with
the few vegetables he found lurking in her fridge. They
had some almond biscuits for afters. It was an odd meal
for one in the morning. She didn't want to sleep. Didn't
want to miss a minute.

She watched him as he ate, wondered how many dinners he'd thrown together out of limited supplies in isolation. 'You don't get lonely when you're alone at sea for
so long?'

'No. I've always been alone. That's the way it is.'

'But you wanted to join in that family Christmas.' She'd
felt that longing in him. She'd recognised it because, if she
was honest, it was echoed within herself.

'I was trying to be a good guest. Helpful.' He winked.
'And I wanted to be near you.'

It wasn't just her.

Liam picked up the belt from her robe and wound it
round his hands, then unwound it. Now he'd refuelled,
he was ready to have every inch of Victoria all over again.
He'd glanced at the clock on the computer and felt a surge

of panic. One night didn't seem so long at all this side of midnight.

'What are you planning to do with that?'

He smiled as he heard excitement tinge her not-quite-innocent question. 'Play with you.'

'Only if I get to do the same to you.'

'Sure. After me.' He turned to look at her.

Gold leaf still glittered on her body, but it was nothing on the glitter in her eyes.

She'd switched her lamp on to partially light the room. The beam from the bulb highlighted a patch on her thigh. He reckoned he'd start there.

'Why do you want to tie me up?' she asked as she offered her wrists for him to bind to the headboard of her bed. That she trusted him so implicitly gave him an immense kick of satisfaction. That she was so willing to be so physically intimate with him. Finally.

'I want to explore you without distraction,' he answered honestly. He wanted to caress every curve, every inch of her skin. 'It's hard to keep control when you have your hands on me.'

He wanted to give her pleasure again and again. To discover her body, her secrets. To understand what it was she liked. Never had he wanted to please a lover more. And that competitive part of him wanted to ensure he was the best she'd ever had.

She shifted—experimentally moving her legs. But she was smiling as he bent over her. 'So I nearly won, then?'

If he was honest, she'd won everything.

'You okay?' He checked again long minutes later as he finally did as she was begging and worked his fingers into her, his thumb circling over her most sensitive spot until she came wet, hot, screaming.

'I'm so doing this to you,' she panted.

'Soon.' He was pushing her over the edge again first.

It was over an hour later when he let her tether his wrists. She smiled at him with such wicked intent he was hard again in a second.

She swept her hands over him, looking at him as if he were something she'd wanted to toy with—and devour—since for ever. She bent over his body—kissing, caressing every bit of him with her hands, her lips, her hair. When she licked her lips and her gaze zeroed in on his erection he knew he was in trouble.

'Victoria.' Part of him wanted her to do it so much, but he also wanted to come inside her again.

But in the end he had no choice. She sucked him so hard, her hands working in tandem, there was no way he could hold back. No way he could resist diving head-first into the generous, seductive attention she was gifting him.

She didn't untie him after—even though he was as limp as a dishrag. Dazed, he lifted his head with a huge effort as she slipped away from the bed.

'Victoria?'

A couple of minutes later she came back to him. She had a fountain pen in her hand.

'What are you doing?' he asked lazily.

'You're missing something all sailors have.' She carefully touched the nib of the pen to his chest.

'What's that?' He twitched at the tickling sensation.

'A tattoo.' She chuckled. 'A heart with 'mother' or something across it.'

He flinched.

'Perhaps not 'mother',' she said quietly and lifted the pen from him.

'It'd be okay,' he said, feigning ease. 'She died when I was very small.'

'I'm sorry.'

'It was a long time ago.' The pen tickled him some more.

'Did your father find anyone else?'

'No. He was a rough man. A stevedore who loaded and offloaded ships. He worked hard, drank hard. Frankly he stank. He didn't have a lot about him to attract another woman.' Except for the ones he paid for.

'So what did you do?'

'Found boats and sailed on them. As often as I could.'

He'd skipped school to sail. Until he'd become so good the schools had come to him wanting him to sail. Scholarships. Performance.

She ran a line down the side of his stomach. He flinched again because it tickled so much. She laughed softly as she dipped the pen in the well again and turned back to him. 'Your abs are amazing.'

He grimaced. 'I'm glad you appreciate them. They don't come easy.'

'Oh, I appreciate them.' She blew, drying the ink.

'Don't put that any lower,' he warned.

She laughed again. 'You don't want me to ink—'

'No, I do not.' He wondered what she'd written. But he wanted to feel her some more first. She clearly ached for more too, as suddenly she tossed the pen and straddled him.

'Release me.' He needed to hold her now—was desperate not just to cup her breasts and stroke her to ecstasy, but to embrace her. He wanted to hold her close. She still had gold leaf in spots over her skin and in her hair. His gilded, branded lover.

She slid off him and reached forward to untie the

knots. On her way back down, she writhed her hips, teasing, freely expressing her enjoyment of him—of his touch, of his body. He shifted again—so his aching need was hard against her lush, wet heat. He arched up into her again and watched the burst of rapture on her face. He inhaled deeply, holding back the urge to dive into the mindless, exquisite release. Not yet.

She pushed on him, levering so she could ride him tighter. He rested his hands on her thighs, letting her. Until he felt her tiring—yet desperate.

'Liam.' Her call came, broken, needy.

He slid his hands higher, cupping her butt and supporting her as he thrust upwards, maintaining her tempo, then pushing it further, faster.

She cried out—pleasure bursting in brief phrases and then moans as words could no longer be formed. He watched the deepening flush and glow of her skin, the red, tight nipples, even redder plump lips and the wild, big eyes.

This was the Victoria he'd wanted—the one he'd caught a glimpse of all those years ago. The lusty, pleasure-bent, hungry woman who'd take what she wanted. Not aiming to please him—but taking pleasure, enjoying herself. Able to give so much—yes. But also able to receive. The woman made for loving.

It satisfied him immensely that she was open, receiving pleasure from *him*. He arched, his spine stiffening as he realised how much he wanted to give her. Passion rushed in his ears as a piercing cry broke from her. He saw it as she shuddered, bearing down on him as the convulsions racked through her body. And he felt it as she collapsed forward, lax in his arms, blanketing him with her soft warmth.

He wrapped both arms around her, gripping her shoulders hard, his forearms pressing down on her back so she was squashed even tighter against him as he finally allowed himself to come.

He found he liked the tiny bed after all. The only way for them to fit on it was if they were locked together, either side-by-side or with one on top of the other.

Mid-morning he fell asleep like that. Still inside her.

SEVEN

———

Sweat had smudged the ink—the words she'd drawn on him, mingled in a mess of blue on both their skins. Liam stood in the shower behind Victoria who had her eyes closed as she rinsed frothy shampoo from her hair. While she did, he scrubbed at the ink with the palm of his hand. He could still see the anchor on his hip.

Stupid to be so bugged by such a common, naval theme. A million guys out there had tattoos just like it. There was no underlying meaning in that symbol. Yet, impossibly, he felt bound—just by the play of last night.

He didn't want to be weighed down. He didn't want permanent ties. Nothing anchoring him—not any one place. Not any one person.

Suddenly a flannel-filled hand pushed his out of the way and tried to scour away the image.

'It's fine.' He grabbed her wrist, uncomfortable that she'd noticed his attempt to wash it away.

'It clearly bothers you.'

He automatically released her on hearing that cold edge

to her voice. He made himself meet her eyes. 'We want different things.'

'Not so different.' An almost-smile twisted her lips. 'Your career is everything to you. So mine is to me. But they're not compatible. *We're* not compatible.'

Except physically. They were *so* compatible there. But that wasn't enough. 'I've stayed too long already.'

One night was all he'd offered her. All he *could* offer her. Yet here it was, late in the day already. He'd not been able to drag himself from her bed and body. The second night was already approaching.

'Yes.'

He hated that she agreed with him. Stupid to feel rejected all over again, as he had those years ago. Even though this was what they'd agreed—what *he'd* insisted on. 'We can't do more than this,' he repeated.

'No.' She glanced at the ink mark again. 'Some turps might help with that. Or nail-polish remover.'

'It's fine. It'll wear off.' Just as this gnawing ache to be near her would wear off.

This was the right decision. They did want different things, in different places. But he didn't like that remote look on her face. He drew her close under the streaming water and kissed her until she relaxed against him. Until she took him one last time.

He left the shower first, needing to recover alone, resenting the power of this pull towards her. He had to run.

Victoria wrapped a giant towel around her. She wanted him to leave. There was nothing she could do or say to make him change his mind and she didn't want to try. A reluctant boyfriend was not what she wanted. She didn't want a boyfriend at all. So it was fine.

When she emerged from the bathroom he was already

dressed, lingering by the door, looking more uncomfortable than she'd ever seen him.

'It's okay, Liam,' she lied.

He tugged at his creased jacket. 'You know it was better than I'd ever believed it could be.'

She looked away. 'But not enough for either of us.' And she'd been a fool. She'd been wrong. This was more than sex. So much more. But only for her. And it wasn't enough to change things for him.

'I'm sorry,' he said.

She put on an unconcerned smile. 'Don't be.'

She wouldn't embarrass them both by asking him to stay. She didn't want to ask him for something he couldn't—or didn't want to—give.

She didn't want him to feel bad, or, worse, pity her. She had more pride than that. She wasn't a pushover any more.

She'd had what she hadn't taken all those years ago. It was done. Finished. She'd get on with her business. She had a new priority in life. She was in control of her life. She was not going to wish or wonder 'what if?'. What was, was. And she'd make the most of every minute.

'It was great.' She forced herself to sound airy. 'But it's all I wanted too. It's time for you to go.'

She just held onto the smile until the door closed behind him. Only then did she release the painful, jagged breath. She looked around her apartment—suddenly it felt spacious without him in it. Anger slowly trickled into the huge gap he'd left behind. She was *not* changing her life for anyone else. Not trying to do anything and everything for someone else.

Never ever.

She had what she wanted—her independence. The strength to do what *she* wanted to do. And she wanted this. She would *love* this.

EIGHT

———

The early morning sun streamed in through the window, the sky as brilliant and as clear as it had been the day before and the day before that. Liam rolled and buried his head under the pillow, totally over the relentless perfection of the weather. Why couldn't there be a storm to challenge him out in the boat? He had energy to release, adrenalin to be used. With a growl he thrust out of bed, tossing the pillow to the far corner of the big mattress. He rubbed his face; his eyes ached, his brain fogged. Yet his muscles leapt and twitched under his skin.

Never had he felt so unfulfilled. He'd sailed for hours this past week, but not even a marathon on the water soothed the inflammation scored deep into his heart. He'd scrubbed every inch of every boat in the shed. Then the shed itself. Even though it was someone else's job, he'd needed the activity—hoped the relentless grind would wear him out enough to sleep.

It didn't.

Nothing could exhaust him enough to stop thinking about *her*. And it wasn't the permanent hard-on causing the restless agony. It was the hurt in his heart. He missed more than her body. More than what they'd shared in bed those too few hours.

The inked image had long since washed away but it was as if the nib of that pen had been poisoned. Leaving him with an uncomfortable—invisible—scar. He didn't think it would ever ease.

Frustrated, he snapped at his crew as they trained. She had him questioning *everything*. What he was doing, what he wasn't doing, what he wanted in the future. Hell, he'd *never* thought too far into the future. He'd always lived for the next race, the next event. Loving the achievement— the solo endurance. The success—sporting and financial. And emotional.

He'd thought he had it so together. His life was perfectly set up.

To fail.

Because less than a week with her back in his life, here he was aching for all the things he'd sworn he'd *never* want. And the thing that hurt most of all was that she didn't want him. She didn't want his lifestyle. Didn't want anything other than what they'd shared.

Illogically—when he'd insisted the same—he wanted to know *why*. Why didn't she want him? He'd never known. She'd been attracted to him from the first moment she'd seen him—just as he'd been attracted to her. But she'd refused him—more than once she'd rejected him. And now, even once they'd shared that incredible night, she still rejected him. It burned his insides as if he'd swallowed a bottle of acid. She hadn't argued, hadn't fought. She'd just so civilly agreed.

Liam stopped winding up the coil of rope as it dawned on him—Victoria *always* agreed.

She always did what she thought the other person wanted. So how was he to know for sure that this good-bye was what *she'd* really wanted?

He shook his head at his fantasy. She'd been so businesslike, so seemingly determined. Matching him in the 'career-comes-first' persona. She'd been legit, right?

But the idea took hold—hope took hold. Had she just been making it easy for him? Doing what someone else wanted the way she'd always done?

His heart thumped at the ridiculous eagerness spurting inside him. He was going to have a coronary if he didn't sort himself out. And it was his own fault. He'd been an idiot—too blind to see what was staring him in the face, too scared to admit even to himself what he'd really like. If he'd given them just a little more time, thought things through instead of bolting—

He tossed the rope to the ground and pulled his phone from his pocket. He wasn't spending another day avoiding the biggest challenge of his life.

Victoria couldn't believe the uplift in her business. It was absolutely as she wanted it—and keeping her busy. But being the scribe who recorded the love notes of other people? Right now it hurt.

But it also kept her faith alive. She'd survived betrayal and divorce and isolation. She could survive this too. Other people did. Other people went on to find happiness. And one night was only one night, right? So she shouldn't be this hurt. Only this wound was deeper than any other. It wasn't only the death of that secret fantasy long locked away—it was the death of the incredible reality of being with him. It had been so much better than *she'd* ever believed it could be too. But she wasn't thinking only of sex. She'd laughed with him, talked with him, felt so content in his company, so inspired. It was so much more than sexual. She was drawn to him on many levels. He worked as hard as she. Was as determined as she. He helped out—and she'd helped out too. They had so much to share.

Only he didn't want to. He didn't want her.

In the early evening she sat outdoors at a café in a trendier part of town, glad to get out of the oppressive feeling of her studio. She had a portfolio with her and a laptop to show pictures of some of her larger assignments. It was safer that way, plus it got her a little 'Parisian café scene' fun.

Her prospective client was a guy wanting to do something romantic for the woman in his life—a beautifully printed series of clues that were going to be part of an elaborate proposal. Lucky woman.

'Do you think she'll like it?' he leaned forward and asked for the fifth time.

'I think she'll love it. And I'd be honoured to do it for you.'

His entire face lit up. 'Merci. Perhaps if she says yes you could do the invitations. I like your work. I think she will too. It's unique.'

'Thank you.' Victoria felt the heat bloom in her cheeks, pleased she'd shown him her personal stationery portfolio as well.

'I must get going or she'll wonder where I am.' He stood and Victoria rose too, slinging her bag over her shoulder.

He stepped around the table and leaned forward to kiss her on each cheek in that polite, Parisian manner. 'I'll call you.'

'I'll look forward to it.' And she would. She smiled as she watched him walk down the street.

'Victoria!'

She turned, put a hand out to grip the back of the cane chair.

Liam was striding towards her. Looking icy. He swiftly got to where she stood superglued to the footpath. He was more tanned than usual, his eyes burnished. Gorgeous.

'It didn't take you long to move on.' He glared after the guy who'd just left her.

Coolly Victoria glared at *him*; the excitement that had burst into being only a second ago was instantly doused at the implication of his words. 'No.' She let the word hang ambiguously.

A muscle in Liam's jaw twitched. 'He's not your type.'

'Who is?'

He looked at her directly, eyes aflame. 'Me.'

She was furious. He was only interested because he'd seen her with another guy—someone he saw as a competitor. 'This was a business meeting, Liam,' she snapped. 'That guy's about to propose to his girlfriend of four years.'

'Oh.' He paused. 'Sorry, I—'

'Anyway, you've no right to comment on who I meet or talk to or sleep with, should I choose to,' Victoria interrupted. 'We had our one night. You left. It's over.'

'You wanted me to leave.'

'Yes.' She didn't want someone ruining her career prospects. She didn't want someone who wasn't going to be there most of the time. She didn't want someone who didn't love her. Not again. And she'd agreed never to see him again because it was what *he'd* wanted. *He* didn't want more.

He'd gone pale beneath his tan. 'I had no idea it was a

business meeting. I misread the signs and thought—' He broke off and visibly regrouped. 'I'd never want to jeopardise your work,' he continued stiltedly. 'That's why I stayed away the week of the wedding. I knew you had to concentrate. Your business is amazing. You're talented. You're making it work and you deserve every success.' He backed up a pace. 'I'd never stand in the way of that.'

Unlike Oliver. Who'd been resentful. Who'd been as competitive.

'So you only called out because you thought that other guy was flirting with me?' She felt even more furious. Because that was it, wasn't it? The only time she got serious attention from guys was when there was more than one on the scene. 'You know, Oliver only wanted to marry me to keep me from finding someone else,' she said bitterly. 'Protecting his investment rather than looking at me.' He hadn't really loved her. Wanted her, yes, but more than that he'd wanted no one else to have her.

Liam's eyes widened—and a second later he frowned. Big-time frown. 'You think I was that someone else?' He leaned closer. 'That my presence somehow forced his hand?'

Had Oliver sensed the attraction between her and Liam? He had to have. 'He hadn't planned that proposal. The ring was a family heirloom. He had access to it any time—it was in the safe in the house.'

'But you said yes.'

'Because they were all sitting there. Because they expected it. Because I wanted to please them, and him. Because I was a coward.'

Liam breathed in deep before stepping forward and taking her by the arm, drawing her away from the café and around the corner into a quieter side-street.

'I didn't come over because I saw you talking to that other guy in some random quirk of fate. I'm not supposed to be in Paris. I just abandoned my training and drove for hours to talk to you. I came to find you.'

This wasn't a chance meeting? Victoria stopped walking, so he did too. 'How did you know where I was?'

There was a long moment of silence. Victoria watched—fascinated—as colour slashed across his cheekbones. Don't-give-a-damn Liam was *blushing*?

'I put an app on your phone.'

She frowned. 'What kind of app?'

'I have the matching app on mine—our phones can track each other. It comes up on a map.'

'You basically bugged my phone?' With some kind of GPS tracking thing? 'That's a first-class stalker thing to do.'

'Yep.' He stared into the distance. Eventually he brought his gaze back to meet hers head-on. 'I didn't want to lose you again.'

Victoria's heart thundered. No. No, this couldn't be. She killed the hope making her heart skip double-Dutch style. 'Liam, I know you had to fight. You've competed against extreme odds to get to where you are. But I'm not some challenge. I won't be a prize.'

She didn't want to be a possession again—someone there to look good and support and not 'be' someone and something in her own right. She wanted to be valued for herself. Wanted. Supported in her own endeavours and not just the one supporting. She didn't want to be a sexualised object or fought over like two dogs did with a bone. Because in the end the bone wasn't of interest. The bone wasn't actually what was wanted.

'Is that how you think I see you? How I treat you?' He

frowned. 'What am I to you? The bit of rough from your past? Am I not good enough for you? '

'How dare you?' she challenged, her voice low and raw as angry tears burned the back of her throat. 'You were the one who said we could only have one night. You were the one who said he couldn't give up his lifestyle for any woman.' She rolled her eyes.

'It's easier not to get emotionally involved when it's only one night,' he said stiffly.

'Well, we couldn't have emotional involvement, could we?' she said sarcastically.

He almost laughed at that; she saw the quirk to his mouth and the flash in his eyes. 'The less expectations, the better. I don't want to hurt anyone.'

'How considerate of you.'

'I like to think so.' A low purr, filled with that old arrogance.

She angled her head and pulled the strap of her bag more tightly to her shoulder. 'Of course,' she said conversationally, 'I wouldn't say that it was because you don't want to hurt anyone.'

'No?'

'I'd say it was because you don't want to be hurt yourself.'

'No.'

'No, you don't want to be hurt? Or no, I'm wrong?'

'You're wrong.'

'I've been wrong about many things, but I'm not wrong about this.' She cleared her throat. 'You're afraid of intimacy.'

He laughed outright at that.

'Not *sex*,' she sighed. 'IN.TIM.ACY. Letting someone in your life. Trusting someone. Being brave enough to rely on someone. You can't do that. And the work thing is just the excuse you give. You don't want to commit to anyone. You even admitted that once. And the reason is because you're too *scared*.' She snuck a breath, starting to get upset. 'But don't make excuses with me. Don't come back and bother me. Don't do that to me.'

'I bother you?'

Of course he bothered her. She hated him for it. For not loving her the way she wanted him to. But she could be okay with it, she could get over it, so long as he stayed *away*. 'All I've ever been is another prize for you to win. And once you've won, you're done—'

'You were *never* a prize to me,' he suddenly shouted. 'You were always—' He broke off, closing his eyes. 'Perfect.' His eyes flashed open again, serious and wide and riveted on her. 'You were the prettiest woman I'd ever seen. And the sexiest. The way you looked at me? And then I *really* saw you. Got to see and know the person you are. The way you did things for everyone. You cared so much for everyone. I wanted you to care for me. You were so lovely. You're still so lovely. Not a prize, but the most *precious* thing. And hell, yes, I feel scared around you— when you only have to look at me to pierce through to my bones. You have always mattered to me.' He paced away from her, then spun on his heel.

'I never wanted to care about what people thought of me. I already knew what they thought of me and where I came from.' He shook his head. 'But I knew that was irrelevant to what I wanted. I'm proud of the way I've made a success of my life. And I won't ever give that up—those wins are mine for ever. And I'll keep winning. But I knew I didn't fit in. Frankly I didn't care. Then I met Oliver and he didn't care at all about my background. No looks or comments. This from a guy who came from a background of such privilege—not just money, but *family*. He invited me to his home—the first real Christmas I'd ever had. Snow and everything—a fairy tale. And there was an angel there too. A porcelain doll with green eyes and blonde hair and her heart on her sleeve. Sweet, compassionate, caring. And when she looked at me? It wasn't disapproval or distrust that I saw. It was desire. Raw, adult desire.' He swallowed. 'I wanted her. I wanted everything she had to give. Like I've never wanted anything from any other person before.'

The pain in Victoria's chest spilled over. 'Did you want *her*? Or was she just a symbol of it all—the family, the Christmas—that whole scene that you'd never had?'

'I just wanted her. And I gave up what I'd found—that brotherly friendship—to try to have her.'

'No, you didn't. You didn't take what you could have taken. You said it yourself—you didn't seduce me. All you did was ask a question and I was too scared to answer it honestly.' She shook her head. 'I was supposed to be perfect,' she said sadly. 'I thought I'd lose everything. And then I lost everything anyway.' She sighed. 'So I'm not what you thought I was. I'm no angel. I'm not some perfect thing to be put on a pedestal. I make mistakes. I can be mean. I can't be perfect.' She couldn't live up to whatever image he had of her in his head. She'd only disappoint him.

'I know that,' he said. 'I know *you*. And I just want you all the more.'

Victoria drew a shaky breath. 'Other women had wanted you.'

'Yeah.' He smiled. 'Other women had. But you were different. You were genuine. You had a softness in you. You were so attuned to other people. So empathetic. So aware of how they were feeling. You care about how other people are feeling. You want people to be happy.'

'It's a weakness. I put off things that I wanted for fear of what other people might say or think or if they might treat me differently. You're so fearless. You don't give a damn.'

'I'm full of fear. And I do give a damn. Both are related to you.'

'This can't work,' she whispered. 'You said yourself relationships don't work with your lifestyle. And you can't change, you can't stop doing something that you love because of me. I couldn't live with that.'

'I'm not going to stop, I'm going to adjust. I want to set up a sailing school. I actually want to settle. If I'm with you. But I don't want to hold you back. I know you've held back because of other people in your life. I know you didn't do things because of your parents and what happened with your sister, and Oliver. I don't want you doing that because of me. But, Victoria, I love you. I've always loved you. I've found myself in tricky situations before—we can find a solution to this. But you have to tell me what *you* want. Don't say whatever you think I want to hear. Be honest. If you want me to leave, I'll leave. If you want me to stay, I can stay. Whatever, wherever you want.'

'I want to work.' She blinked back tears. She couldn't give up her job. She needed the stimulation, the security. But she also needed love. 'And I want to be with you. I want *you*. I love you too.'

His arms wrapped tight around her, pulling her in close. Noses bumped before lips touched and clung and her tears fell. He leaned back against the wall, taking her with him, so they both rested against the solid structure.

The most incredible feeling of relief swept through her. Relief—and disbelief too.

'I understand you don't want to move.' He spoke fast, his warm breath stirring her hair. 'I have money. We'll get an apartment with a nice view of the river.'

Left Bank? She pressed her face against his tee before pulling back to shake her head and laugh—albeit a bit watery. 'I'd prefer an apartment with a view of the sea or the ocean. Whichever one.'

He frowned. 'But what about your work?'

'It's transportable,' she admitted. 'I just need a work-space with good light and an Internet connection and a post office nearby.' She looked at him. 'I don't want to lose you again either.'

'You never will.'

She curled her fingers into his tee. She nearly had lost him again. But he'd come after her. He'd held onto her.

His heart pounded against hers. She felt his tension, realised that he truly had been afraid. As vulnerable as she. She leaned closer into him and let him soothe her with the gentle strokes of his hand down her back, the light kisses he pressed into her hair.

'It's taken us so long to get here,' he said softly.

'I can't regret it. I won't. I don't. I'm not the girl I was when I first met you. I couldn't have handled you then. I can now.' She lifted her head and looked at him, brushed her fingers on his jaw. 'We weren't right for each other then.'

'You agree we are now?' He pulled her closer. 'I'm not letting you go again. Not ever.'

'Are you sure?'

'Don't doubt it.' He shook his head. 'There was always

something about you. There was always just this. Just us. You make me want everything.'

He kissed her. Exquisite tension built between them—delicious torture, free of undercurrents and uncertainties. Nothing forgotten, but now, there was nothing forbidden, nothing hidden. Glorious desire surged as pure happiness filled her. She loved him. And he loved her.

She leaned closer, positively clinging. His hands clamped on her hips, an iron grip, stopping her instinctive circular sway against him.

'We need a room. Now.' He groaned, muttered a short swearword or three. 'I can't breathe for wanting you.'

She laughed, enjoying the heated agony in his eyes. 'Don't stop breathing.'

He frantically dug a hand into his pocket. 'I've got an app on my phone.'

She lifted her brows and teased, 'Another one?'

'Hotel finder.' He swiped and tapped at the screen. 'I'm locating the nearest.'

'Liam,' she chuckled. 'We're leaning against the wall of a hotel right here.'

'We are?' He glanced up at the flag hanging on the corner of the building. 'Thank God. Let's get in there.' He peeled away from the wall and took her hand in a death grip—but she was the one who led the way.

'Together.' She turned her head back to smile at him.

He stopped, tugging on her hand so she stopped too. He planted a kiss on her lips and then whispered, 'Finally and for always.'

ONE

———

'No. No, no, no, no, no.' Vivi Grace shook her head at the woman who owned every minute of her existence.

'Too bad,' Gianetta growled, stretching out her hand, her fingers crab-snapping. 'No option. She's throwing one of her worst.'

No kidding. The current hissy fit would be heard three streets away and Vivi was only five feet from ground zero, her ears basically bleeding. Gritting back a helpless giggle, Vivi unclasped her bra and wriggled the straps out from the sleeves of her shirt. Good thing she stayed out back— she'd never be seen in public without boob containment. 'The things I do for you.' And for the spoilt brat who was the bane of her life.

'You're paid ridiculous amounts of money to do them.' Gia took the bra and glided across the room in her inimitable hovercraft style.

Vivi watched, grinning at the woman's *élan*. Impossible as it was, Gia was more mesmerising and unique than her million-dollar creations. But what she'd said was true and, not only did Vivi need the money, she was driven to nail every aspect of this job. It might be completely crazy at times, but she loved her work. And given her relative youth and inexperience, Vivi still felt compelled to prove herself. She had to be better than brilliant and she worked hard to be—twenty-four/three-sixty-five.

So if the brat wanted to wear Vivi's bra, she'd wear her bra. Definitely one of the more mortifying things Vivi'd been asked to offer up in the last four years, but no real surprise. For the biggest events of the season—New York, Paris, London and this, Milan—she did whatever it took. Tonight Alannah Dixon, global supermodel *du jour*, would wear the ultimate haute couture design of Gianetta Forli, supreme fashion queen and Vivi's 'every-minute-you're-breathing' boss. It was the grande finale of the most fab collection and not a thing would go wrong. Not on Vivi's watch.

As Gia handed Alannah the bra Vivi was unable to stop herself from stating the obvious. 'You'll need to sew it or something, I'm way wider round the ribs.' She really shouldn't apologise. Only an eight-year-old starving orphan would be narrower.

'The point is you're fuller,' Gia muttered, already working a needle. 'The dress needs breasts.'

So why had Gia designed it for boobs when she'd known it would be ironing-board Alannah wearing it? Vivi bit back the bitchy thought. 'Got some stuffing?'

'Plenty.' Gia growled. 'You've lost weight, Alannah.'

'I couldn't help it,' Alannah whined as Gia deftly sewed a few last stitches into the fantasy frock. 'I couldn't eat last week.'

Vivi rolled her eyes. It was a guy. Alannah had lost her heart and her appetite with it. Again. She was master of the 'crush from afar', actors or musicians her favourite *ob-*

jets de lust, but when she actually met the guy in question, she was invariably disappointed in the reality. As a result, the world knew she was impossibly hard to please—which made her all the more attractive to many, *many* successful and overly assured men. Alannah the Unattainable.

If anyone bothered to think about it, they might call Vivi unattainable too. She didn't do crushes, flings or fullblown affairs. She didn't do anything. Definitely not during Milan Fashion Week. And she'd not eaten that much these last few days either, she'd been wired on nervous energy and a 'to do' list centuries long.

Braless and feeling as if she were bouncing all over the place, she stepped out to the main changing area to ensure everything else was going to plan. Some of the stylists saw her and immediately straightened and moved faster.

Good.

As Gia's personal secretary she had serious kudos. She was the person responsible for organising absolutely everything and everyone knew it. If anyone wanted to get to Gia, to impress Gia, even talk to Gia, they had to get through Vivi first. She was Girl Friday, Bouncer, Therapist, Exercise Buddy, Travel Agent, Punch Bag, Publicist, Chauffeur, Cook, Calendar, Cleaner, Censor, Enforcer, Enabler, Receptionist and more, all rolled into one.

Vivi turned away from the hordes of hairdressers and stylists, mentally preparing for the clean-up and postshow party mayhem. She rolled her shoulders, uncomfortable without her bra. Not physically, but because she worked hard to maintain her scary 'fail-me-and-you-die' persona. There was only success or failure and she ensured all staff and contractors knew it—from her attitude, speech and image. Her crisp white shirt and tailored black skirt reflected her all-business approach. Inoffensive, unobtrusive, efficient—it wasn't her job to look out-rageous. Although just this second Vivi wished she'd worn some scarlet lace number that would've shown through the dress. But Gia knew Vivi always wore skin-coloured support under her starched exterior. She was nothing if not reliable.

Right now A-listers lined the front row, trying not to rip into the goody bags Vivi had ordered. She always had her pick of gifts to include; many companies sought an af-filiation with Gia's label. Most were rejected. Only the elite were accepted—ensuring they became even more sought after. For another company, getting Gia's nod was like striking gold. Vivi didn't go to watch their glee, she stayed out back, clipboard, laptop and phone in hand—one eye on the security screens, one eye on the models before they went to Gia for final inspection, one eye on the techni-cians, one eye on the clean-up already. Yeah, she needed a lot of eyes, a few ears and several extra arms as well.

Quickly checking the nearest monitor, Vivi saw the models strutting evening-wear. One second 'til Alannah claimed centre-stage with her Vivi-bra boobs. She walked back to the private dressing room to get ready for the next phase. The monitor in there didn't capture audio but she could hear the applause thundering through the walls anyway. She paused from her manic paper-shuffling and smiled at the screen as Gia then appeared, owning the catwalk alongside Alannah, taking the adulation.

Vivi frequently pinched herself, still unable to believe she'd had the luck to land a job with Gia and then be pro-moted to such a coveted position. Hundreds would kill—or worse—for her job. She met amazing people, went to incredible places. But as the applause faded she sat on the leather sofa, more than a little tired. Her post-show crash was hitting too soon.

'Vivi!' Gia's strident tones echoed down the corridor. 'I need you.'

Naturally. Vivi inhaled deep, hoping for a hit of energy. Gianetta needed her for the most basic things. Not merely organisational skills and people management—being secretary to a creative genius meant hand-holding on a whole new level.

Other voices grew louder. A burst of Alannah giggles was underscored by deep male laughter. Great. Vivi frowned. Guests were coming already too? She glanced round for her jacket but it was nowhere to be seen and her bra was still sewn to Alannah's dress.

'We need drinks, Vivi!' Alannah sang. 'I've found a friend.'

Of course. Vivi shook her head. Time to forget about her boobs' bounceability. She lifted one of the already opened bottles and filled a couple of the flutes on the nearby tray, briefly wondering about Alannah's human appetite suppressant. Was he her usual elite A-list actor type, or an extremely wealthy benefactor? To be invited into the exclusive room meant he was *someone*. But still, he ought to have been vetted by security.

The door opened.

'Champagne?' Glasses in hand, she turned to offer one to the latest five-minute-flirt—and nearly fainted with shock.

Oh, no. Oh, definitely no, no, *no*.

Rigid—to stop her faint—she stared at the tall figure who'd stepped in after Alannah.

'Thanks.' Alannah pried one of the glasses from Vivi's clawed fingers.

Vivi didn't answer. Couldn't. She just kept on staring.

'This is Vivi. She does everything.' Sweeping past, Alannah didn't bother to tell Vivi her date's name—managing to compliment and insult Vivi at the same time. But Vivi didn't need Alannah to tell her who he was.

Liam Wilson.

Her long-time-ago lover. The one she'd worked relentlessly hard to forget about. *Entirely.* Yet faster than the burst of a champagne bubble, every memory, every sensation, every sigh, flooded back.

They'd run away together. A reckless, passionate impulse. She'd turned her back on everything—her family, her almost fiancé, her carefully planned future. And for what?

Her affair with Liam Wilson had changed the course of her life. Mostly for the better, right? But it had also brought heartbreak.

He'd broken her heart.

'Excuse me a moment,' Alannah purred, walking further into the room and pulling across a small screen that she'd get changed behind. Gia disappeared behind the screen too. Alannah was usually completely at ease with nudity, but never with a possible flirt in tow. She knew how to work mystery.

So Liam was Alannah's latest crush? That'd be right— because Liam loved nothing more than a challenge. And that was fine. Of course. Because Vivi was so over him— light years over him. She'd not given him a thought in aeons.

But now he was right in front of her, a smile slowly curving his lips. Vivi remembered that smile and it hit her exactly as it had five years ago. Like the loud beat of a bass drum, one stroke set her heart on a new rhythm—

led by him. But she wasn't listening to it this time, certainly not dancing.

She turned, looked at the glass in her hand, tempted to lift the thing and drain it—and then the rest of the bottle. But that would be telling and she wasn't letting him know how much his appearance had thrown her. Nor was she ever letting him know how badly he'd hurt her—not when he was here chasing someone else. Not when he was looking so, so...*fine*.

She turned back and offered him the glass. 'Champagne?' she repeated, pleased her voice sounded almost normal.

He was still looking right at her and his smile deepened. 'Thank you.'

The tips of his fingers brushed hers as he took the glass. She suppressed the shiver, turning to pour herself a glass with a slow, careful hand. She took a very small, very controlled sip. She drew a breath but her throat was totally dry—as if the liquid she'd just swallowed had evaporated. Actually it probably had, because she was unbearably hot.

So hot.

It would be rude not to look at him, right? Not to talk. Swallowing, she went back to staring.

Tall, dark—and, you got it, handsomer than any of those pretty guys who'd been strutting it down the catwalk all week—Liam Wilson exuded more masculinity than all of them put together. More rugged, more raw—nothing but muscle and determination, all but breathing fire. He was slightly thinner than when she'd last seen him and his hair might be longer, but his edges had hardened—leaving him leaner and, yeah, meaner. His smarts were still visible—splinter sharp in his gold-flecked brown eyes. More than intelligent, he'd been calculating. And, in the end, ruthless. Doubtless he still was.

Mr All or Nothing. The 'all' had been fierce intensity. The 'nothing' had meant absolute abandonment. He'd enticed her—claimed her completely. And then ditched her.

Well, that was okay. She'd moved on—higher, further than she'd ever imagined she would. So she had pride, right? Good defence. She'd argue the heat in her cheeks was because she'd been working hard.

'Hold still,' Gia snapped louder than the steel scissors she was using to free Alannah from the frock.

Neither Liam nor Vivi moved. But the amusement in his eyes deepened, as did the intensity of colour. Too gorgeous for any woman's good.

'Did you enjoy the show?' she asked, trying to suck back some cool. Failing.

'It was stunning.'

How had he come to Alannah's attention? Vivi didn't know what he did any more. Five years ago he'd been on the competitive sailing circuit. Teaching on the side, taking wealthy types like Oliver out, getting them some skills and himself money, status—building a reputation that led to demand. Alannah didn't seem the type to want to learn to sail.

But Liam had other talents. And he was clearly good at whatever he did now, given the fabric and fit of his suit. Bespoke. Emphasising the bold, beautiful body beneath.

Hot enough to combust, Vivi wrenched her gaze from him, hideously aware that beneath her white shirt her breasts were unfettered and right this second straining towards him.

Stupid body.

But it remembered. Everything. She'd had the hottest sex of her life with this guy—incandescent passion fraught with guilt. Three weeks of burning up bedroom after bedroom, barely surfacing to breathe and travel on. Intense. Insane.

Unsustainable.

Because it ought to have been forbidden. She'd broken all the rules and she knew it. Doubt had wormed its way into her heart. In the end the old cliché was true: lust was not enough. It was no foundation for anything solid to be built on. Even though she'd given him everything. Given up everything for him.

But he hadn't wanted it. All he'd wanted was—

'Don't move too fast—you'll wreck it.' Gia's words rang in the scorching room. Vivi snapped back to the present.

'Gia's work is incredible.' She produced a smile, determined to break the hot-ice moment and fill in the wait for the others to re-emerge.

'Yes, she's amazing.'

'As are the models, of course.' Vivi couldn't help an acidic tinge filtering through.

'Indeed,' he agreed, his voice deepening.

Of course. Back then she should have known he was nothing but a flirt, but she'd been so young—she'd believed in the happy-ever-after fairy tale. Fool.

'So, you're Vivi now?' he asked.

'Yes.' She lifted her chin. It had taken a long time and a lot of effort to become Vivi and she was proud of what she'd achieved.

He angled his head, watching her far too close for comfort. 'You'll always be Victoria to me.'

She froze at the friendly tease. 'Naturally you'd be unable to do something that I'd prefer. You've only ever done what *you* wanted to.' She covered the slight bite with a laugh and a superglued-on smile.

His smile also flashed wider, but his eyes sparked. 'Well, I'm still Liam. In case you'd forgotten my name.'

As if she could ever forget his name. As if she could ever forget his face, his mouth, his hands, his body and the way he used it...

She blinked and halted her thoughts. She'd been there, done that, burned the tee shirt. She had self-control now. Grown up, mature, she wasn't the bowled-over idiot she'd been. And once bitten, she was now ninety-nine times shy of this guy. She should turn tail and run. She couldn't lose herself again.

Except she was no longer a coward. She was a highly paid, valued and skilled assistant to one of the world's most iconoclastic talents. And she wasn't going to let him get to her or cause trouble at a time that was far too important. And that was the point. She was being paid to be here and do a freaking awesome job. So here she'd stay. But she sure wished she could get her bra back on.

'It's been a while.' He offered another easy conversation starter with another too easy smile.

Okay, that was how they'd play it—like vaguely friendly, old acquaintances. 'I suppose,' she agreed, as if she'd not really noticed. As if she couldn't tell him down to the last minute.

He looked amused. 'You look different.' His attention lifted to her hair. 'And yet the same.' His lids fluttered as he swiftly looked down her body and back to her face. There hadn't been a blatant stare at her boobs, but she knew he noticed them—she felt it in their response.

'Still beautiful,' he added quietly.

Oh, hell. She wasn't going to let him seduce her with

his soft-spoken, smiling wickedness—especially when she knew all it ever had been was words. No matter how sincere he could sound, there was no genuine emotion behind them.

'While you're looking as wolfish as ever.' She deliberately glanced at the screen Alannah was changing behind. 'You still love a challenge and a chase?'

He laughed. 'Possibly.'

There was no 'possible' about it.

'So you work for Gia?' he asked.

'Yes, I'm very fortunate.' Vivi maintained her composure. She hadn't spent the last few years working around models not to pick up a few points—like the ability to smile on demand no matter how you were feeling inside.

At that moment, Gia materialised, the steel scissors still in her hands. 'Tell me more about your plans,' she said to Liam.

Vivi leapt at the opportunity to duck behind the screen. Alannah was just pulling on a stunning minidress that should by rights be a tee shirt. She had no bra on either.

'It seems to be the look tonight.' Alannah winked.

Yeah, well, it was all right for Alannah—she was the definition of pert'n'petite.

'Where's my bra?' Vivi violently whispered.

'That ugly thing was a bra?' Alannah answered excruciatingly loudly. 'No idea.' She breezed out from the curtain to sing at the others. 'Comfort stop, won't be a sec.'

Vivi stayed hidden, hunting for her bra and acutely aware of the quiet—inaudible—murmuring between Gia and Liam. How had Liam met Gia? Victoria had control of the calendar; she knew everything Gia was up to, didn't she?

He had to be here for Alannah. He must be the guy the

model reckoned was the love of her life. Vivi grimly hoped that the usual pattern was followed and the 'Unattainable' would eat him up and spit him out.

Finally she found remnants of her bra on the floor. Unlike the dress, no time and care had been taken to preserve it from the sharp shears. There was nothing for it but to go back out there and face him—headlights on full. Straightening her shoulders in pure defiance, she stepped out from the small screen.

'Vivi, hurry up.' Gia frowned.

She had no intention of hurrying anywhere with them. She still had work to do—thank heavens. 'Gia, I can't come with you now. I need to supervise the—'

'One of the others can do it.'

Oh, she had to be kidding. But Vivi recognised the hard light in Gia's eyes. The woman might be a genius but she was notoriously difficult when consumed by her latest idea. It seemed inspiration might have struck in the last ten seconds. Vivi kept her tones calm and sensible. 'All right, but I need to go by the hotel to—'

'There's no time for that,' Gia snapped. 'I need you with me now.'

No mistaking that tone. While Vivi was used to Gia's imperious orders, others were often shocked by her supersonic switch to demanding Diva-Of-Them-All. Vivi glanced at Liam and saw the slight tightening around his eyes. But he looked from Gia to her and his momentarily forbidding expression shattered as he turned on a smile.

Vivi turned away and drew breath. Great, so now she got to go to the glamorous after-party in the clothes she'd been wearing all day, without half her underwear, and in the presence of an ex-lover whom she'd never quite got out from under her skin. The one guy in front of whom, if she had to ever see him again, she'd want to look hotter than hot.

Well, doubtless she looked hot—her face felt as flamed as a tomato on a grill. Her frigidly efficient persona had melted and she was mortified. Given the field she worked in, maybe she should be less conservative sartorially, but her attire was part of her armour and at this moment she needed all the steel she could get her hands on. What she really needed was a chastity belt. She wasn't getting sucked under by the tsunami of sensual power that was Liam. Not again.

A bunch of paps loitered by the limo. Vivi put on her best secretary face and acted as bodyguard for Alannah. She'd long since learned the best way to ensure the photographers didn't bother taking a picture of her was to look as if she were on a mission and hold a clipboard or something. Tonight she clutched her bag to her chest.

Liam had also stepped ahead of the two stars and now held the car door for them—looking like a much more efficient bodyguard than she as she brought up the rear. Clearly amused, he looked right at her bag as if he knew exactly what it was she was really trying to hide. She got into the limo, painfully aware of him getting a face full of her butt as he waited to get in after her.

He took the seat opposite hers, the one next to Alannah. So she got to watch as he conquered the Unattainable? Okay, she didn't need the chastity belt, but a paper bag to stick her head in would be really welcome right about now. Because he *would* succeed where all others had failed. Wasn't that what Liam was all about? Winning what no one else could.

'So, what's so special about this boat you were telling me about?' Gia picked up on the conversation she'd been having with Liam while Vivi had been bra-hunting be-hind the screen. 'Sell it to me.' She went into bottom-line businesswoman mode.

'Everything. Sleek lines, luxurious fabric, simple de-sign. You get comfort but elite performance. The speed over the water is unlike anything in its class. I think you'll find it an exceptionally good fit.' Liam didn't do plain busi-ness-speak. The way he spoke evoked the sensuality of the design he was discussing. It was obviously still boats for him, then. Still that 'freedom' that was so important to him and that he could never find on land. Glancing at Gia, Vivi could see his effect in action. He always spoke with that smile in his voice, with the kind of confidence that had everyone leaning forward and listening.

'Will you take me out on it?' Alannah asked with one of her coquettish giggles.

'I'd love nothing more.'

Goosebumps feathered over Vivi's hot and cold skin. She was hyper-aware of him sitting so close, but she point blank refused to look at him. She studied the plain fab-ric of her skirt instead. Once she'd had the freedom to touch him when and how she liked. And she'd liked—too much. But it wasn't just the possibility of touch making her squirmy; he managed to attack all her other senses too—most especially with that scent.

Vivi wasn't wearing perfume, nor were Gia or Alan-nah. The models used nothing to stain the delicate fabrics used, nothing that would interfere with the understated scent in the catwalk salon—Gia's shows were carefully de-signed multi-sensory experiences. So that subtle scent in the car wasn't coming from anyone but Liam.

Musky, masculine, delectable.

Once he'd smelt of sea and sun, even in mid-winter.

Now that was masked with a splash of something expensive—and every bit as devastating.

'I think it could work,' Gia said. 'I want to see it. We can go from there.'

Vivi's muscles screamed with tension. Liam and Gia were working some deal? It was Vivi's job to have all potential business partners screened by Gia's financial advisers. She could have had this nixed had she been aware of it. Because no way on this earth did she want to have to work with Liam on anything. She was getting through this car ride and then leaving him and Alannah to it. She just did *not* want to know.

'We're looking at using Liam's new boat for a one-off fashion shoot.' Gia coolly confirmed the worst. 'You arrange it, Vivi.'

Vivi glanced at him, stiffening as she encountered his watchful eyes. He had an annoyingly amused look on his face, as if he suspected how much she *didn't* want to arrange it. As if he knew she wanted to tell him to go jump off one of his precious boats. But she didn't tell him. Instead she pulled on her tough-nut, impervious-to-stress persona.

'Of course.' She smiled. What Gia wanted, Vivi did. She was professional and she had no problem working with someone equally professional. She'd calmly navigate these waters with Liam's own secretary. 'No doubt you have an assistant I can liaise with, Liam?'

'Not here,' he answered with a roguish drawl and a deliberately *un*apologetic shrug. 'I'm afraid you're going to have to *liaise* directly with me.'

TWO

———

The extravagant hotel in Milan had more bouncers roaming the rooms than the fashion magazines had models. There were roped-off areas within roped-off areas—screens protecting the most rich and famous from the merely rich and famous. And, in the central, most holy, V.V.V.V.I.P part of the place stood Liam Wilson.

He didn't let it go to his head. He was only here because of mystery, reputation and mutual benefit. Because the world's most sought-after designer was happy to work with him and her pet, the world's latest 'It' model, was happy to use him. He wasn't afraid of using contacts to get ahead either—not in the professional sense. But this wasn't just about business. This was personal too.

He'd wanted to catch up with Victoria Rutherford—the woman now named Vivi Grace. He'd known she'd be somewhere behind the scenes at the show tonight but, even so, finally seeing her again had taken him by complete surprise. It was that gloriously sexy, uptight outfit. He'd had to freeze as if it were a game of musical statues to stop from hitting on her as he had five years ago. In less than a second the urge had bitten all over again. Red hot, rampaging lust.

Rot. He gritted his teeth. He did *not* still find her attractive. It was merely her braless state. Finding real curves in this particular environment was heady stuff. Plus, he'd been single—i.e. sex-starved—these last few months. He'd been working vicious hours. His juices were flowing because he smelt business success in the air... Oh, he could come up with a hundred excuses for the instant rock-hard reaction he'd felt.

But he couldn't help looking at her. Drinking her in. She had the same beautiful curves—swollen breasts, slim waist, sweet hips. Her white shirt and black skirt were clearly intended to give off the uber-efficient, frigid school-mistress stereotype, but they totally failed. The knee-length skirt simply emphasised the legs on show beneath and made a man itch to slide the hem higher to see the thighs Liam already knew were supple, strong and yet soft. The fabric curved tight over her hips, giving her a slim roundedness that was so much more attractive to him than the bony frame of the supposed supermodel.

On her feet were the instruments of torture that were uniform in this industry—the highest of heels. He'd no idea how she could walk in them but he liked how they brought her face nearer to his. Not quite eye to eye but tantalisingly not far from mouth to mouth. They were a superficial sign of change—so different from the slip-on things she'd worn that winter. Her hair was different too. Gone were the long waves of blonde. In their place was a sharp-edged cut just to her chin. Very French. He'd seen the style a lot. On Victoria it looked good, but so different from the style she'd had those years ago. A veneer of sophistication had replaced sweet innocence. She'd topped off this change with her new name. *Vivi*.

But none of those changes wiped the image he had of her in his head—with her naked and able only to breathe through the moments beyond climax. The most beautiful woman he'd ever known.

And he'd known plenty in the last five years.

Yet none had left the same impression. None had left this residual irritation—like a barb beneath his skin. None had led to another moment of madness—the one that had brought him here. Liam tried to rein in the energy building in him—the very, very red blood pulsing round his body. Victoria Rutherford.

Too hot to handle. Too hot to last.

For a moment his mind was so fogged with tumultuous memories he couldn't speak. It could have been an hour ago when she'd been soft, warm, willing and he'd lost himself in her. He'd not meant to get that physical that quick once they'd walked out on everything. But she'd stunned him with her sweetness and he'd been unable to resist. Taking what she'd offered. Stupidly, he'd become more jealous of Oliver than he'd been before. She'd drilled him open until he'd never felt so unsure in his life. He'd asked her stupid, insecure questions, needing to know that what was between them was better. But whatever had brought them together eroded—again more quickly than he'd imagined it could.

She'd left and he didn't just lose his heart. But everything he'd achieved.

Business contacts, work, his world. She'd no idea how much it had cost him. No idea what he'd brought himself up from only to be dumped in an even worse place. He'd had to start all over again—from below the line he'd started. Because he then had the reputation, the ostracism, to overcome. He'd betrayed someone who should have been like a brother to him. But Liam had never had a brother. Never had anything anyone could call a family. And that was the way it would stay—no long-term lover, certainly no marriage. Career came first and always would. It was the one constant in his life and what gave him greatest satisfaction.

Which wasn't to say he didn't like sex. Usually he pursued plenty of it—and won. Now he had the money and status that came with success, he won even more. Which gave him more reason to doubt a woman's motivation. Because back in the day when all he'd had to offer was himself, it hadn't been what she'd wanted. It hadn't been *him* at all. Victoria Rutherford had used him all those years ago and he'd suffered through hell because of it.

He took another sip of his drink and told his imagination to settle and his pulse to slow. It wasn't that she'd broken his heart. It had been a *crush*. He'd been tempted by the forbidden and by hormone-fuelled fantasy. And he'd recovered what he'd lost. He'd worked round the clock. He'd had to leave the UK and try Europe—doing anything and everything. Clawing his way back up the ladder. In truth, he'd probably done better than he would have had he stayed, because he'd had to reach round for other business opportunities. It had cost him hours and hours of sheer graft, struggle and sweat but he'd done it. Single-handed. And single he would remain. Always. He'd never risk his security again.

So, for now he'd sort out this photo shoot deal with the designer. It was a win-win proposition and the old bird already knew it. He could handle a few meetings with Victoria. He'd pull a satisfactory outcome from this lame burst of curiosity. But right now that curiosity bit harder. Liam looked across the room to where she stood in the corner, yapping into her mobile phone. He pegged it as defensive—a way of disengaging from the scene in the room and the threat of a scene with him.

Too bad. He started walking. Because it was time for the kind of scene Victoria had once loathed.

A frisson of awareness skittered down Vivi's spine. She turned and watched Liam walk nearer. He watched her in a way that set her teeth on edge. Compelling, confident he'd get her attention. Of course he bloody would. He got everyone's attention. She'd done some quick research as soon as she'd got Gia ensconced centre stage in the room with her favourite drink on tap. Liam hadn't hidden the way she had. So now she knew—he headed a luxury boat-building firm based on the Italian coast. He'd turned the ancient, once-family-owned company around. In only a few short years he'd pulled them out of the red and into the utterly desirable. He'd fended off an aggressive take-over threat from a far bigger rival and come out on top. He had people queuing for orders and celebs calling in favours to get in first—almost as many as Gia. Vivi knew to have achieved that much in such a short time meant he'd worked every hour there was. He simply had to have a team with him now.

'Are you sure you want to organise this shoot yourself?' she said the second he got within earshot, a bright smile pinned to her lips. 'You wouldn't prefer to have an assistant work out the fine details with me?'

'The thought of dealing directly with me really does bother you.' He stopped walking an inch over a socially acceptable distance from her.

'Of course it doesn't.' She maintained her smile through gritted teeth and resisted the urge to take a step back. 'I'm just surprised you have the *time to waste* on something small like this.' She less than subtly emphasised the 'time to waste'. That was what he'd said to her in the heat of one of their many arguments in the last few days they were together.

I don't have the time to waste on this.

On you.

'It's a very precious boat and has yet to be revealed to anyone,' he said lazily, not taking his eyes from her face. 'It's under tight security until the Genoa show in a couple of weeks. This is my absolute priority.'

'You don't think you're leaving it a little late to get promo shots?'

He laughed. 'I already have promo shots. But when you get the chance to have the world's most popular designer and her model work with you, you take it.'

'Yes,' Vivi mused, her bitch-claws flashing out. 'You were always good at taking every chance you got.'

'It is a skill of mine. And I'll continue to take full advantage of every chance I get until I have all that I want.'

'And what do you want?' She stared right back at him, refusing to think that there'd been any subtle suggestion in his tone. 'Global domination?'

'Why not?'

'Why indeed?' she answered lightly. 'All the money, the travel—'

'Don't forget the women.' His smile was lazy but his eyes were sharp.

'Oh, how could I forget the women? So you have everything you desire—fame, fortune, fawning minions?'

'Minions?' He chuckled. 'Is that what you are?'

Anger flashed—white-hot, rapid—but she controlled it, using everything she had to preserve an almost unruffled exterior. 'I'm no minion.' Certainly not his. 'I'm the puppeteer. I organised this party—this whole decadent circus was on my instruction.'

'Really?'

Something about that answer set her on edge—as if he was indulging her. She was proud of who she'd become, what she'd done. 'Absolutely. You know—' she stood taller '—I really ought to thank you. This job, my life—' she waved a hand at the opulent room '—all because I walked out. My leaving home, leaving you—it was the best thing I ever did.' She lifted her chin, emphasising her bravado. Masking the tendril of fear that was uncurling in her stomach—fear that one chink of her armour had loosened from one little *look*.

There was a moment of silence.

'Well.' He paused again. 'Congratulations.'

Caution niggled—something in his tone alerting her. His face had shuttered again, his lashes lowered, hiding the warmth in his eyes.

'I want you to meet with me first thing in the morning,' he said.

'That's not possible.' She smiled an insincere apology. Thank goodness she was having a few days off. She'd arrange his shoot once she got back. 'I have—'

'But Gia promised you'd take care of everything and meet every single one of my demands.' His shoulders lifted and his eyes widened as if in total innocence.

Vivi mentally counted to five. Because she recognised the single-minded obstinacy beneath his good-humoured façade. She couldn't let him muck up her rep with Gia and she suspected he would. 'As long as every single one of your demands is *professional*, then of course I will.' She smiled. For Gia.

'You think my demands might not be professional?' he leaned in to murmur.

She angled her head back, aware she exposed her neck as she did—ignoring the secret flare of desire within for him to kiss her vulnerable skin. 'I think the professional and the personal are intertwined for you.'

'Oh?'

He moved forward and she backed up a pace before thinking better of it and locking her knees tight. 'Nothing matters to you more than the professional and you're more than happy to use the personal to get there.'

She ignored the battling urges within her—flee-or-fornicate. Crass it might be, but those had always been her only options when it came to Liam. But she was doing neither tonight. She was in *control*. She'd never been in control of her feelings around Liam before, but she'd grown up plenty since then.

'Then it's just as well you're still so eager to please, isn't it?' He angled his head bringing him to a way more personal than professional distance—a kiss distance. 'How ironic that the girl who was so determined to achieve independence has become the ultimate in slave.'

She blinked. 'Excuse me?'

'Running around after your boss. Never saying no. Definitely a *slave*.'

Oh, that was rude. But worse was her melting reaction to the way he lingered over that last insulting word. The dreadful thing was she'd felt enslaved all those years ago—so in love she was all but bound to him. Being that enthralled was what she'd run from. Especially when that depth of emotion had never been reciprocated. She fought harder to hide the electrical current running red-hot between them now. 'I'll *never* be your slave.'

'No?' He lifted his hand and brushed the back of his finger along the edge of her tightly clenched jaw before he stepped away. 'Seven-thirty tomorrow morning. My hotel.'

Liam walked away before he did something really stupid—like pushing her back to the wall and kissing the sass out of her. Since when did Victoria Rutherford talk back like that? Since when did she deny what was so obvious between them? She'd never been able to before.

And *he'd* been unable to help stepping closer just then. Drawn like an idiot moth. Again. And she'd admitted that she'd used him—that what had happened had been the best thing for her. Just as he'd suspected. All she'd really wanted was to get out of that small village and the life her parents had mapped for her. He'd been the convenient taxi driver—one that gave her a few thrills along the way. Now she was Ms Independent and so happy about it?

She'd got more than some lip with her sophistication. She'd got bite. And frankly, she made him want to bite back. His teeth were already sharpened, thanks to the driving attraction that had surged back within a second of seeing her again. But here she was acting all uninterested? All cool and calm and unaffected? Little liar. He'd read the signs—he'd heard the husky edge in her voice, seen her flush and the tension in her body. Sexual tension. Well, he wasn't letting her deny it. She wasn't rewriting history. That attraction had been insane. It still was. Those hormones still crazy powerful—but not uncontrollable. At least, not for him.

And he'd prove it.

He smiled as he raided a tray of hors d'oeuvres. But it

was another appetite he was planning to sate. He hadn't felt driven to prove a point in a long time. But this was irresistible. He'd play. He'd take such delight in teasing. And in less than a week he'd have Victoria Rutherford begging him to bite her.

Vivi tried not to watch him from across the room but she was viciously aware of him laughing with Alannah and Gia and everyone else having a jolly good time.

She *wasn't* anyone's slave. She was paid a mint and she deserved to be. Gia was lucky to have her. But for once she didn't want to stay sober and sensible and on the sidelines. She stepped forward, grabbing a glass of champagne from a tray being carried straight past her. She'd participate, she'd prove how she belonged right in the heart of this society.

She took a sip and heard a laugh from nearby. She turned. Nico, one of Gia's fave photographers, was watching her. 'You're in a strange mood tonight, Vivi.' He stepped closer.

'You think?' She took another deep sip of the champagne. She was infuriated with Liam for showing up. As for standing that bit too close, speaking that bit too soft—as if it were yesterday that they'd been shagging as if there were no tomorrow? There hadn't been a tomorrow, of course. There hadn't been anything for him but blind lust and she wasn't falling into that trap again.

Nico nodded, his gaze roaming over her. 'You have an aura about you.'

'An aura?'

'A lot of energy.' He looked her up and down again. 'There's definitely something in the air tonight.' Nico looked surprised. 'You really do look different. More liberated.'

'That would be my lack of bra,' she said bluntly. 'Alannah used it in the show and now it's shredded.'

'Alannah seems to be interested in another of your possessions at the moment.'

Her *possession*? Vivi followed Nico's gaze and looked over to where Alannah was hanging on Liam's every word. 'She can do what she wants with that.' Vivi determinedly turned back to Nico. 'He's not mine.'

'Vivi.' Nico looked amused. 'You forget I record expressions for a living. I understand every flicker of emotion on someone's face. My trigger finger knows when to snap that flash of pure, personal honesty. You *own* that guy.'

'As if.' Vivi damped down the violent surge of feminine satisfaction at the possibility. It was ludicrous. 'You don't understand emotion—you deal with blank canvasses and give the *illusion* of emotion with make-up, staging and lighting.'

'Vivi—' Nico put his hand on his chest '—you wound me.'

'It's true. And then you tweak the fantasy pictures even more on the computer.' She teased with a smile. 'You're not a photographer, you're a two-bit magician using sleight of hand and trickery to deceive the eye.'

Nico laughed with relish. 'Definitely a blazing aura. I wonder just what—or *who*—it is that's set you on fire tonight.'

'I've already told you.' Vivi shrugged. 'It's the lack of bra.'

'When stripped, Victoria's a completely different person,' Liam drawled behind her.

Vivi stiffened and turned.

'*Victoria*?' Nico laughed again. 'Who *is* this woman?'

Liam stepped between her and Nico. 'The one I want to talk to.'

Brows sky-high, Nico lifted his champagne flute in a silent toast and slinked away.

'That was classy,' Vivi admonished Liam lightly, but her fingers were so tight around her glass it was a wonder it didn't shatter. 'What if he was my boyfriend?'

'He'd have stayed,' Liam answered in a 'duh' tone. 'Anyway, it's obvious he's not. The cow-eyes he was giving me...' He grinned, unabashed.

Everyone in the room was sending that look to Liam. It was grossly unfair of him to be more attractive than all the models in the room. And all the models were looking at him as if he were the predator they hoped to be prey for. They preened and posed, but to no avail. Liam didn't seem to notice them, certainly didn't do the same. He'd no need to conform to some code of coolness. He wasn't afraid to throw his head back and laugh freely. In short, he was so comfortable in his own skin he drew everyone towards him. Which infuriated her—because he affected her most of all.

'What did you want to talk about?' she asked, trying to regain her legendary efficiency.

'I had another thought about the shoot.'

'We can discuss it at the meeting you scheduled first thing tomorrow.'

But he grabbed her wrist as she turned away—his large hand wrapping around her, branding her skin.

'Don't tell me you've clocked off for the night? Rumour has it you never stop working. But...' he leaned closer '...I'm happy to go personal if you'd prefer.'

She hoped he couldn't feel her frantic pulse. She rolled her eyes. 'See? Some things don't change.'

'Such as?'

'Leopards, spots...'

'Hmm.' He nodded. 'Nor do the laws of physics, right? Magnetic attraction.'

Vivi smiled sweetly. 'And let's not forget repulsion.'

He laughed. This time it was a warm burst of infectiousness that lingered a long time after he'd fallen silent. He let her go. Yet she didn't step away. Didn't want to. Because there was something about him that called to her—that sensuality, yes. But also that sense of *fun*. So very inviting.

'You're even more arrogant.' She shook her head.

'I wasn't arrogant,' he denied oh-so innocently. 'I was a callow youth caught in the throes of his first love affair.'

'First?' She choked—one quarter outraged, three quarters amused.

His eyes twinkled. 'The first that counted.'

She let her brows shoot to the ceiling. 'Have *any* counted?'

'You've changed,' he mused. 'You talk back.'

Hell, yeah, she did. 'Well, I am five years older.'

'Wiser.' He nodded. 'More experienced.' A whisper of a wink. 'And at pains to point out how perfect your life is now.'

'Because it is.' It was. And, yes, she wanted him to know it.

His eyebrows did a dance then. 'There's always room for improvement.' His voice dropped. 'A tweak here and there.'

What kind of 'tweaks' was he thinking of when he spoke in such a wicked way? 'Are you flirting with me?'

He spread his hands wide, his shoulders lifting an inch. 'You have a problem with that?'

'We now have a business relationship.'

'What's with all this emphasis on boundaries? You were happy to ignore other kinds of relationships five years ago.'

Oh, that was low. 'Well, you can flirt all you like, but I'm not playing.'

'No?' He laughed. 'You challenging me? Don't you remember I find those hard to resist?'

She swallowed. 'You're saying you haven't changed? You're not older and wiser and more experienced?'

'Two out of three isn't bad.' He shrugged.

'No prizes for guessing the two,' she snapped back.

He smiled—easy, amused. 'I can't wait to catch up more at our meeting tomorrow. Seeing you first thing was always a pleasure.'

She suppressed a shiver but there was no hiding the attraction was still there. That chemistry. She had to mentally grip every muscle and *not* move. Not preen or lean towards him. Not lick her lips. Not shift her legs apart.

There was a moment where she just stood before him— her gaze locked in his, her thoughts chaotic. Then, thankfully, he stepped back. She watched him walk away. Then she forced her eyelids to shut and she pivoted—like an owl, to stare in another direction. To her surprise Alannah was standing beside her.

'What'd you do to get him to look at you like that?' Alannah's mouth was hanging open.

For a moment Vivi panicked that the diva model was going to have some kind of petulant fit. But then she realised Alannah was serious—as if genuinely amazed. Vivi grimaced. Was it so far-fetched that a guy might think she

was attractive? Well, yeah, this would be the first time
in history that a guy had looked at her when Alannah or
any of the other models were anywhere in the vicinity.

'I tied him up and whipped him,' Vivi quipped, wishing—just for this second—that she really could.

'He's submissive?' Alannah's eyes went watermelon
wide.

The idea of Liam being submissive to anyone was totally laughable.

'Um...' Vivi felt a shift in the atmosphere as Alannah
gazed at her with a weird intensity.

'Oh... My...' A nodding Alannah looked her up and
down and spoke in a theatrical whisper. 'I can see it now.
It makes total sense. You're a domme.' She paused and actually fanned her face with her fingers. 'Wow. You know
I can be submissive too. I love it when a lover makes me
beg.'

'Uhhh...' Was Alannah for real?

Alannah giggled so hard she all but doubled over. 'You
should see the look on your face.'

Vivi groaned. 'You're a brat.'

'But such a good one. Dontcha wanna whip me?'

'Go away. I was kidding.'

'Oh, I don't think so,' Alannah teased. 'But honestly,
Vivi, you should take the boots off and do whatever he
tells you to. Let him take the reins—and the whip.' She
winked and sashayed away.

Uh huh. Tried that once already and look where that
had got her. Pain so wasn't her thing.

Back in her hotel room she sat at the desk program-
ming appointments and updating Gia's schedule. Except
Liam's image kept sliding into her mind.

Damn.

She'd not thought about him in years. She'd done a brilliantly good job of training her brain not to dwell on men at all. She knew what they were about. And a guy wasn't part of her life at this point in time. She was all about work this week, this month...this whole year.

She didn't need a lover and was decades off marriage and kids. Because she'd learned that what *she* wanted was never of importance in a relationship. She always came in second. Always had to be the one to sacrifice and put her wishes behind his. That had been how it was with Oliver. Liam was supposed to have been different, but he'd turned out to be the worst. The few guys she'd dated since had just added a few ditto marks to her scoresheet. So she wasn't going there for ages yet—not when she had an amazing career to make the most of.

She'd do this meeting, set up this shoot, prove herself to be the professional she was. But as she slipped into bed and switched out the light she had to sternly remind herself. She would not remember. She would *not*.

THREE

———

His lips brushed hers. Gentle. The barest rub, back and forth. She tilted her chin and heard approval rumble deep in his throat. The kiss deepened immediately. She opened and he took what she offered—claiming her with his tongue, caressing the roof of her mouth. Startled, she shivered. So quickly seduced.

She'd already been seduced. She'd been his from the first moment she'd seen him in the guest bathroom when she'd been in nothing but a towel and he'd been all steam, strength, sex—and fun. Such fun. That kiss had started with a smile, an intimacy she'd been unable to resist.

With her lips parted, her mouth his to own, his hands roamed, moving in time with the tease of his tongue. He swept a broad palm down her spine, pulling her closer to him while at the same time pushing her against the cool, concrete wall behind her. His other hand teased, feathering strokes against her hip, up her side, feeling out the soft swell of her breast. His thumb scraped over her nipple. This time the moan of approval was hers. She arched into him, rising on tiptoe to get closer.

She wanted more. Needed so much more.

Vivi opened her eyes and stared at the dim ceiling. It was more than a dream. It was a memory.

That first kiss had been outside some motorway services restaurant. She'd been excited but slightly scared at the same time. She'd never kissed anyone but Oliver before. Liam was taller. Broader. Stronger. Liam was more everything.

He'd pressed her up against that wall of the building for what had to have been hours. Until some blushing security guard had interrupted and asked them to move along.

They'd moved to the nearest hotel.

Finally unleashed, the simmering passion between them had meant there was nothing else they could do. They didn't leave that room for three days. Then it was further south only as far as they could be bothered before falling into bed in another hotel. A few more days. Another hotel. Slowly travelling, hungrily seeking that physical satisfaction.

Frustrated, Vivi threw back the sheet, got out of bed and got some chilled water from the minibar. Her memories were fantasy enhanced, right? Dreams highlighted, magnified…It hadn't been all that fabulous. Five years was a long time. She was over it.

But now five years didn't feel like long enough.

She got to sleep ten minutes before her alarm rang. Thank heavens Gia had taken the day off from her usual schedule. The last thing Vivi felt like was managing her as well as Liam.

She stood beneath a cool shower spray and gave herself the pep talk. She *could* handle him—she'd handled way worse with ease. She'd meet him, arrange things beautifully with an utterly businesslike manner. No more laughing and almost flirting. This had to be a quick, efficient strike. It'd all be over in half an hour or less. And she'd be sure to arrange things that meant she didn't have to see him again. Ever. Piece of cake.

Liam's hotel was only a short walk from hers but she took a taxi. She didn't want to be in the least bit flushed when she met him again. Nothing like the blushing schoolgirl she'd been last night.

He was in the hotel restaurant in loose chinos, a white cotton tee and an amused smile—the kind a cat circling a broken-winged bird would wear.

'You want to eat?' he asked.

'No, thanks, but some orange juice would be great.'

As she took her seat he ordered for her. Oh, Lord, the guy was temptation enough without suddenly switching to Italian and sounding all seductive first thing in the morning.

He caught her staring and raised an eyebrow. 'So how does this work?' he asked.

'Basically, you tell me what you want and I arrange it.' She ignored the widening smile on his mouth. 'Gia instructed me to do whatever it takes for this to happen.'

'Whatever it takes?'

She sighed. 'Your little mind's still in the gutter.'

'But I've got the rest of me out.'

'I never thought the rest of you was in it,' she said simply. 'Now tell me what you want.'

His smile slowly widened again. 'So, this is what you do all day? Arrange things for Gia?'

'That is my job.'

'It must be exhausting.' He sat back as the waiter served them both a glass of fresh juice. 'What are the perks? You obviously don't get to wear her designs.' He gave her fresh white shirt and black skirt combo a cursory glance—clearly uninspired.

Good. That was the point. But she couldn't stop a little defence seeping out. 'Men wear suits—why not women?'

'In a creative industry?'

'It's not my job to be creative. I need to be efficient.'

'Why not both?'

She shook her head. 'Around Gia I need to be unobtrusive.'

He laughed. 'Doesn't matter what you wear, darling, you can never fade into the background.'

He was doing it again. Making her laugh. Paying her attention. Making her feel warm and alive and so easily attracted to him.

'So your life is nothing but work? No boyfriend?' he asked.

Her eyes narrowed. It was tempting to say there was. To invent a wildly passionate lover. To be as in love as it was possible to be. To be *safe*. But her wayward body dominated. Answering while she was still mulling her options—her head slowly shaking.

'Don't tell me you've been living like a puritan all these years?' He chuckled. 'You still feel guilty about what happened?'

She sharply glanced at him. He'd known she felt guilty?

His smile softened at her expression. 'You were such a 'good girl', Victoria. You'd never gone against your parents' wishes.'

'I went against everyone's expectations that day,' she pointed out with a touch of heat. She hadn't been that much of a child.

'True. But that's nothing to feel guilty about.' He paused. 'You didn't cheat on him.'

No? Where was the line? Just by looking at Liam she'd been all but cheating.

He shook his head. 'You broke up with him before anything happened with me. You'd already said no to me before you broke up with him.'

But then it hadn't taken her long to change her mind. How had this happened? She'd been in his company less than five minutes and already they were talking past and *personal.* 'Don't worry, what happened between us hasn't scarred me for life or anything.' Vivi laughed lightly. 'I'm so over it.'

'So you've had other boyfriends since me.'

'Of course.' Not a lie this time.

'But nothing serious?'

She didn't have to answer that.

'And no boyfriend now?'

She ran her fingers over the cool glass. 'Not during the show season.'

'What, you put relationships on hold for that?'

'Of course. I can't be bothered with a man moaning about being neglected.'

He chuckled. 'Neglected? I can't imagine you ever neglecting a lover—you were always so generous...'

She chose to ignore *that* reference. 'Well, *you* know how it is, Liam—people tend to feel ignored when their partner is wholly focused on work. I find it's easier to be single at the busiest times.'

'I would have thought a true partner would understand when his lover has a huge crunch on at work. Wouldn't he be supportive? Offer an end-of-the-day massage?'

'Is that what your girlfriend does for you?' Vivi smiled, oh, *so* sweetly.

He chuckled. 'No, I'm every bit as single as you. I've had

girlfriends but it never seems to work for long. I guess long-term relationships don't fit with my personality.' He sounded careless.

'It's not that you're having too much fun enjoying the *variety* in your high-flying lifestyle?'

'I know you love to think the worst of me, but I'm actually not a slut.'

'What?' She paused for effect. 'You mean you don't sleep your way to what you want?'

He bridled. 'Aren't you getting a little desperate to score a point?'

'No point scoring, just an honest assessment. Isn't it an extension of networking and schmoozing?'

'I guess it could be but I think you've been hanging around the Hollywood types too much. You know, most of the people I need to network with are guys,' he said dryly. 'And you know I'm not gay.'

'So you're telling me you don't all get together at lap bars and do your deals amongst breasts and legs?'

'You're really trying to have the lowest opinion of me, aren't you?' He looked way too amused. 'Why so determined to talk yourself into disliking me? Dreaming up the worst dirt your mind can dredge? Sorry, darling, but I'm not going to help you out. Fact is I'm an all right guy. That's not to say I don't have sex, but it's always good and it's always with a woman who's as happy about it as I am.'

'I'm sure she is,' Vivi ground out poisonously.

'And naturally, any man lucky enough to date you would be very, *very* happy,' he added.

She bit back a bitchy retort. She really needed to steer them back to business.

'Or are you holding out for Mr Right?' he asked with a laugh.

'There's no such thing,' she growled, provoked. 'No hero on the white charger. No love of your life.' No grand passion. There was companionship and good sex. Neither of which she had time for right now.

'No.' He said it with such finality and, even though she believed it herself, she was somehow wounded.

'Shall we get back to business?' Vivi forced herself to back away from the boggy territory they'd wandered into. 'We have a limited time frame. Alannah has a shoot in Venice today and tomorrow. Gia was supposed to be having a few days at a spa.' And Vivi had been longing for three days' solid sleep.

'You can get Gia into the spa a few days later and I have a plane that can get Alannah from Venice as soon as she's done.'

'You want Alannah that much?'

His gaze lifted. 'I want her in the pictures for my company.'

No man just wanted Alannah on paper.

Liam openly laughed. 'I don't think I'm her type anyway. She was looking at me very oddly last night.'

'You mean not in the usual total adoring way you're used to? Women just fall at your feet, don't they? Well, men just fall at hers. So perhaps she's the perfect challenge for you.' She glanced at him to see his reaction.

A smile played around his mouth. 'She's not a challenge for me.'

'Oh, please. Every man on the planet sees her as the ultimate score.'

'Not me. As far as I can see there's no discernible personality there.'

'It's there. She just hides it.' Vivi reckoned she had to, in order for her to survive the insanity of her life. 'So you only like women you see as a challenge?' It was all about the challenge.

'Not a challenge to get into bed. I like a woman who challenges me on every level. Physically, intellectually.'

'Emotionally?' she mocked. 'You'll never get me to believe that, Liam.'

He kept looking at her so long she grew uncomfortable with the silence.

'Maybe Alannah looked at you funny because I told her you like me to tie you up and whip you.' She cleared her throat and sat back, waiting for the explosion.

But he didn't blink. 'Well in one way you did. I was only a toy for you.' His eyes met hers. 'You used me.'

'Excuse me?' Vivi's temperature rose so she worked hard to keep her tone calm. '*You* used *me*. You wanted in. You wanted acceptance.'

'Stealing you away from your family and almost-fiancé was hardly going to gain me acceptance,' he said, equally cool. 'I was some kind of escapist fantasy—the bit of rough. But once reality hit, you couldn't wait to get away. You used me, Victoria. Not the other way round.' He leaned over the table. 'You wanted to escape the nice middle-class prison you were in. You didn't want to marry Oliver but you felt trapped. I was your escape route. Nothing more.'

How could he possibly think she'd used him like that? 'You've no idea how hard it was for me to walk out of that house and go with you. I walked away from everything.'

'Which was exactly what you wanted.' Obstinately he stuck to his warped view of what had happened.

'How would you know what I wanted?' He'd never asked her. 'You weren't interested in anything I wanted to do. You just expected me to fall in with your plans. I was supposed to sit on the beach or something while you were out sailing. It was all about *your* dreams. You had no clue what mine were and you didn't want to know.' She didn't want this—to go over what had gone wrong. 'Look, I'll rebook Gia's spa and get her to Genoa and rework Alannah's schedule. Given your inability to stay on track with any kind of serious planning this morning, and given the pressure on *my* precious time, I'm going to leave now and will keep you updated with plans via email.' She stood up from the table and looked at him. 'Anything else you need from me right now?'

'Just one thing,' he answered blandly, following her out of the restaurant.

Vivi kept walking. 'What is it?'

'A kiss goodbye.'

What? She lurched to a standstill and turned, scraping up a laugh. 'That's not appropriate in a professional relationship.'

'Yeah, well, this relationship was never going to be professional.' He stepped closer. 'You're going to have to get over that.'

She opened her mouth but he put his finger on her lips.

'A kiss makes for a better goodbye than harsh words, don't you think?'

Five years ago goodbye had been a doozy of an argument. He'd got wild with her and she equally so. She'd never been so angry in her life. He'd made her lose control of her emotions in more ways than one. She'd lost him. She'd already lost her family. And she'd kept all her emotions under control since.

'You can't reheat old soup.' She tried to ignore the sensations of his finger on her mouth as she spoke.

'You think? Don't things taste better when the flavours

have had time to infuse or ferment? Isn't that the difference between grape juice and wine?'

She didn't need to get drunk on Liam again. 'You're incorrigible.'

'But you know I'm right.'

'No.'

'Then prove me wrong.'

'You can't tease me into this.'

'No?'

'Public displays of affection are tacky.'

'This isn't affection.'

'Then what is it?'

He moved so fast she didn't stand a chance. His hand dropped from her mouth and slid round her waist, pulling her close against him. His head dropped.

His lips didn't brush, they bruised. But only for a moment—they softened almost immediately, caressing, then the pressure increased again. He teased—always such a tease. And then he lifted just a fraction. She knew he was going to pull away.

No. That wasn't enough. She reached up and stopped him stepping back. She kissed him.

He met her again, his arms swiftly coming tight around her, and she clung right back. Her mouth parted, her tongue seeking greater intimacy—to stroke and torment as good as she was getting. Memory and reality slammed together.

She felt the rumble deep in his chest. He pulled her tighter into his heat. She felt him hot and hard. Her heart ripped open. No one had ever made her feel like this. Not just lust—not just turned on. But *touched*. Somehow he woke something so deep within her, something she'd never been aware of until him. And he made her want more. Always more. She wanted everything.

No.

She pushed back, her breathing choppy—wildly waving a hand in the air, seeking some stability. He reached out and held her hand hard—allowing her the distance but supporting her at the same time because he knew just how close she was to stumbling. Falling. For him.

Oh, no.

'That shouldn't have happened,' she said firmly.

For once he wasn't smiling, his chin was lifted, determination written in the intensity of his eyes. 'You wanted it as much as I did. You wanted more. You want me.'

She did. But she shook her head. 'This can't happen, Liam. I can't let this happen.'

FOUR

———

Liam stared sightlessly at the designs on his screen, unable to stop thinking about Victoria. He'd had his victory, right? He'd teased her. Traded barbs. And it had happened—he'd drawn her in. He'd kissed her. But even better, *she'd* kissed him back. She couldn't deny their explosive chemistry. And she hadn't. So he'd proved the point, right? But the second he'd taken that success, she'd stolen it back with her decree—she couldn't 'let this happen'.

Why not? The need to know drove into him. But his need to follow through did more than dominate. The desire to have her—to win—consumed. He didn't want her to 'let it happen' either. He didn't want her in passive mode. That was what bugged him most—her lack of honesty. She hadn't just 'let' that kiss happen. She'd pulled him close—*taken* for one hot moment. And now he wanted it all—it was pure chemistry. Undeniable and so strong. He wanted her to push for all of him. Not to be the one pleasing, the one offering, or 'letting', but the one taking. He wanted her to admit it—to ask. To demand.

And he'd answer the only way he could.

* * *

'No, we have to have that fabric sample by Tuesday morning at the latest. Needless to say, if we don't receive it by that time we won't be looking at your supplier again.' Vivi, on the warpath, ended the call and immediately placed another. Typing with one hand while texting with another and talking on her earpiece to someone else altogether. Clients were melting down at the prospect of Gia extending her time in Italy; one reporter was psychotic over her not being back in London in time for some interview.

'Could she do an interview on Skype?'

'Gianetta doesn't Skype. You'll have to reschedule.'

Liam's last-minute photo shoot had caused an almighty headache but Gia seemed determined for it to go ahead, meaning Vivi was busier than ever on the day she should have had as a break. Usually being busy was good. But being busy for something Liam-related? Not so much. It meant she thought about him *all* the time. Most especially in the too few hours she'd had to snatch sleep. Memories stole into her mind—like wicked little elves breaking into a locked garden to frolic and play and torment. She remembered the slide of his hands, the steel of his body, the intensity of his expression...

She tossed, turned. Gave up.

Maybe she should hit the nearest open-all-hours sex-aids store and grab a vibrator? But she was in Italy and had no idea where or how to find one. Besides, she already knew the thing wouldn't work it for her. She wanted hot, real touch.

With just one look, one smile, she'd been bitten again. Just as she had five years before. But their affair couldn't be repeated. She'd not just walked away from her family, she'd lost *herself*. That was a huge part of what she'd run from in the end. Looking back, she knew she'd been shel-tered. Her relationship with Oliver had been sweet—in truth a little cloying. With Liam it'd been fevered, uncon-trolled passion. But he'd been right the other day. She'd felt guilt and it had worsened as those weeks passed. Leaving Oliver for Liam made her conscience burn—un-necessarily maybe—but it had. Worse had been her *need* of Liam. Conflicted—insecure—her emotions flailed and never found the foothold she'd needed. Not from him. She'd never get it from him.

The 'goodbye' kiss the other morning told her. She couldn't touch him again. She had to turn her back on temptation. He'd always be too much for her to handle. She'd fought too hard to make something of her life. She wasn't losing it for another short-lived affair. So she forced focus. Sent him a very brief, businesslike email explain-ing the shoot details she'd arranged.

His reply came back within ten minutes. For twenty more she stared at it, her blood heating, until finally she picked up her phone.

'You can't call me 'darling' in an email,' she said as soon as he answered.

'Why not?' he asked innocently. She could hear the wicked smile in the words.

'It could be considered sexual harassment.'

He snorted. 'Doesn't everyone in the fashion industry call each other darling?'

'Not me.'

'Why? You give them a frosty look and scare them off?' He chuckled. 'Is this the phone equivalent of that?'

'Yes,' she said firmly.

'Hmm,' he murmured. 'Am I allowed to sign off my emails with a kiss? A little 'x' like they all do?'

'Not me,' she repeated, regretting calling him now because the wretch always seemed to make her smile. To make her take a step closer.

'Of course not. I'm thinking you're more triple 'x', right?'

'Liam, *you* are my ex,' she said pointedly. 'And you're staying that way.'

'It didn't feel over the other morning,' he answered softly. 'Is it sexual harassment to say I'm looking forward to seeing you again?'

She gritted her teeth. 'I guess not.'

'I think sexual harassment would be something much worse than a 'darling',' he added thoughtfully. 'Explicit suggestions...instructions maybe.'

She closed her eyes, her flush blooming, her body five steps ahead of her brain even though her brain was on overtime—sending images that were way worse than triple X-rated. He wasn't saying anything bad. Not really. It was all in the *way* he said it.

'I *am* looking forward to seeing you again,' he repeated in that deceptively soft, dangerous voice. 'Watching you come...here. Watching you work. And seeing you satisfied when all is done.'

In the echo of his words all kinds of explicit suggestions—instructions—filled her head. And she wanted them. She did. She'd always wanted him. She wanted what they'd had. She wanted more. She probably always would. But she could resist. She *would*.

'You're not going to answer back?' he prompted.

'No.' She forced herself to say it to him.

Practice made perfect, right?

* * *

'You really need me to go with you?' she asked Gia later that day, trying to hide the high-pitched 'please say no' edge in her voice.

'Of course.' Gia barely grunted her reply.

Twenty-four hours later Vivi landed in Genoa with Gia, Alannah and a couple of male models, Nico, a pair of stylists and scores of bags.

The coastal city was beautiful, but the boats in the marina were mind-blowing. Vivi was used to excess. Working for Gia, she met pop stars and actors, oil barons and media moguls—all of whom loved to have pretty models surrounding them. So she'd seen some fancy boats and apartments in her time. But this was something else again. But they were whisked past far too quickly for her to really appreciate them, and taken to a large shed on the furthest side of the facility. They went through another round of security and were finally allowed in. Liam's boats were locked away, carefully hidden from view.

He was waiting for them. Vivi tried to stay at the back of the group. Tried to stay busy helping one stylist manage her bags. But she couldn't resist looking as he relentlessly watched her *coming* nearer towards him. His eyes were dark. The longer cut of his hair didn't soften him any, or make him look casual. He looked like a pirate. She tried to stop the slither of her body towards him, it was so unfair of him to be so irresistible. She'd never seen him sailing all those years ago. It'd been winter, Christmas. He'd been covered up until she'd stripped him in that hotel room. But now? All bronzed and in shorts and boatshoes and standing easily along the wooden deck of that beautiful cruiser? There was too much skin on show, too much *man*. He looked every inch the warrior who knew how to fight, how to seduce, how to win.

She turned away. Gia was in raptures. The boat 'in the flesh' was even more marvellous than she'd expected. Nico was an over-the-top nightmare, already barking orders and deciding on angles. Vivi hadn't even noticed the boat. Now she forced herself to pay attention.

She stepped onboard, drawing breath as she did. He'd designed this? She carefully gazed around, stared at the boat and then him. He'd been so competitive. So ruthless in achieving what he wanted. She'd have thought he'd be all function over form. But this was beautiful. Elegant. Simple. Every feature well thought out, sleek and stylish. No wonder he'd become so successful so quickly. He deserved to be. She felt a bubble of pride. Astonished, she realised she was pleased for him—and she couldn't hold back her smile.

He looked at her, his eyes mirroring her smile. 'You're surprised.'

Reluctantly she nodded. 'Don't be offended. There was a lot I didn't know about you back then.' She had a feeling there was still a lot—back then she'd been too self-absorbed to realise it.

He nodded briefly. 'You need a hand with those bags?'

'No, I have it covered, thanks.'

But she didn't. Nico was bellowing orders, as was Gia. Alannah was tired and demanding caffeine. Vivi needed thirty extra helpers to carry all the gear to where it was needed. She glanced at Liam, who was standing too close and watching with a far too amused look on his face.

'Can't those pretty boys help, or are they scared of breaking a fingernail?' he asked.

She refused to laugh. 'They're getting their make-up done.'

'Ah, well. Since I'm handsome enough without make-up...' He stepped forward and took a heavy bag in each hand. 'You tell me where to put them.'

Well, she wasn't a total idiot. If he wanted to help, he could help. And she? She'd...try really hard not to watch too closely as his muscles worked, not stare at his butt as he bent down, not feel the itch in her fingers to touch. And not dwell on just how handsome he was without make-up. Without anything.

Dear heaven, she was going to need so much help not to do those things.

It took over an hour for Alannah's hair, face and body to be made-up—slightly less for the two male models, and slightly more for Nico to decide on how he wanted them draped in his first scene.

Finally they got to taking some pictures—meaning Vivi could have a moment to step back and organise refreshments. Good thing—she didn't want to watch everyone start sweating as they took in Alannah posing in a teensy bikini.

'You want some help?' Liam caught up with her as she stepped off the boat.

She sent him a suspicious glance. 'You don't want to go watch the models writhe on your deck?'

He shook his head.

Oh, she didn't believe him. 'You'd really rather do the coffee run with me?'

'I'd rather writhe on my deck with you, but sadly that isn't an option.'

She choked back both her blush and a laugh. 'We need to be quick.'

'Do we?' he asked idly. 'Shame.'

Oh, he was naughty. So much naughtier than he'd been all those years ago. And even more irresistible. 'You're appalling.'

'I'm not as bad as you,' he argued mildly. 'Here's you spending your life doing everything to keep everyone else happy. When do you do what you want? Take what you want? You've got the give, where's the take?'

He might sound as if he were teasing, but she got the less-than-subtle criticism. 'This is what I want. I have everything I need.'

'Everything?' His brows arched and he waggled an admonishing finger at her. 'No boyfriend. No orgasm.' His expression reckoned she was missing out big-time.

She rolled her eyes. 'What was I thinking?' she played along, sarcasm dripping. 'Of course, no life is complete without sex.'

'You said it.'

She sent him one of her stern-secretary looks. 'I do not need a man to have an orgasm.'

'Oh, my.' His laughter rumbled. '*So* independent now.'

'That's right,' she said loftily, walking down to the doorway to collect the coffees she'd ordered to be delivered. 'From meek and mild to self-sufficient and successful.'

'And sassy,' he noted. 'But still someone else's slave,' he called after her.

'Secretary,' she corrected, giving him a kill-shot look over her shoulder.

'Same thing.' He shrugged it off.

'Insult me all you like—it's not going to work.'

He grinned and stepped in front of her to take the tray for her from the delivery boy. Easily dealing with the transaction in flawless Italian for her. At least it sounded flawless.

It sounded gorgeous.

'Where did you go?' he asked as they walked back to take it to the others. 'After we split?'

For a moment she tensed, then consciously relaxed. Why not talk about it? They were adults now, right? They could hold a conversation about the past without getting worked up—neither flirting nor fighting.

'London.' She gestured for him to put the coffee down until the current crop of pics had been taken. 'I had no money, no skills, three quarters of a degree, nowhere to live.' She'd fought hard to get a foot in the door. She hadn't had the time to think about him. Not ever think about him. But she was proud of what she'd achieved.

'What about your parents?' He frowned. 'You didn't go back to them?'

'Why would I do that?' she asked. After the way they'd spoken to her—making their opinion of her crystal clear? After what had happened to Stella, she'd known what she was in for when she'd walked out of that door with Liam. When her sister had left home as a teen, all record of her existence had been obliterated. Her parents were unforgiving. No memory of Victoria would remain in their home.

'But...' He picked up a coffee but didn't take a sip. 'You see them now?'

She hesitated. 'I send them a Christmas card.' Because there was that tiny part of her that ached.

'Do they send you one back?'

She didn't answer.

'You're kidding.' He looked appalled. 'They really did

it, then? Cast you out? They don't even acknowledge *Christmas*?'

'Well...' Vivi shifted uncomfortably '...I don't put a return address on the envelope.'

Liam paused, then his left eyebrow lifted. 'You haven't told them where you live? Or what you do? Or anything?'

Vivi unnecessarily brushed her fingers through her bob, knowing it would fall perfectly back into place. Hooray for working with the world's best hairstylists.

'You haven't given them a chance?' he pushed.

'What was the point? I know exactly what would happen. Look at Stella.' She was too scared. If they didn't have her address, she wouldn't hope for contact. She couldn't be disappointed.

'Right.' He nodded. 'Well, what about her? Have you tried to get in touch with her?' His voice raised enough for Nico to turn and frown at them.

Vivi took a step back from the others and sent Liam a frown of her own.

'I thought about it.' But she hadn't wanted to come begging. She'd wanted to succeed on her own first. And she had. Then she'd made some friends at work. They'd become her family. And why would Stella want to get in touch with her? She'd walked away and never looked back. Never once thought to call her little sister.

'But you never did?' Liam had an intent, almost disapproving, solemn look on his face. 'You're so unforgiving.'

Vivi folded her arms across her chest. 'No, I'm not.'

'You are.'

'Stella never once tried to get in touch with me. My parents told me that if I left, not to bother coming back.' Hell, hadn't Liam heard that? Her mother had shouted it so loud half the world must have.

'You've never said anything awful in the heat of the moment?' Liam asked quietly.

There was a silence and she sent him a look. Then sighed. 'Trust me. I know they're not interested. They're the ones who are unforgiving. When Stella left, I saw what they did to her stuff. Why would I do that to myself? Why would I knock on the door only to have it slammed in my face?'

'So you're afraid,' he said softly.

'No. I'm just not stupid. Besides, I don't have the time. I'm too busy—'

'Doing everything for Gia.'

That again? 'Gianetta's been more of a friend to me than anyone in my family ever has,' Vivi pointed out. 'And believe me, I understand that the relationship I have with Gia is a business one. If I annoy her, I'm out the door.' She knew what she had to do to survive. And survive she would.

'Okay.' He blew out a big breath and then cleared his throat. 'So what do you do for Christmas?'

Oh. She couldn't help the guilty grin. 'I work. What about you?'

'I work.'

She laughed. So not surprised. That Christmas they'd had together had kind of killed the spirit. When you had people screaming at you, it didn't make things festive.

'Can you two be quiet, please?' Nico glowered at them.

Vivi bit back her smile and went to ensure the lunch caterers were going to make it past security. It seemed the monsters needed feeding.

An hour later she was exhausted—having checked and double-checked that all the special orders were fulfilled. She'd lost sight of Liam for a while, presumed he'd gone to do some work somewhere. She wished she could escape for a bit too. The constant demands from the 'talent' were wearing.

'Hey, have this.' Liam appeared at her side and offered her a steaming cup.

'Oh, thanks.' She took a careful sip and smiled as the flavour hit her taste buds—peppermint tea? She couldn't believe he'd found some. What surprised her even more was that he remembered it was the only tea she drank—that he'd noticed she'd not had any of the coffee. He'd sat up with her that night she'd been making Christmas decorations for Oliver's mother. He'd kept her laughing. He'd teased her about the tea. He'd offered...more than he should have.

'Not everything changes, right?' He stood beside her, dangerously intimate.

'No,' she said ruefully. 'I guess not.'

Another hour went by. Another change of bikini for Alannah, new trunks for the men, more adjustments with the lighting and the spray-on mist-to-look-like-sweat. Vivi fetched, carried, stood——all with Liam at her side making amusing comments and general chat. Until Nico was fully engaged with another set-up.

'I thought you'd gone back to Oliver,' Liam said quietly.

She went completely cold. 'Oh, no.' She shook her head. 'No.'

Liam turned away from the models, angling so he could see her face. 'Do you wish you'd said yes to him that day?'

'No.' She didn't hesitate. 'He wasn't right for me either.' She braved looking at his face as she said that last.

He looked thoughtful. 'I saw him recently.'

'*Oliver*?'

'Yeah.' Liam grinned at her squawk. 'He bought one of my boats.'

'Oh. Great.' Vivi swallowed back her shock. 'He's well? And happy?'

Liam nodded. 'Married and climbing his way to the top of an investment bank. Exactly on the track he'd always wanted to be on.'

Yeah, it was that same life plan. Just with a different woman.

'So he's done okay through the recession?' Vivi shook her head at her own stupidity. 'Of course he has—he's bought one of your boats.'

And he was happy. That was good. She wouldn't have been happy with him and she knew she'd have made him unhappy too. 'I'm glad he's doing well,' she said, meaning it. But she was thrown that Oliver and Liam were still... *friends*? Well, she supposed it figured. Mates before dates, right? Then she remembered. 'I'd forgotten you'd gone to work for his family friend...' She frowned, confused. 'But when did you move to Italy?'

Liam had straightened up and faced back towards the models. 'I never worked for the friend.'

'Yes, you did.' She turned towards him to read his face. 'That's why you were there that Christmas. How you got the visa to come to England. Oliver got you that job. You were starting in the new year—you were going to Cowes.' Oliver's family had pulled strings to get Liam a job with a close contact in the yachting industry there. She'd thought it would be okay—truth be told she hadn't thought about it at all.

'They rescinded the job offer. I found other work.'

Her blood ran cold. 'When?' She fought the churning sensation in her gut. 'When did they rescind the offer?'

'A couple of days after we left.'

'But—' She broke off, oddly breathless. 'You'd signed a contract.'

'They found some loophole. What was I going to do—fight it?' He laughed.

But it wasn't funny. She stared at him, a horrible hurt feeling inside. 'You never told me.'

Liam kept looking beyond her, at the scene Nico and Gia had staged. 'I hadn't seen him for years until he came to buy the boat. He asked after you.' Liam sighed. 'He wondered how you were getting on.'

Had Oliver thought she and Liam were still together? 'What did you say?'

'I didn't. I thought you'd gone back to him, remember? I was totally thrown when I found out the wife he'd been going on about wasn't you. Turned out neither of us knew a thing about you. Then I did a couple of searches, but it seemed you'd vanished.'

So Liam had then searched for her? Why?

'How did you hide?' he asked.

She grasped onto that—trying to keep the conversation light, trying not to dig deeper into something that seemed a lot like a giant can of worms. 'With all this social media it's supposedly easy to track anyone down. From the fifteen kids in your first ever class at school to the three hundred in your uni lecture hall. You can find anyone and everyone with a quick Facebook look, right? Unless you consciously change. I shortened my name. Shut down all my accounts. Cut my hair. Became someone new.'

'Vivi.'

She nodded. 'It took a while, but I became the person I wanted to be.' She'd worked in a stationery store to start with but wanted to get into design. She'd loved drawing and doing graphic design on the computer. But it wasn't for her to do fashion at university. That was a hobby, not a career, her father had lectured. Doing French hadn't exactly been much of a career option either. But she could type and organise and she'd picked up computer systems quickly. She learned to get what she needed from other people simply because she had to. 'I got an admin job in Gia's office.'

'And then you showed them what you could really do.'

'I worked so hard,' she said. *How* she'd worked. 'And it's been worth it.'

'So you've proved yourself?' He gazed at her.

'For *myself*. Not anyone else.' She frowned. 'When was it you saw Oliver?'

'A couple of months ago.'

Her heart thudded. 'So, is that why...?'

'I never liked how it ended between us. I thought it'd be interesting to see what had become of you since then.'

Interesting. 'So you're combining business with something personal. Looking up an old flame? This is merely curiosity?' It was silly but somehow it hurt. What was he going to do now—report back to Oliver and the others?

He stepped closer, turning to face her again. 'I don't think this is *merely* anything.'

'Vivi, where the hell is the bag with the power strips?' Nico's shout echoed around them.

Vivi tore her attention from Liam, turned away. And tried to stay away while she processed what she now knew of the past. Liam losing the job offer and never telling her. He must have been so worried—she'd known he didn't have money, didn't have a family... He didn't have much of anything.

And she'd shouted at him. She'd left him.

Eight hours later she was so, so tired. The shoot was taking for ever. She walked off the boat, walked down the back of the boatshed where it was dark. She could hear Nico ordering Alannah about, Gia adding her views. The stylists flitted around like moths. A cast of thousands—and Vivi was supposed to be the one at the back ensuring every single one of them was happy and had all they needed.

Too bad. Right now she needed a break. From Gia's demands. From Alannah's. From Liam.

From the way he watched her. From the way he made her feel—so hungry, so yearning, so turned on all the time. It was insane. She sank into a pile of sail bags in the furthest corner she could find. Her body ached from tension and sleeplessness. She'd steal a few minutes. Five. Then she'd be ready to handle them all again. Handle him.

Liam grimly stopped himself hunting round for Victoria. He didn't need to stalk her. But fifteen minutes later she hadn't come back to the spot where she'd been watching the shoot. He wanted it to be over. He wanted to be alone with her. Truth? That was all he'd wanted. He didn't give a toss about publicity photos and magazine spreads.

He'd been a fool to think it was a stint of celibacy that had made him so hot the first night he'd seen her again. No woman had ever had the effect she had on him. The minute he'd found out Oliver had no clue where she was, that no one knew anything about her... He'd needed to find her.

Ten minutes later he couldn't cope with her absence any more. He went searching. He found her right at the far corner of the boatshed, curled up in a pile of gear, sound asleep but looking horribly uncomfortable with her head at that angle.

Very carefully, quietly, he bent down. Holding his breath, he gently lifted her and slid in beside her, pulling her back to rest against him. He gazed down at her pretty but pale face. She hadn't stirred. Which meant she had to be exhausted.

She worked too hard.

That was something he understood. He'd been working too hard for too long as well. He'd been obsessed with building a company, a basis for a future. Security. She had too. They'd viciously fought that last day—her wants versus his. But it turned out they were incredibly similar.

He'd not realised how much she'd sacrificed and risked to go with him. She'd not understood how desperate he was for money. He'd not told her about the email rescinding the job offer—it had landed in his email account two days after they'd left Oliver's family home. It had meant he had nothing to offer her. He'd felt utterly useless and absolutely determined all at the same time. He'd been so desperate to secure something for his future. For theirs.

But he'd been too proud to admit it all to her. And she'd got angry with him—that he was expecting her to just 'fall in'. He'd thought she was full of bravado that last day when she'd yelled that she didn't need him or anyone and she'd prove it. He hadn't believed her. He'd thought she'd gone back home. Back to her stifling parents. Back to Oliver.

But he'd been wrong. And she had proved it. Changed her name, her look. Built a career. Worked incredibly hard. Turned her back on everything.

He frowned. You couldn't turn your back on everything for ever.

And at heart Vivi Grace was still Victoria Rutherford—generous, caring torment who spent her life pleasing others. He'd tried to tell himself it was just sex that drew him to her. But it wasn't lust filling him now. There were so many more, conflicting, emotions. Amusement, annoyance, *concern*. He'd thought he had this figured out. Now he didn't know what he was going to do with her.

Well, he did. Kissing her the other morning had brought it home. He wanted her. But what he wanted, even more than that, was for her to want it. For her to ask.

Just once. To complete their history.

Vivi wasn't just warm and comfortable, she was lax and hot. She breathed in deep, the scent filling her lungs. Salt air, strong man. She opened her eyes and gasped. He wasn't just with her, he was beneath her—encircling her. His arms were around her, his chest below her cheek.

She looked up at him, trying to read his beautiful eyes. They were dark, but lit by that fire. The sharp planes of his jaw roughened by short stubble. She wanted to stroke it with her fingertips to feel it; she wanted to touch her lips to his.

There was nothing she wanted more than his kiss.

'Something you want?' His voice was so low, she felt it more than heard it.

She said nothing. He knew already.

'Victoria?'

She lived in London. He lived in Italy. She didn't want a relationship. Nor did he. This time she was certain of where this would go, when it would end. With such firm parameters, she'd be okay, right? This would bring closure. She'd expunge the remnants of that lust, reveal it really wasn't that good, and she could prove she had control of her emotions. Able to enjoy a moment.

It could only be a moment.

'Something you want?' he repeated.

'Kiss me,' she breathed.

'Nico?' Alannah's piercing voice shattered the moment just as she lifted her chin to press her lips to his.

'I'm just finding Vivi.' Nico's voice sounded way too near.

Vivi turned her head so quick she almost got whiplash. Nico was a few feet away, his camera in his hands. 'Gia needs you,' he said.

'Of course,' Vivi said.

But she couldn't move—Liam's arms were too tight around her. She looked back at him as she heard Nico walk away. Liam's expression hadn't changed—still trained on her. Still hot. Still determined. And she liked it.

It seemed some things didn't change.

FIVE

———

Gia, the models, Nico left.

Liam didn't.

Vivi was usually the last away from a shoot, the one to ensure all had been done. She was aware of him silently working beside her. Carrying things to the truck for the stylists. Until they too left.

'You need to get back to your hotel.' He finally broke the silence between them. 'I'll give you a lift.'

'Thank you.'

He didn't speak on the drive. Nor did she. At the hotel she got out of the car, hyper aware that he did too—that he tossed the keys to the valet, that he was right by her side as she walked through the reception and to the elevator. That he took the key card to her room from her and opened the door.

'I owe you a kiss,' he said, standing just back from the doorway.

Stepping through the doorway, she turned her head to look him in the eye. 'Then you'd better come in.'

To her amazement a tinge of colour slashed his cheekbones.

She walked on, suddenly smiling. Suddenly sure. She wouldn't say no tonight, didn't want to. Denying what she so badly wanted wasn't going to protect her. Walking away in the morning wouldn't hurt as it had before. Last time there'd been shattered dreams—she'd grown up quickly, painfully. This was merely fun, right? The kind of fling she knew she could handle. She turned in the centre of the room—a half-metre from the bed—and faced him.

He kept walking until he was right in front of her. She lifted her chin and waited. Slowly, too slowly, he pressed his lips to hers. The touch was too careful, too light—but her body went incandescent anyway.

'Anything else you'd like from me?' he breathed.

She gazed into his fire-lit eyes and down his beautiful body. 'One night.'

'Doing what?'

'Everything.'

This time the kiss wasn't light—but it was still full of care. Steeped in passion. She clung to him—he to her. Hands clutched, caressed, swept—pulling bodies closer, stroking. Needing.

'You mind taking off your clothes?' He tore his lips from her neck and gasped. 'I'm likely to rip them if I try to do it.'

She sent him an amused glance.

'It's not funny. I'm serious.'

'Oh, in that case.' She stepped back and slowly undid each button of her white blouse.

'A bra today,' he mused, his eyes twinkling. 'I wondered.'

'You didn't wonder. You already knew. You've been staring at my chest most of the day,' she said tartly, letting her shirt fall to the floor.

'It's not because of your breasts that I'm here.'

'No?'

He shook his head. 'It's your legs.'

She chuckled.

'You mind taking the skirt off?'

She complied. Quickly as she watched the fire in his eyes burn brighter.

'Actually,' he amended, 'it's everything about you.' He backed her up against the bed. 'Always was.'

He kissed her. Vivi leaned into him, curling her arms around his neck and giving into it. All was unleashed. She'd always been so carried away in her passion for him. Stunned by the sensations he'd made her feel. How could it be like this again? How so quickly?

'It's been a while.' She pushed him away for a second so she could breathe. Regroup. Focus. Narrow-eyed, she frowned at him. 'Why aren't you naked?'

His laugh had a desperate edge. He rubbed his fingertips over his forehead. 'It's been a while for me too. I need to keep myself in check somehow.'

'No constant stream of girlfriends?'

He hesitated. 'Not constant. None constant. Long term not my thing. Never will be.'

She didn't doubt it. She knew he was reminding her of that line in the sand. And she had to accept it. There was no changing him. And she didn't want to, right? She only wanted this one night too. Now she understood he'd been emotionally alone for a long time—and he only wanted fun. Well, so did she.

'What do you want me to do?' he quietly asked.

She picked up on the subtle meaning—he was giving her the chance to change her mind. She didn't want to think about the past any more. Or the future. Instead she focused on the present. On the present that he was to her. 'I want you naked. Take your tee shirt off.'

He removed it immediately. Suddenly she felt confident. A confidence she'd never had all those years ago. Back then she'd just been overwhelmed. This time it was going to be different. Maybe he was right. This time she'd take all she needed from him. Do everything she wanted to. After all, it was only sex.

She reached for his shorts, deftly undid them and shoved them—together with his boxers—down to his knees.

'And now?' He stood there, all bared magnificence.

'Touch me.'

He stepped out of the clothes and reached for her. And as he caressed her she caressed him. Running fingers over the body she'd once known so briefly, but so well. Still knew. Still admired…adored. She glanced back to his face, touched light fingertips to the smile that always melted her. He stepped closer, feathering kisses down her neck, to her breasts, his hands leading the way—tender, savouring, tormenting, until she was hot, restless, breathless.

'Liam?'

'Anything.'

She whispered, her confidence growing still. And he answered in action—quick, devastating action.

'We need to…' He broke away for a moment and found his shorts, swiftly fitting the protection. Then his hands returned to her—sought out her sensitive parts. He listened, but too soon she couldn't speak. It didn't matter. He seemed to remember her as if it were yesterday. What she liked. What she *really* liked. What she discovered that she now adored.

She shivered and tried to slip away from his touch as

she got too hot, too quick. 'I don't want to come without you. I want you to be in me.'

He laughed, again that edge of desperation. 'Be over too soon.'

His fingers trailed more, teasing until she was sighing and rocking and escalating towards the peak way, way too quickly.

So now she needed to do more than speak; she had to *seize* control. Before she'd always lost control. Always been swept away. She shoved, her hands slapping on his chest. To her delight he fell back, letting her straddle him.

'You gonna break out your whip now?' he teased.

She laughed but then shook her head. 'No pain,' she whispered. 'I don't want this to hurt.'

His laughing expression sobered completely. 'No.' Suddenly he moved, sitting up, his sky-high erection solid between them, rubbing against her in a way that had her squirming to lift and slide straight onto him.

But it was the kiss that killed her. He thrust his fingers into her hair, cradling the back of her head in his broad palm, holding her in place as he kissed her in a way she'd never been kissed before. Not just passionate, not just deep.

But somehow almost desperate—as if he were pouring a part of himself into her. She felt it raining down inside her, filling the gaps with warmth and sweetness.

Giving.

Oh, dear Lord, she couldn't cope with this. She wanted this to be *sex*. Hot, sweaty, wild sex. She didn't want something that seemed so much more.

Trembling, she wrenched her mouth away. That was too savage, too tender, too much. How could it be even more intense than it had been before?

She pushed away, slipping onto the middle of the big mattress. There had to be a way she could control this better, could put this into the purely sexual box she needed it to be in. She bent her head, trying to cope with the yearning of her body. And heard the hiss of his indrawn breath.

Smiling, she leaned further forward onto her fists, sending him a glance over her shoulder and registered with pleasure the way his fiery gaze travelled down the length of her—to the part of herself she'd exposed.

Yeah, that was what he wanted.

She bent further, presenting herself to him, pressing her face into the pillow, her knees apart, her hips rotating in bold invitation.

'Oh, wow,' he growled. His hands lifted, smoothing over the curves of her butt as if he couldn't resist touching.

And that was what *she* wanted. Nothing but sex. To be nothing but the receptive female. To feel a mate's strength pound into her. All animal. Hot, satisfying. Over.

She waited, feeling him move into position. She groaned as she felt the strength of his thighs lock against hers. She quivered, her body shaking already in a precursor of ultimate pleasure.

He leaned forward, his hands sliding up from her hips now—up the length of her spine. He slid one hand around her ribs, boldly sweeping, and tweaked her nipple, while his other hand continued up her spine to massage the base of her neck. She angled her head as his fingers worked, she arched her rear up higher, rocking back and forth against the hot, hard erection he was holding back just out of her.

He gave her nipple another tweak, half laughing as she moaned. But then he slid that hand lower—his hand spread wide, firm down her stomach. Down, down, to the part of her that was burning, ready for him.

One touch was all it took to make her beg. 'Oh, please,' she sobbed. 'Please, please, please.'

He thrust hard inside her. The force pushed her face harder into the pillow, muffling her scream. Her fists tightened as she tried to absorb the pleasure as he growled and then rocked into her, again, then again. Oh, he was good. How could she have forgotten just how good? How had she ever thought anyone or anything could ever match up to this? This was the *ultimate* pleasure for her.

His fingers toyed, teasing over her too sensitive nub until she was bucking like a wild pony. But his other hand clamped onto her shoulder, holding her in place so he could continue to thrust into her with brute strength, such masculine force, she thought she was going to break apart with the pleasure.

She closed her eyes, her face locked hot against the feather-filled pillow. She could hardly breathe. But it was good. He couldn't see into her eyes and take everything from her. Not all her secrets. She just wanted the sex. Wanted the orgasm.

His fingers tightened on her skin. She relished the slight pain—recognising how close he was to losing control. She wanted that. She wanted it to be a raw, physical, *fast* explosion. She groaned again and again as he pushed her higher, further until she was so close she—

'*Damn it.*' He pulled out.

'What—?' She fell forward, bereft.

But he deftly flipped her onto her back. Her lax legs fell apart and in seconds he'd covered her. His chest to hers, his pelvis to hers, his nose to hers. His eyes boring into hers. 'What do you want? Tell me what you want.'

'You can't figure it out?' she growled at him.

He shook his head. 'You're offering, giving. Don't just offer—*take*.'

'You didn't like that?'

'Of course I did,' he roared through gritted teeth. 'You make it so easy to take from you. But what do *you* want?'

So excited, so exposed, so needy, she was pushed beyond limits—beyond self-preservation. 'You!' she breathlessly screamed, her eyes watering. 'I just want *you*. All of you.'

He didn't move for a moment. Didn't answer.

Then he lowered his mouth that last inch and kissed her. Another kiss of the kind before—the one she'd been unable to bear. Explicitly sensual, yes, but also warm and sweet. *Loving*. And as he kissed her he thrust—slid—straight back inside. So deep, so full, so right.

He didn't stop kissing her—his tongue stroking, the rhythm matching that of his hips. He hadn't just settled over her, he'd sealed them together. So nearly satisfied, she wound her arms tightly around him, her hands spread wide over his muscles, her fingers digging into his tight, flexing butt. She could feel the power of him, but she could also feel the slight trembling, the oversensitive spasms of *his* body as well as those of her own. The sensations battered her defences, his grip on her body—her heart—too strong.

She screamed in his mouth, her body clamping around his. Finally, finally, finally he pushed her over the edge—and caught her. And she clung as if he were her life raft. As she convulsed and cried his name over and over, he lifted his head, gazing down at her with absolute satisfaction in his eyes, a beautiful smile on his lips, before he let out a glorious growl of release of his own.

Vivi collapsed in his embrace. She'd drowned again.

SIX

Something was screeching in Liam's ear. Loud, electronic, incessant.

'Is that your phone?' Aghast, Liam sat bolt upright in bed, rubbing the gritty feeling from his eyes.

He blinked in time to see Victoria's wincing nod as she swiped up the gadget to answer. 'Hi, Gia. Of course. I'll be there in three.' She ended the call and grimaced. 'I must have slept through.'

Liam reached out and grabbed her wrist, stopping her slide from the bed. He didn't want her to leave. 'Be where?' he asked, an ominous feeling in his gut.

'In Reception, waiting for her to turn up.'

'To do *what* at this hour?'

'She likes to keep fit. She runs for forty-five minutes every day.'

Liam didn't let her go as he glanced at the illuminated numbers on the clock on the bedside table. 'You're kidding. She wants you to go running with her *now*?' At three in the morning?

She freed her wrist with a sharp twist and stepped away from the bed.

'Gia doesn't like the paparazzi taking pics of her exercising so she goes out when the world is asleep.'

Liam's heart started thudding as if he'd been running for two hours already. 'Why doesn't she use the hotel gym?'

'She prefers to exercise outdoors. Fresh air. Like many people.'

'Why doesn't she take a bodyguard? Why does it have to be you?' He frowned, concern obliterating the remnants of his sleepiness. 'It's not safe for the two of you to be out running in the dark streets at this time of night.'

But Victoria chuckled. 'She does take a bodyguard. But she likes to talk to me. She gives me instructions.'

'So what, you're taking dictation while you're out jogging?' Appalled, he watched her pull running shorts from her case. 'You're prepared for this?'

'We run most mornings.' She tossed the shorts and sports-singlet on the bed and walked through to the bathroom.

'But you worked so late.' And she'd got to sleep so *much* later. He slid out of bed to follow, watching as she efficiently flicked on the shower. Part of him wanted to step in after her so he could soap her up. Most of him wanted her to come back to bed. *Now.*

'It's the way she works.' She lathered the soap. 'She doesn't need a lot of sleep.'

'What about you? Don't you need sleep?'

'I can sleep later.' She swiped soapy bubbles around her body.

'But you won't.' He frowned and pulled a towel from the rail for her. 'You're too busy organising Gia's life and running errands and keeping Alannah out of trouble.'

'It's good for me to keep fit too.'

'It's not good for anyone to have their sleep interrupted like this. This is the middle of the night. This is bad for your body clock.' And bad for every single one of his internal organs. He didn't want her to go.

She rinsed off and plucked the towel from his fingers. 'My body clock is just fine.'

His blood was running cold; he gritted his teeth but it didn't stop the chills spreading down his spine. He didn't want her to walk out on him. He didn't want to lose what he'd just found. He wanted her to stay. He'd do whatever he had to to make her stay. 'We only got to sleep half an hour ago, you know.'

Oh, Victoria knew. He'd asked her again and again what she wanted. And she'd told, she'd taken. She'd indulged so many fantasies. Only now she had so many more. And, man, she wished he'd pick up a towel to put around his hips. He was distraction incarnate. She bent to jam her feet into trainers and tie her laces and avoid looking at him. Then she made it to the door.

But he was waiting there for her.

His hands swept over her body—one around her waist, one sneakily slipping up her thigh. She couldn't resist another look at him. He was as hard as iron.

'You're panting already,' he drawled in her ear. 'How are you going to run for forty-five when you're already as breathless as this?'

'Don't tease.' She leaned against the door for support, letting herself enjoy this last touch.

'I'm not teasing.' His grin proved him a liar. 'I'm seriously concerned for your welfare.'

'I—' Her phone chimed again. She glanced at the screen but didn't take the call. 'I'll tell her I was in the elevator and didn't have reception.'

The last thing she wanted to do was go running and listen to all the things Gia wanted her to do today. Not to mention do all the soothing, calming talk if the boss was panicking about something. Which no doubt she would be. Because she always was. But Vivi had to go.

'Victoria.' He settled both hands on her waist. Firmly. His smile fading. 'No job is worth this.'

She narrowed her eyes. 'This one is.'

'Really?'

'I'm Gia's longest serving assistant. We have trust. I'm not letting her down.'

'You have trust? What would happen if you didn't go?'

Vivi didn't answer. She didn't want to think about that.

'I don't care how much she pays you, she's asking too much.'

'You can't accuse me of being a workaholic.' She deflected the argument back on him. 'You're way worse than me.'

'I *had* to work. There were people relying on me. Pulling a company back from the brink is almost harder than building one from scratch.'

'You don't think I *have* to work?' Her temper flared. 'I'm the one who ended up alone in London with no money, no friends, no family. I got this job on my own and I'm damn well going to keep it. And what makes you think I can't cope with working as hard as you?'

'Of course you can.' He let out a frustrated growl. 'I admit I worked like a dog. Most of the time I still do. Every bit the same kind of crazy hours as you. But there's a crucial difference. This company is *mine*. It's all my effort. It's *my* baby. I'm in control of it.'

'So working for someone else isn't as good?' she snapped. 'Is that what you're saying?'

His frown was quick, so was his attempt to explain. 'You're a talented person. You had design ideas of your own back then. Maybe you should be doing more for yourself.'

More? More like what? 'This may be hard for your feeble brain to compute,' she said crossly, 'but I find it rewarding to support another person.'

'*Exactly.*' He leaned forward. 'And it seems to me you've ended up in the *exact* same position you were in five years ago. Running around doing everything anyone asked of you. Doing everything for other people and not for yourself. Not taking care of yourself. Answer me this—do you really want to go?'

'It's not about what I want.'

He looked frustrated. 'You're already regressing? Unable to say what you really want? Too scared of Gia's disapproval?'

'I have *responsibilities.*'

'Unreasonable ones.' He looked furious. 'If you go, I won't be here when you get back. And I won't come back.'

Vivi froze. 'Is that a threat?' She glared up at him. 'Because *that's* unreasonable.'

Just who did he think he was? She couldn't give up her life again. And that was what this would be. If she refused Gia now, she'd be sacked on the spot.

'Can you put what you want first?' he asked. 'Not what I want. Not Gia. But you.'

'No, this is only about what *you* want. You say I can ask you anything? You only mean sexually. You still don't *listen*. You don't respect what I do. What I want.'

He still only wanted to win. To be the one she chose. And for what?

Of course she wanted to remain locked in his embrace.

But she wanted more. *Already* she wanted more. Being intimate with him only worsened her attraction to him. He was like a drug. Her absolute addiction. Addictions were never a good thing. Too much led to bad. And here it was already—the request to bow to his will. And the thing was—he *didn't* want more. He'd made that crystal clear.

He'd stilled, his hands at his sides. Fisted. 'You said one night.'

'Yeah, and my night is over. The day has begun.' And she really needed to get moving—away from him. She needed to get on the first plane back to London.

'Whereas my night has a few hours left.' He stepped back into her space. His fingers skimmed the edge of her shorts.

She couldn't hide her instinctive shiver—not just from his touch, but the determination, the intensity in his eyes.

'Victoria,' he asked softly. 'How long do you think you can last?'

She stiffened—he knew, didn't he? How much his touch affected her. This was a deliberate attempt to seduce her. Too bad. Because she'd lasted *years* and she *wouldn't* be bowled by him again. 'It was only sex, Liam.' And she'd had other sex. Good sex even.

His eyes narrowed. 'Only the best sex of your life.'

'All right, yes. The best. That satisfy you?' She paused, admitting the truth hurt. But it was true. It had always been there, had never gone away, never died. It had only taken one look, one fraction of a second, to burst back to life stronger than ever. But it was all he wanted and it wasn't enough. 'It's lust. It's purely chemical. For some reason my body thinks yours is the best one on the planet to procreate with. But *you're* not the best person for me. You're not Mr Right. We want different things.' She shored up her defence—reminded herself of what she'd worked so hard for. 'We're both career driven, we live in separate countries. I can't give up my life again. And you wouldn't want me to. You've said it yourself—you don't want more. This has to stop. I can't let this happen again.'

When she'd been with him, it had been as if the rest of the world could crumble around them. Such a cliché. He'd been her escape. But he'd also been her prison. In the end she'd needed to be free of that too. The intensity still frightened her.

He stepped back, looking oddly pale under the dim light from the bedside table. 'You regret it.'

'I think...' She hesitated again. 'Yes.'

'This life you got going isn't that great,' he said. 'Not when you have to go on freaking training runs at three in the morning. But you can't say no. You're afraid to stand up for yourself for fear of rejection.'

'There's a major point of difference you're missing. Gia *pays* me.'

'You're still scared of her. Of disapproval.'

'I *choose* to work for her. You're as hot-headed as ever, like some bulldozer barging into a situation and not getting the subtleties. Doing and getting what only *you* want regardless of the impact on anyone else. Did you know Gia was due a holiday after Milan? Your demands ruined it.'

'Gia is a machine who never needs rest,' Liam scoffed. 'The person who missed out on the break was *you*. And you can't ask her for it because you're completely afraid. You're still too scared to be honest.'

'Oh, I can be *honest*. But you can't seem to *listen*. Here's some honesty for you. I want you out of my room. Out of my life.' She couldn't cope with him—with the power of her emotions. Not when it wasn't reciprocated. When for him it was just sex and for her it was *everything*.

She heard his indrawn breath, felt his muscles brace as he lifted his chin. She swore as her phone beeped again. She opened the door. 'I have to go.'

She had to run.

SEVEN

———

From Victoria's hotel room Liam watched the rising sun compete with the streetlights. He'd not been able to think of anything but Victoria for days. Even in the few moments when true concentration claimed him, she snuck in somehow. He'd wonder what she'd think of a new design feature. Whether she'd smile if he repeated the lame joke a salesman had told him. Her opinion mattered. It always had. He'd been boyishly nervous about her seeing how he'd refitted that boat. He, who never had wanted to impress anyone, had wanted to impress her. And what had she done once she'd got inside his prized shed?

Fallen asleep.

A rueful smile crossed his lips. She'd been so tired. So tense. So wary.

Because of him.

Five years ago he'd doubted he could live up to her—his youthful ideal. He didn't think she'd understood the dire situation he'd come from. He'd clawed his way up—scholarships, the dreaded networking. Using every skill he'd had to gain some kind of footing. Then he'd met her and thrown it all away. Landing them both in the worst position either had been in.

On the road with her, he'd *had* to get some kind of security behind him because he knew relationships didn't work when life was impoverished. It wasn't so much dog-eat-dog, but an isolated hand-to-mouth existence. No one had energy to spare for caring.

He hadn't wanted her to experience that. He'd wanted to protect, care, provide for her in the way that she should have been provided for. That she was used to. But all he'd done was cast her adrift and leave her alone to face exactly those kinds of trials.

Him too. He'd had to start from an even worse position—he'd killed his 'team player' rep. He'd broken the unspoken honour of fraternity by betraying Oliver. The shame he'd felt when he'd got that email rescinding the job offer—the realisation he had nothing to offer her. Nothing that she'd want for long.

And now? Now—for all the success he had, the money and the success she had—it still wasn't going to work.

Because he still wasn't enough.

In all his life he had never felt so alone—not even when his father had left for hours, days at a time, or when he'd spent months sailing alone at sea, when he'd spoken out and betrayed his best friend...none of that was worse than this moment.

He'd moved on from his past. But now he'd lost the most precious *possibilities* for the future.

He bowed his head, hating how ripped apart he felt. How stupidly vulnerable he'd allowed himself to get so quickly. No one central to his life had stayed with him—neither mother, father, nor the girl he'd once thought he loved.

Now he knew he loved her. He loved the strong woman she'd become—the generous, loyal, smart, beautiful woman. Because tonight, what had started as something of a game—a challenge—had become something so serious. So much more. For him.

He'd opened up to her. He'd offered her all he actually had to give—himself. Not just his body, but his support, his humour, what compassion he had...whatever else there was in him to be wanted. He'd wanted to give it all.

And he'd wanted her to take all of him. To embrace him. And she had—for one moment he'd been what she wanted. And it had felt so good he'd wanted her to hold on tight. He'd wanted to be her first choice. He wanted everything.

He'd pushed. Asking too much, too soon. *He'd* been the one to regress—to the insecure, needy youth he'd once been. Selfish. And, yes, unreasonable.

So she'd pushed him away. She didn't want what he had to offer. He didn't blame her for that. He was just going to have to learn to live with it. Again.

He still believed she deserved more to her life—for all the fabulousness of her career. She shouldn't remain so isolated from her home, her history, her family. The wistfulness in her eyes when she spoke of them told him that. So did her need to be integrated into a community—to be necessary—that was why she'd made herself so indispensable in her work.

How much of an idiot he'd been no longer mattered. All he wanted was for her to be happy. Maybe, from a distance, he could help her reconnect.

But he had to leave now—because that was also what she wanted. And, frankly, he couldn't stay to face her rejection again. She'd said no and she was right; it was time he *listened* to her.

So Liam did as she'd asked. He dressed. He left.

He didn't look back.

EIGHT

———

Vivi wasn't paying attention to Gia as they jogged. She clutched her phone so she could leave herself voice messages if Gia gave orders. But she was half hoping for a message or something from Liam. There was nothing, of course.

Her whole body ached but she mentally beat herself up all the more. Why had she lost it like that with him? Why'd she have to get so melodramatic and scream at him? Why couldn't she just chill out and go a few more rounds with him? Have a whole night fling and take it for what it was? Sex that good wasn't easy to find…

But she was deluding herself and she knew it. She wanted so much more from him. Always had. Always would.

Her nerves shrieked as she swiped her card to get into the room. But before she stepped in she knew. She sensed the void. For once he'd done as she'd asked. He'd listened. He'd left.

She couldn't feel hurt by that—it was what she'd wanted, right? And he'd got what he wanted too. But all that emotion she'd thought she'd felt in those kisses? In that connection? To her it had felt as if he'd stopped them from having sex. He'd switched it totally. He'd made love to her—making her love him. He'd opened up to her, offered so much to her. And he'd held her as if he never, ever wanted to let her go.

But it seemed all that had only been her imagination.

A week later, back in London, winter had arrived early and Vivi felt the chill to her bones. Gia was on a bender—she'd been hit with inspiration after the boat shoot and wanted to design a whole range with a nautical theme in time for the following spring. Vivi couldn't bear it. When Gia was in full-on create mode she shut everything else down, leaving Vivi to deal with every inquiry, every problem. So her hours were worse than ever and the ache in her soul worsened with every sleepless second. Nights were interrupted not just with the runs with Gia, but with memories of Liam—the building of an ache so great she didn't see how it could be eased. And the more tired she became, the worse it got, the less she could sleep.

Finally one morning after a run that had gone on way too long, she glared at the bland monotony of her wardrobe, then turned her back on it. She stomped into work in ancient jeans and a huge jumper and went straight to the room where samples were kept. She found a scarlet shirt that was almost large enough. Gia wouldn't stand for her wearing another designer's outfits. Then she marched into Gia's design room without knocking.

Gia lifted her head and stared frigidly.

Too bad. Vivi tossed the dictation machine she'd had couriered that morning onto Gia's desk. 'If you need to make notes for me, the bodyguard will hold this. I'm not getting up at three any more. I need my beauty sleep.' She totally snapped.

Gia just kept staring at her. 'Anything else you'd like to address while you're here?' she asked, her face completely impassive.

Vivi barely thought about it before biting the bullet. 'I need another assistant to work on the new online distribution project. It's getting too much for me to handle alone. Plus I need to take the next few days off work. Sorry for the short notice but I missed my holiday for the Genoa shoot and I need the time now.' She needed to go and sort her head out. Get away completely, lick her wounds in private. Come back refreshed and ready to take her career to the next level—on her own terms.

If Gia didn't like that, if Gia sacked her, then she'd just find work somewhere else. She had a name—a rep in the industry that she'd worked so hard to build. It was time to call on it. Only now, now she'd had a second to breathe... She held it in and waited for the bomb to blow.

But Gia just blinked. 'All right.'

Vivi blinked back. 'Really?'

Gia actually laughed. 'Really.'

'Okay.' Vivi breathed out, then turned and walked across the room before Gia changed her mind.

'The red looks good on you,' Gia said as Vivi got to the door. 'I've been wondering when you were going to get as bossy with me as you are with everyone else,' she added.

Now Vivi chuckled. 'Not bossy.' She paused, lifting her chin. 'Just...balanced.'

'Bossy. But I like it.' Gia's eyes went slightly glassy. 'And I really do like that red... Can you get me some—?'

Vivi held up her hand. She'd won a point here and she wasn't conceding it the next second. She was going on in her new, fully sorted style. 'I'll get someone else to come in and take notes. I'm away the next few days, remember?'

Gia's eyes snapped back into focus and she laughed. 'Okay. But no more than four days—I can't cope longer without you.'

Four days was longer than Vivi had had off in one stretch in the last four years. But she grinned at Gia's genuine appeal—at the realisation that her incredibly demanding boss did actually recognise that Vivi was great at her job. But she also deserved more.

Back in her own office she drew a deep breath. If she could manage Gia, she could figure out the rest of her life, right? She could take it on.

'Can you sign for these, please, Vivi? They're both on your sig. only.' The receptionist looked nervous as she came to the door. Yeah, Vivi had been grumpy these last few days. So she smiled sweetly and signed. 'Thank you.'

Two parcels. She picked up the top one—the smaller. It was addressed to her, with 'private and confidential' typewritten on the front of it. Inside was another packet—with only her name on the front. This packet she unwrapped slowly, her heart thudding. Because she recognised her mother's delicately perfect handwriting. She'd never really appreciated how beautiful it was before.

Inside was a whole bunch of envelopes, bound together with a rubber band. Her name on each envelope, but no address. She opened the top one. At first she couldn't read the words, she was too nervous. Goosebumps rippled down her arms and she sat in her chair, her legs wobbly. The letter was signed from them both.

Her parents were in touch with Stella? Her parents wanted to get in touch with her?

And inside all those envelopes were all the letters her

mother had written over the years and never known where to send them. The Christmas cards. The birthday cards. All kept. All written. Some short messages. Some longer.

Vivi's heart beat so violently it was a wonder it didn't burst from her chest. How had they got her address? This was marked so clearly—to Gia's private bag. Someone had known to address it to Vivi not Victoria.

Liam had been right. She was afraid. She'd run from her problems and she'd never stopped running, never turned to face them. It was beyond time she did.

She put the letters to the side. She'd read them later—she needed to regroup now.

The next was a parcel from Nico. She frowned. She didn't want to see the prints from the Genoa shoot, but he'd addressed this packet to her personally with a private note scrawled across the corner in his hand.

Thought you might like this. Snapped it the other day when you were snoozing.

It wasn't just a print. He'd blown it up and framed it. In the black and white portrait, she was curled against Liam's chest. He—like she—was oblivious to the photographer. Liam was looking down at her, his arms cradling her. It was the second after she'd woken. The second she'd looked into his eyes. That perfect moment just before he'd encouraged her, when all emotion flowed simply and purely. Wordlessly. So incredibly obvious.

It was what Nico was revered for—capturing the essence. No Photoshop magic needed here. No wonder the guy won every award there was.

She'd no doubt that the shots of Alannah on the boat were magnificent, but none could be as beautiful as this.

This was art. And what was most important was there for anyone to see. Love written all over her face. And on Liam's?

That intensity, yes. But also, in his beautiful eyes, that slight strain of vulnerability.

Pain shafted through her. She wanted to believe in that image so badly. All those years ago he'd been the one to help her through the night when she'd been insanely making Christmas decorations. Because he'd wanted that one thing? He'd wanted to win her from Oliver?

Or had it been more than that? He'd come from nothing, from no family, no love. She'd never really understood how neglected he'd been—on so many levels. He'd worked hard to fit in—using his humour, his sporting ability. But he'd fallen for her. He'd wanted her. He'd given up everything he'd gained in his pursuit of her.

That humbled Vivi now—hurt her—as she realised he'd wanted to help her again. This time knowing there was nothing more. Putting her parents in touch with her was a gesture of generosity—of compassion, caring. The only way left to him to show it. Because she'd pushed him away. She'd rejected him. Once more they'd failed to communicate properly.

He'd listened. But she?

She'd not been honest. She'd not done as he'd challenged her to—she'd not asked for what she'd truly wanted. And she could have.

Vivi stood. She'd go and see her parents. Yes she would. She'd meet Stella. She'd sort out her past. But there was something else she had to do first. She had to lay claim to her future.

* * *

Eighteen hours later she locked her wobbly knees as she knocked on the door, clutching the parcel under her arm. Back in Italy, hoping like crazy he was in his office.

A woman opened the door. She wore shorts. Incredibly stylish shorts that showed off incredibly slim and toned legs. Vivi tried not to panic and asked in painful Italian to see Liam.

'He's not here.' The woman answered in English.

Vivi blinked, her blood chilling. 'Where is he?'

'London.'

'London?' Vivi felt faint, then frustration kicked in. 'When did he go to London?'

The pretty woman looked at her oddly and then called to another worker out of Vivi's sight.

'When did he go?' Vivi repeated, her tone rising. Why had he gone to London? Her heart leapt but she tried to jump on it. He wouldn't have gone to see her. It would be for business. That was it.

'He goes later today.' The man had come to the door.

'Then where is he now? Is he at the airport?' Had she just crossed paths with him in some mean twist of fate?

The Italians exchanged another glance.

'I think he's in his rooms,' said the man. 'If you'll fol-low me.'

Of course she'd follow. After the mad packing, the long flight, the crazy taxi ride...

'Liam?' The guy broke into a string of super-quick Ital-ian.

But Vivi stepped past him and her guide went quiet.

Liam looked up, leapt to his feet. Then froze.

The Italian disappeared, shutting the door behind him.

'Victoria?' Liam's face shuttered the second he said her name. So carefully bland.

'Yeah.' Vivi swallowed and walked further into the room, tightening her grip on the packet in her hands. She noticed the bag on the floor near the door. It was small. Just a short trip, then? 'Am I stopping you from getting somewhere?'

A very faint smile tweaked the corner of his mouth. 'No. It doesn't matter.'

Okay. She breathed out. She'd never felt so nervous in her life. Not even in that moment when Oliver had asked her to marry him in front of everyone, when she'd been so terrified of the reaction and so unsure which way to go.

This was a million times worse. Because this time she knew exactly what she wanted, exactly how much it mattered.

It meant everything.

'I got sent a parcel,' she began. 'Actually I got two.'

His brows flicked.

'You told them my address, didn't you?'

He said nothing. Didn't ask who she meant but she knew he understood exactly.

'I know it was you,' she said, managing a smile. 'There's no one else it could have been.'

He rubbed his lip with his index finger. 'What was in the parcel?'

Her eyes filled before she could get the words out. 'All the letters they've written to me over the years and never been able to send.'

'Have you been to see them?'

She shook her head.

He jerked. 'Don't you think—?'

'I had to see you first,' she interrupted roughly. 'I needed to see you.'

He froze, his gaze riveted to her.

Vivi stepped forward. 'The second parcel was from Nico.' She cleared her throat and pulled the portrait from its bubble wrap and put it on the desk between them. 'Did he show it to you?'

Liam slowly lowered his gaze to look at the picture. Vivi watched his face, saw the flicker of a muscle in his jaw before that rigid control took over again. He looked at the picture for a long time.

Finally Vivi took that last step forward. 'I don't want a picture,' she said, suddenly feeling liberated at putting it all on the line. Her heart thundered and chills feathered over her skin but adrenalin pushed her on. Finally saying what she really wanted—and knowing that at this moment he was *listening* so intently. 'I can handle people in a business sense. But you were right—I wasn't asking for anything for my personal life. I was avoiding anything very personal. But not any more. Not after...the other night. I've contacted my parents. I was scared but I offered the olive branch and I think it's going to be okay.' She breathed in deep. 'And then there's you.'

'Are you offering me an olive branch?'

'No. For you...' she paused to draw in some steel '...I'm fighting.'

'Fighting me?'

'If I have to.' She walked around the desk.

He leaned away slightly, letting the desk take some of his weight as he regarded her. 'I was an idiot,' she said. 'I'm sorry I lost my temper.'

The smallest smile appeared on his lips. 'I was glad you weren't afraid to with me.'

'I was afraid,' she admitted softly. 'That's why I sent you away.'

'It hurt.' He barely moved as he spoke.

'I'm sorry.'

'No.' He shook his head. 'I deserved it. You accused me of not listening to you. And you were right, I didn't. Not back then. Back then I was too busy trying to figure solutions on my own. It was what I was used to and I was too proud to let you in. I'm sorry about that. But last week I should have. Then you put the words in my mouth—that I wouldn't want more from you—'

'Words you'd once said.'

'But it's not only women who're allowed to change their minds.' The corner of his mouth curved. 'And honestly, for me it wasn't a change of mind, it was more a recognition of what's been true all along.'

Vivi's heart was almost bursting from its speed. 'What is it that's true?'

'That I love you. I realised I'd never actually told you. But I do.'

'I never believed you felt for me as strongly.' Her eyes filled again, this time the tears spilled.

'How could I *not*?' He jammed his hands into his pockets. 'I fell so hard. I gave up everything for you.'

'So did I.'

'I know that now.'

And she'd just thought he'd done it because it was a challenge. And that once he'd had what he wanted he'd got bored. She hadn't ever realised he'd been as flipped out by it as she'd been. That he'd lost as much as she.

She glanced at the picture and then looked back at him. 'I'm still scared, Liam, but I'm not going to let that stop me from asking for what I want any more. And I'm asking for you to come over here.'

'I can't.'

'No?' Her heart smashed.

A small, rueful smile softened his mouth. 'You know what will happen if we touch.'

'Well...' She bit her lip, relaxing a smidge as she saw that smile. 'I was kind of counting on that.'

'We're not making the same mistake as we did then. We touch now, it'll be all on. We have to talk this through first.'

'What more do you need to know?' She gazed at him. 'I love you. I've always loved you. And it totally scares me.'

His rigid stance melted; in a step he was there, his arms around her. 'Okay,' he muttered into her hair. 'There's nothing to be scared of now.'

He kissed her. Kissed her the way he'd kissed her the other night. With all the love in the world, until her toes curled in the crazy high heels she'd worn specially to get tall enough to see eye to eye with him. And she kissed him back—as fervently, deeply, sweetly.

'I can't let you go now.' He groaned. 'You know I was going to London this afternoon.'

She knotted her fingers into his shirt, keeping him close, and failed to answer coolly. 'Your assistant mentioned it.'

'I was coming after you. I've never felt so bad. Hurt. Furious with myself. I realised I'd never been honest with you either. I'd never let you in the way I should have. I never told you...so many things I should have. Especially that I was in love with you.' He pulled her closer into his heat, a pained expression on his face. 'I should have opened up to you all those years ago. I should have come after you.'

'No. We weren't ready. Way too young. I had baggage to get over. I had to grow a spine.' She smiled. 'And you had a business to build. It's better now.'

He bent, resting his forehead on hers. 'I love you. Always have.'

A feeling of utter contentment seeped into her bones, but as she leaned against him reality—logistics—bothered the bliss. 'How are we going to make this work?' she voiced her fears. 'We failed so badly last time.'

'No.' He framed her face with his hands, tilting her so she had to meet his gaze head on. 'Failure is making the same mistake twice. The first time wasn't failure. It was merely a mistake.'

'Merely?'

'Merely.' His eyes twinkled. 'We won't fail now. So long as you ask, I listen.'

'And vice versa.' She nibbled on her lip, clutching his shirt more tightly. She never wanted to leave him but there was no choice. 'We can make distance work.'

'No,' he said softly. 'I've had enough nights without you already. I've done what I can with the business here, now I'm ready to sell it on. I'm ready for the next project. That will be wherever you are.'

Shocked, she dropped her hand and stepped back. 'You can't sell your business.'

'I can.' He chuckled, capturing her by the waist and moving in close again. 'Darling, I'm bored. I need a new challenge.' His eyes sharpened. 'And, no, I will never get bored with you.'

That wasn't what she was worried about. 'Your career

matters. I won't let you sacrifice anything for me. You'll resent me.'

'This isn't a sacrifice. I came looking for you and as soon as I saw you again, spoke to you again—it was all over. It just took me a bit to get my head around. I'm never losing you again. You're what matters most in my life. This time I need to give us the chance. This time I can. I can't afford not to.'

'But your business—'

'What is it that matters to you—the financial security I have or me?'

She stared at him—at the vulnerability in his eyes, the same that had been caught in that portrait. It was real. Now she understood—part of him was as afraid as she. 'You.' She tightened her arms around his neck. 'You, you, you.'

She felt the tension ebb from his body—and another kind of hardness steal in.

'Then if you don't mind risking it with an entrepreneur, you'll be fine. I'm ready for new challenges. Business challenges. Family challenges.' He grinned. 'Trust me, Vivi.'

'Vivi?'

'That's who you are—my Victoria, my Vivi. My life.'

She smiled, glowing inside. Knowing, believing that he loved her the way she loved him. Suddenly she saw that the overwhelming passion wasn't going to drown her. Their bond was so much more than sexual, it had humour, support, substance. Being with him would enhance her life, not diminish possibilities, but expand them. He'd never stifle her. And she'd never hold him back either.

'If you like,' he muttered, 'I'll even come with you on your three-a.m. runs with Gia.'

'Actually, there's no need.' She grinned, feeling a sense

of strength and pride rippling through her. 'I stood up to her. Handed her a dictation machine and told her to go with the bodyguard.'

Liam laughed and kissed her. 'How'd she take it?'

'She basically high-fived me.' Vivi giggled. 'But you know, there's still a problem.'

He looked concerned. 'What's that?'

'My body's used to a really tough workout in the early hours of the morning. I'm going to need some kind of activity to replace that run...something really, really energetic...'

He bent, sweeping her into his arms, that wicked smile on his mouth. 'You know, I think I can come up with something that might wear you out...'

'When can you come up with it?'

'Oh, it's up now.'

She chuckled at the lame innuendo, delighted in being carried off by the one true love of her life.

Long, quiet moments later he gazed into her eyes—his own free of tension, alight with love and passion.

'It was only ever you,' he promised.

'And you,' she answered.

Finally. Always.

For ever.

* * * * *

THE WEDDING DRESS DIARIES
Aimee Carson

ONE

———

'Can I get you a drink?'

The busty brunette behind the bar at the exclusive Manhattan restaurant was addressing the guy at the end of the counter. And, when Amber spied the man, she did a sharp double take that would surely leave her with a crick in her neck.

Parker Robinson.

Blinking, Amber adjusted to the sight as the sounds of Reese's engagement party faded.

When Parker didn't respond, the bartender repeated, 'Can I get you a drink?'

Attention finally caught, Parker drew the sexy smirk like a gun from a holster. No doubt he wasn't even aware. It was more like an automatic response, like most people would say please or thank you or mutter an excuse me when they accidentally stepped on someone's toe.

'Why, yes, you can,' Parker said.

The brunette puffed up her chest, clearly pleased she'd finally earned an attentive smile, and Amber resisted the urge to roll her eyes. Apparently Reese hadn't exaggerated; her half brother's attitude toward women hadn't changed much since adolescence. Amber had witnessed that grin directed at girls often enough, that knowing twinkle in his eye communicating that females liked what they saw, and he knew it.

A cocky confidence that, on Parker Robinson, was more endearing than annoying.

The sun-streaked blond hair of his teens was now a light brown with leftover golden highlights, like keepsakes from his childhood. He still wore it tousled with soft spikes up front, and the little-boy, rough-and-tumble look totally suited him, hair begging to be tugged. Years ago she'd longed to do just that, to pull him in for a kiss. Had fantasized about him teaching her how. And while his hair hadn't changed much, his masculine features were better defined, cheekbones and jaw now sharp enough to cut cold butter. Yet he straddled youth and maturity with an ease to be envied, that cocky teen housed in the bad-boy adult making a killer combination.

His gaze collided with Amber's and held, and a pit yawned wide beneath her stomach. The brilliant green eyes hadn't faded with time. Pulse pounding, she realized, belatedly, that he'd caught her staring, and the shameful memory barreled into her. The day when he'd called her out on exactly that. But she wasn't the besotted little preteen anymore, the one that had followed him around like an adoring puppy.

'You a friend of Reese's?' he asked.

Amber was proud she didn't laugh out loud. Amazing. Ironic that the guy she'd spent every summer in the Hamptons with from the ages of seven to twelve—the guy she'd loved from the ages of eight to fifteen—didn't even remember her.

Though, in his defense, she'd been in the sixth grade the last time he saw her.

In jeans and a leather jacket the color of burnt butter, Parker picked up his glass and came closer, moving with that easy earthy stroll that came with a confidence few could dream of. It had been captivating on Parker the teen.

On Parker the man, it was absolutely breathtaking.

He slid onto the bar stool next to hers and leaned his elbow on the counter, facing Amber. Parker cleared his throat and lowered his head a little to look up at her face— most likely a *stupefied* face—as if worried her lack of response meant she wasn't completely sane.

Parker seated this close was definitely threatening her sanity.

'Are you a friend of Reese and Dylan's?' he repeated.

It had been fifteen years since she'd seen him, had been close enough to *touch*. She gripped her glass and sipped her wine, hoping she looked more sophisticated than she felt.

Amber managed a nod of her head. 'I've known Reese a long time.' *I've known* you *a long time.* 'Why would I be at their engagement party if I didn't know them?'

'Could be a party crasher, here for the expensive food and free drinks.'

It was surreal to be having this conversation with her childhood crush, protected by her unknown identity. Because she had plenty to be embarrassed about when it came to Parker.

From the time Reese had asked her to handle her wedding, Amber had been dreading the moment she had to measure this man for his tux—an event that needed to occur soon. But she'd thought she could relax tonight because Reese had said Parker would never show. He hadn't attended any of the other parties for his half sister and her fiancé. So why had he come now?

'Is that why you're here?' she said with a smile. 'For the free food?'

Parker let out a bitter scoff. 'If only.'

He didn't want to be here.

The realization hit her with all the force of a sledge-hammer on steroids. It fit with what Reese had told her, the man who refused to have anything to do with the Michael family anymore. Not that Amber could blame him. But ever since her engagement, his sister had been trying to pull him back into, well, if not into the fold, at least within touching distance.

He tipped his head with an almost boyish curiosity. 'Do I know you?' he said, and Amber's heart froze. 'I definitely think I know you.'

He pursed his lips contemplatively, and Amber wished her memory of his mouth hadn't been so spot on. He *did* have the most gorgeous lips in the world. Full. Sinful. Utterly kissable. Pretty savvy of a stupid twelve-year-old to notice, if she did say so herself.

Enjoying the rare sense of power in Parker's presence, she sent him another smile. 'Maybe.'

'A name would be helpful,' he said.

Amber let out an overly thoughtful *hmm,* as if she were seriously considering giving him the information. But suddenly, the moment she'd been dreading, her first meeting with Parker, was more about fun than fear.

'That would be too easy,' she said.

Parker's understanding smile at her tone set her pulse fluttering. 'Okay,' he said, settling in as if for a prolonged conversation, the light in his eyes sizzling. 'I'll bite.'

God, she wished he would.

'Do I know you through your work?' he said.

Amber bit back the smile. 'Could be,' she said with laughter in her tone. 'I used to be a seamstress, but now I own my own bridal shop.'

He actually recoiled as if slapped, and the look on his face as he backpedaled made her laugh. Clearly, Parker Robinson was offended at the thought of frequenting an establishment that dealt with weddings.

'Definitely not through your work,' he said gruffly. 'Maybe through mine?'

Amber pretended not to know. 'What do you do?'

He narrowed his eyes at her. 'I work Homicide down at the fifty-seventh precinct. Maybe I interviewed you as a witness before?'

'Maybe I was once a suspect,' she said as coolly as she could.

The roll of his eyes, that sarcastic 'yeah, right' expression made her suddenly sentimental. She remembered that look from her childhood, and a small part of her was glad he hadn't changed too much.

'Do I look too innocent?' she said.

'No,' he said bluntly. 'I just remember all my perps.' His face grew tight, and a harsh laugh escaped his mouth, and he slid his eyes to somewhere beyond her shoulders. 'And yeah, you look too sweet. But, trust me,' he said with a light tone that he didn't quite pull off. He took a sip of his drink and carefully set the glass down, his tone distant. 'No one is as innocent as they look.'

There was a hard set about his eyes, the crinkles at the edges more about experience than age. A bitter fatigue that had started in his teens and now was fully realized.

That bold green gaze was back on her, intrigued. *Interested.* 'Maybe we attended the same school?'

She shook her head.

'Did we meet at a party once?' he asked.

Enjoying his frustrated curiosity, she sipped her wine. 'Try again.'

His eyes narrowed in thought. 'Well, I know we haven't slept together,' Parker went on, sending her stomach plummeting to her toes.

God, only in her teenage dreams.

'Because, although you're certainly attractive,' he said, 'you're definitely not my type.'

Amber ignored the sudden surge in her pulse and maintained an even tone. 'Is that the *only* reason we couldn't have slept together?' she said. 'Because I'm not your type?'

The reflexive sexy smirk lit up his face.

And as the words finally sank in, she drew back a touch in surprise. 'Wait,' she said. 'What type do you think I am?'

His gaze traveled down her body, leaving her hot in places that normally...weren't. Her A-line dress was simple, with a classic cut. Nothing seductive. No overt 'I'm yours for the taking' in the way it clung to her body.

He hiked a brow dryly. 'You own a bridal shop, which means you believe in the institution of marriage.'

'And you don't?' she said softly, only pretending the statement was a question.

Sure enough, a bitter sound escaped those beautiful lips. Not that Amber could blame him.

'Hell, no,' he said.

Heart bleeding a little for him then, she remembered the day she'd found him by the dock, devastated by his mother's words.

You were a mistake.

Amber had grown up knowing she was wanted. Secure in the knowledge her parents had been devoted to each other, were devoted to *her*. Her dad had died when she was a child, and her mother had loved him so much she'd never remarried. And Amber's bridal store revolved around proving that love existed every day, with every client.

But Parker...

Well, Parker's experiences were opposite in every respect.

And the boy who'd given Amber her first taste of romantic love—*unrequited,* but love nonetheless—had grown into a man who mocked its very existence.

'You've made weddings your business,' he said. 'So, obviously you believe.'

'And that's how you've concluded I'm not your type?' she said. 'Because of the dress I'm wearing and what I do for a living?'

He sat back a bit to study her, no teasing, seductive tone now, but a kind of gaze that could see through your soul. 'No,' he said, shaking his head softly. The thoughtful look on his face was deep and, for the first time, he actually looked at her. *Really* looked at her. 'It's the light in your eyes,' he said with a simple shrug. 'You still believe.'

Her lungs slowly collapsed, forcing the air from her body. Believed in what? In love?

In *life?*

The thought instantly drained from her mind when he shifted closer, and the scent of his leather jacket drifted in the air.

'I can't remember who you are.' Simmering gaze on hers, he said, 'How about throwing a poor guy a hint?'

'Okay,' Amber said. After the years of crushing on Parker the teen, now that he was looking at her as a desirable woman, she wanted to work the moment for all she was worth. 'You once pressed your lips against mine.'

Parker's eyes widened, and he dropped his gaze to her mouth, pulling all the oxygen from the atmosphere. Amber's breathing increased in an attempt to suck in enough air.

'Awesome.' His voice slid lower, like heated silk. 'I approve of my choices.'

He leaned close, his eyes glowing, sparking embers she'd thought long dead—those secret pieces of a young girl in the throes of her first sexual attraction. Not really understanding the full extent of what she felt.

His teasing grin was hot enough to light the Christmas tree at Rockefeller Center. 'Did I get to second base?'

Skin vibrating at the thought, her smile was strained.

'Sorry, only first,' she said.

And technically, it was probably only *half* base, but she was having too much fun to clarify the exact nature of how their lips had touched.

'Did I slip you the tongue?' he said.

'No.'

'My loss,' he said, and his mouth parted a bit, as if imagining righting that previous wrong.

The tiny peek at his tongue sent a shot of adrenaline through her body, surely leaving her glowing. Fine hairs standing on end.

'And as first kisses went,' she pressed on, 'it could have been better.'

Mostly by being *real*.

The offended expression on Parker's face was comical. 'Could have been— Wait...*first* kiss?' He shot her a skeptical look. 'Either this was a really long time ago or you've confused me with someone else.'

'I definitely don't have you confused with someone else.' When he looked at her as though he was beginning to suspect she truly *wasn't* sane, Amber sent him a smile and gave up the pretense. 'I practically grew up at your mother's house because my mom worked as her personal assistant,' she said. 'Which was the fancy title for glorified gofer girl.'

There was a three-heartbeat pause that felt like thirty as Parker's expression remained blank.

'I'm Amber Davis.'

'Amber Davis,' he said slowly, as if pulling the name from a memory long buried. Recognition finally shot through his face, and his shoulders snapped back. 'Well, hell,' he breathed out. 'You're the one who tried to drown.'

TWO

———

Fifteen years earlier
The Hamptons, Long Island, New York

Swimswimswim

Eyes fixed on the dock, the chant rang on and on in Amber's head. She'd lost sight of her paddleboard ages ago, swept away by the Sag Harbor current. Crap, she was *so* getting in trouble for this.

Mom's gonna kill me if I drown.

A fresh slice of panic surged. How was she going to marry Parker now if she died? At the stupid age of twelve. Jeez, she'd never even been kissed before! Frowning, she paddled harder. She should have played Spin the Bottle at Nancy Kruger's last month. Okay, so Amber probably would have been stuck kissing Jimmy Stevens, better known as lizard tongue, but at least she wouldn't be drowning with virgin lips. An epically lame end to the suckage that was her life.

All except for Parker.

Parker.

So what if he was in the eleventh grade and she was

only in sixth. She'd loved him since she was eight years old. He'd briefly been replaced with Justin Timberlake from 'N Sync, but even she knew that was pretty unlikely to happen. And Parker was cuter. She wanted to marry him so bad that she'd picked out her wedding dress ages ago. Course, it had taken her four months to whittle it down to her top five favorites. Her obsession with tulle and satin and lace was growing pretty strong. This summer, in a fit of boredom, she'd planned the whole ceremony. Reese would have been her maid of honor cuz she was Parker's half sister and Amber's sort-of friend.

Stupidstupidstupid

Sneaking off and forgetting the life vest. But she'd really *really* wanted to get better on the paddleboard. Mostly cuz she wanted to impress Parker. Last summer he'd taught her how to stand and maneuver a turn, but this summer he was more interested in kissing Susie Frances. Amber scowled. And he never helped her bait a hook or capture crabs anymore.

The current was scarily strong, and the dumb dock was slipping farther away. The chill from the water seeped deeper with every passing minute, despite how hard Amber swam. Teeth chattering, her arms and legs grew heavy. So much so it was a struggle to control them now.

A sob ripped from her throat, and she fought back the fear, closing her eyes.

Giveupgiveupgiveup

Her muscles screamed for a break, her lips quivering, the taste of salt a mix of seawater and frustrated tears. The furious pounding of her heart was now just as much about terror as tiredness, and she was sure her chest was gonna explode.

Her thoughts began to drift and grow foggy. She knew

there was something she was supposed to be doing. Swimming? Finding Reese?

'Amber!'

The call shook her out of her daze. God, she really *was* drowning. Was she already in heaven? Now she was hearing Parker calling out her name.

The voice grew closer, the tone urgent. *'Amber.'*

Exhausted, she turned and spied Parker sprawled on his board, sleeves pushed to his elbows as he paddled toward her like a madman. She sucked in a breath, getting a mouthful of salt water that burned her throat, and she coughed and gagged, slipping beneath the surface. The cold closed over her head and she stopped fighting for a moment. It was peaceful. Quiet. And she was so, so tired; it was nice not to fight so hard to keep her head above water.

She drifted, floating, until an arm circled around her chest and heaved her up. She had a vague sensation of being hauled onto something hard, but she couldn't move. It took too much effort to breathe.

And then there were lips on hers and warm breath filling her lungs and she had an overwhelming urge to cough again. She rolled, gagged and then threw up a bunch of salt water that stung as much coming up as going down. Shattered, she collapsed again, drifting in and out, only half-aware as Parker paddled the board for shore and dragged her up on the beach.

That was when the shivering started for real. Water dripped down his nose as Parker gathered her close, fear making deep lines in his forehead. She gazed up at him, dazed, her heart pounding from the feel of his arms cradled around her. The feel of his breath, *Parker's breath,* on her cheek was awesome. But the close-up of his face was just...was just... And as she blinked, her mind clearing, it hit her.

Parker had kissed her!

Her heart fluttered like a hummingbird stuck in a cage. Okay, true, it was more like he'd given her mouth to mouth, but still... She closed her eyes, remembering the hard press of those soft lips she'd been obsessing about for years. Pressed against *hers*.

OMG...it was almost worth drowning for.

His dark blond hair looked brown when wet. A smattering of freckles bridged his nose, and thick lashes framed the prettiest pair of green eyes in the history of *ever*. Eyes that always did funny things to her stomach when they locked on hers. Used to be they'd look at her with patience and, when she was *really* lucky, a hint of fondness. Now that Parker had gotten older there was a lot of irritation. But it wasn't *her* fault his mother made him watch out for her and Reese when Amber's mom wasn't around.

She clutched his arm. 'You can't tell my mom,' she croaked out.

'Aw, come on, Amber.' Parker's face scrunched up tight. 'You nearly freakin' died.'

'I did not.'

He rolled his eyes in that ever-sarcastic 'yeah, right' way of his. 'What if you get sick or something?' he said. 'She needs to know.'

And be grounded? Amber had been looking forward to summer vacation for *months*. As the daughter of Ms. Michael's personal assistant, Amber had practically grown up in the Michaels' home. Parker never visited his mother in the city anymore, so summer at the Hamptons was the only time she got to see him.

She pulled harder, panicking now. 'If you tell, I'll—I'll—'

Her mind sputtered as she scrambled to come up with a good threat. And then a memory filled her mind. A vision of Parker, lids rimmed red, sniffing as she stumbled on him down by the dock. He'd yelled at her, of course, scrubbing at his face as he'd told her to scram. As always, her heart hurt when Parker got that look in his eyes. And the only person in the world that could make Parker that upset was his mother. It had been a long time since she'd seen him sad about his mom. Lately, his reactions more often resembled anger.

She straightened up. 'I'll tell Susie Frances that I caught you crying like a baby.'

His gaze flashed to hers. 'I was not crying,' he said. 'I got salt water in my eyes, is all.'

They both knew it was a lie, and she fought the temptation to look away. This was too important.

'Fine,' he said. And then he jabbed a finger in front of her face. 'But you have to stop the creepy stalker stuff.'

Heat flaring up her face, she was horrified by the words. Had she been that obvious?

Suddenly, she wished she'd been swallowed up by the waters of Sag Harbor. 'Fine,' she said, mimicking him. But then her bravery ran out, her voice growing small. 'I don't suppose we can find the paddleboard?'

Parker stood, and right away she missed the heat of his skin. He swiped a hand through his hair, leaving it spikier than usual. 'The board's long gone.'

Jeez, it all seemed so *unfair*. Blinking back the tears, she looked across the water. Petrified Parker would see her cry, she dragged her hand across her eyes and sniffed.

Another shiver racked her body, and the rustle of clothing brought her attention back to Parker.

He'd taken off his hoodie. 'Don't worry about it, Ace,' he said gruffly, pulling his sweatshirt down over her head.

Her heart soared, both from the touch and the words and the protective tone in his voice. And she'd always adored his nickname for her. She jabbed her arms into the damp sleeves, savoring the heat from his body, the smell of *Parker*.

'I'll take the blame for the board.' Those too-beautiful lips flattened grimly. A dark look crossed his face. 'My mom already hates me, anyway.'

A needle pricked her heart, the sharp pain familiar. Ms. Michael was all *Reese Reese Reese*, spoiling her daughter rotten. But Parker? He barely even existed in the Michael household. No wonder he chose to live with his dad.

'Thanks,' she said, hoping she wasn't tearing up like a baby again.

His lopsided smile appeared, leaving her weak in the knees as he said, 'Let's get you home.'

Parker gripped his whiskey glass.

Amber Davis.

Discovering the redhead's identity had been like a cattle-prod shock to Parker's nervous system, his mind reeling with the memories of his youth. He struggled to ignore the beautiful woman who'd trailed after him as a kid, hanging on his every word. His every move. The one who'd witnessed his most humiliating moment.

You were a mistake.

Tossing back the rest of his drink, he tried to focus on his goals for tonight. Avoid his mother at all costs, speak to Reese and tell her no and then get the heck out of here.

Attention firmly on him, Amber asked, 'Do you re-member—?'

'Yeah,' he said gruffly, fixing his eyes on his empty glass. No way was he letting her finish that question. 'I remember.'

He could feel Amber's gaze, but he needed a minute to adjust. Several of them, actually. Because he sure as hell wasn't ready to face the lady who, years ago, had found him sniffling like a wussy little girl.

Thank God for his cell phone.

Parker glanced at the incoming number flashing in time with the vibration, answering with his pat 'What's up, Robby boy?'

'Why aren't you at Rosie's Bar?'

Parker let out a discontented grunt, longing for the bar that was the watering hole for most of the fifty-seventh precinct. His gaze swept across the elegantly attired guests at the restaurant, the fancy venue most likely chosen for its bird's-eye view of Manhattan. The only bright spot had been the pretty redhead that he'd known was too sweet and *all* kinds of wrong for him. Resisting a little harmless flirting had been impossible.

But, man, was that ever a freakin' mistake.

'I'm busy,' Parker said to his partner as he shot a look at Amber.

Creamy skin, wide mouth and eyes the color of maple syrup. Her auburn hair was pulled back in some sleek knot that looked more professional than dressy. If he'd known she was gonna turn into a stunning redhead, he might have actually paid more attention. But she had been all knobby kneed, gap-toothed, with gangly arms and legs. A quiet kid.

A lamb among wolves at the Michael household.

He'd always felt a little sorry for her, a bit protective. Some of that had been drilled into him, to watch over Reese and Amber when Amber's mother couldn't. And more than anyone, he knew how it felt to be an outsider in the Michael household.

Now Amber was gorgeous, but there was still a lingering sense of the innocent openness that she'd had as a child. He could see it in her clear, honest eyes, the face that left everything on display. Parker couldn't remember ever being innocent.

Had stopped *believing* in innocence long ago.

Gaze locked with the redhead's, Parker spoke to Rob, who was waiting patiently on the other end of the phone. 'Trust me,' he said. 'I'd rather be spilling a beer with my partner at Rosie's Bar than at this fancy restaurant.'

'Get your butt down here,' Rob said.

'Sorry, Robby boy.' *Christamighty* was Parker sorry he was here instead of there. 'Got something I've got to do first.'

There was a long pause on the end of the phone. 'This isn't about the Miller case, is it?' Rob asked.

Parker's insides felt as if they'd been hooked to two tractor trailers racing in opposite directions. Shoulders tense, he rolled them back. 'No,' he said, careful to keep his voice casual. 'I've done this job long enough that nothing shocks me anymore.'

He knew his partner thought the turn of events had affected him. Was worried, somehow, that Parker was burning out on all they dealt with day to day. But he was more disturbed by the fact that he *wasn't* affected. The latest case had taken a twisted turn that most people could never fathom and, yet, Parker hadn't felt a speck of shock. Zip, zilch, nada.

The hollow darkness surrounding his heart expanded, and Parker refused to admit how much it scared the hell out of him.

Rob cleared his throat on the other end of the phone. 'I hate that our number one suspect is a teen, especially given his parents are total dirtbags,' he said.

Parker huffed in agreement. 'Yeah, sometimes family sucks.'

Eyebrows tenting at his words, Amber frowned.

And as he said goodbye to Rob, Parker let out a sigh and addressed the redhead. 'You got something you want to say?'

'Just wondering if you've spoken with your sister yet,' Amber said.

'Haven't had the time.'

'Haven't *made* the time.'

As if on cue, a feminine voice called his name, and he turned to face Reese. She was crossing the hardwood floor in a cocktail dress, her blond hair in a delicate twist.

'Be nice,' Amber whispered.

Parker frowned. 'I'm always nice.'

As Reese drew closer, he slipped his phone in his jacket, bracing for the upcoming conversation. Confronting his sister and telling her no appeared to be the only way to get her off his case. Emails hadn't worked. The phone calls had been a failure. Seemed the only way to get her to accept his no was a face-to-face conversation.

You can do polite.

But when Reese went to hug him, for a moment he panicked. Freakin' *panicked*. A master at deflection, he shifted on his feet, subtly placing his shoulder forward, blocking her attempt. Fortunately she interpreted his body language accurately and abandoned her attempt.

He didn't do public displays of affection.

He'd learned long ago not to do affection *period*.

'I'm glad you came,' Reese said with a small smile. 'I hope this means you've changed your mind about the wedding.'

Parker bit back the urge to say *hell, no*.

Now that she was getting married to her supposed dream guy, Reese was suddenly all 'peace on earth, good will toward men.' More persistent in her insistence they pretend they were a real family. They lived in the same town and hadn't seen each other in two years.

Mostly his fault, sure, but *still…*

'I came to talk to you in person,' he said.

'And to catch up with old friends?' Reese said.

His sister shot the redhead at his side a curious look before addressing Parker.

'So…' Reese said. 'Are you and Amber setting an appointment time for you to get measured for your tux?'

Parker's lips quirked in surprise as he slid his gaze back to Amber. She was watching him as if assessing his every move, the beautiful woman's attention sending a thrilling shimmy down his spine. *Amber* was supposed to measure him for his tux?

Interesting notion, but not enough to get him to change his mind.

'Come on, Reese,' he said, trying to be the diplomat he wasn't. 'Can you really picture me in a monkey suit?'

How many more times did he have to say no?

He wasn't a part of the Michael family, had never been welcomed. And at the age of thirty-two he wasn't going to start pretending now.

'Of course we want you there,' Reese said. 'You're my brother—'

'Half brother,' he said bluntly, knowing he sounded callous and trying to care. 'With emphasis on the half.'

Amber briefly touched the back of his hand and flashed him a disapproving look, and he chose to ignore the warning and the stimulating warmth of her touch, the fleeting feel of soft fingers. Reese eyed him warily. As if, after knowing him forever, she was still trying to figure him out.

Yeah, well…good luck with that one. He was still working on that himself.

'Listen,' he said. 'I'm happy that *you're* happy that you and that fiancé of yours are finally tying the knot.' He did his best not to scoff out loud. 'Not that I believe in the whole marital thing. But you know, to each his—or her—own delusion.'

'Parker,' Reese said gently, and he hated the worried look in her eyes. 'Love isn't a delusion.'

'Oh, yeah?' Parker screwed up his face, hoping he looked more doubtful than like the caustic bastard that Jessica had called him before breaking it off. After four months, a real record for him, it was almost a relief to have her gone. 'If I remember right—' he studied his sister '—you've pledged 'till death do you part' before.'

Amber's fingers returned to his wrist, gripping him hard. The contact briefly short-circuited his brain, bringing to mind better reasons she could be holding on to him so tight.

Not your type, Robinson. Not your type.

He discreetly pulled his wrist from Amber's clasp. 'Mason was your ex's name, wasn't it?' Parker said, lifting a brow at his sister.

Pink staining her cheeks at the mention of her first

husband, Reese ignored his comment. 'Being in the wedding doesn't mean you're endorsing the institution.'

He plowed a hand through his hair, not caring if it stuck out in all directions. 'Reese—'

'Please,' she said, her face the picture of sincerity. 'You're family.'

Every muscle in his gut tensed with the hit. As far as he was concerned, his family died the day his father had passed away.

And the void that had started with his mother's *you were a mistake* had grown through the years, only to expand to unbelievable depths the day his dad had died. Since then he'd felt numb, as if nothing touched him. Detached. A black hole that threatened to consume everything.

Amber shifted slightly on her feet, and his eyes went of their own volition to land, *again,* on the pretty tagalong from his youth. She pressed closer until their shoulders brushed, a distracting touch. But she was giving him an emphatic stare that screamed *Don't you dare break her heart.*

Because Reese didn't deserve it, not really.

It had taken him years as an adult to realize that his sister wasn't responsible for the way their mother had treated him. That Reese's precious-princess status in the Michael household was her parents' doing, and not his sister's. She'd been a clueless, pampered kid adored by her mom and dad. And wasn't that the way life was supposed to work?

But Parker Robinson wasn't a fake.

He puffed out a breath. At this point, he was just gonna have to let her be disappointed when he didn't show up for the Big Day.

'I told you,' Parker told his sister. 'Dylan needs to pick someone else for his fifth groomsman.'

Parker headed for the elevators, and Amber spied the crestfallen look on Reese's face.

'He's never going to say yes,' Reese said.

Amber hated seeing her so down. Helping her childhood friend plan her dream day—complete with a reunion with her three college roommates as bridesmaids—was vital. Because she'd watched Reese work hard at her marriage to Mason, had *seen* how devastated she was when it failed. It had been painful to watch her friend suffer. Reese deserved her happily ever after with Dylan.

'Parker will say yes,' Amber said. 'Because deep down he knows you care about him.'

'You care about him, too,' Reese said with a knowing look in her eye.

Her stomach lurched. 'That was a long time ago.'

'And you're both grown-ups now,' her friend said, tone riddled with subtext.

Shooting Reese a look, Amber said, 'Anyone who chooses to get involved with Parker is a glutton for punishment.' She cast an eye at the man as he waited for the elevator. 'And I don't chase men.'

'No,' Reese said with a sigh. 'You just sit back and let life pass you by.'

'Hey,' Amber protested. 'Romance will happen when it's good and ready.'

Her mom had always said loving her father had been easy. Reese and Dylan's relationship always looked effortless, too. They were the perfect couple. Amber's other friends chased love as if it were something to be hunted down and captured, torturing themselves in the process.

Amber knew when she met the right man, love would happen naturally.

Until then, she'd help others plan their perfect day.

Reese let out a *hunh*. 'Maybe you should be more pro-active in getting what you want.'

'Listen,' Amber said, changing the subject. 'I'll talk to Parker about the wedding.' Amber gave her friend a hug. 'You go find Dylan and enjoy the rest of the party, okay?'

Heart pounding, Amber followed in Parker's path. But who was she, really, to try to convince Parker Robinson of *anything*?

The elevator doors were beginning to shut, and Amber picked up her pace and slid inside just before they closed.

Tension bounced off the walls, making the space feel especially small.

Parker sent her an overly tolerant look. 'Did Reese send you to try to change my mind?'

'No,' Amber said truthfully. She knew she needed to ease her way into this conversation. Years of resentment weren't going to be undone with a one-minute elevator ride. 'I was hoping you could give me a lift home.'

He straightened up and stared at her.

'Are you coming on to me?' he said. There was no seductive tone. He actually sounded amused by the thought.

Amber sent him a disgusted look she didn't feel. And why did he find the idea *funny*? 'No,' she said. 'Will you give me a ride, anyway?'

'I'll give you a ride because you're *not* coming on to me,' he said. Before she had time to process the unsatisfying words, Parker pushed the button and went on.

'Where do you live?' he asked.

'In a loft above my shop,' she said. 'Down under the Manhattan Bridge overpass.'

An emotion she couldn't quite place swept up his face. 'I would have thought Reese wouldn't be caught dead in a shop anywhere other than on Fifth Avenue itself.'

Affection flared across her heart. Reese's wedding to Dylan Brookes was one of *the* social events of the year. The Michaels and the Brookeses were two of the most prominent families in the city. Handling the account was going to put her shop on the map, and she would forever be grateful for her friend's business and her trust.

'Reese has changed,' Amber said as they exited the elevator. She knew that better than anybody. 'I know she was a little oblivious as a teen...'

Parker chuckled at the understatement, though there was no malice in the sound.

They entered the lobby and Parker held the door open for her, and Amber passed through onto the busy, night-time sidewalk. Traffic whooshed by, the smell of rain heavy in the air.

'Honestly, I don't care how much she's changed.' And as he gave his ticket to the valet, he shot Amber a sharp look. 'I'm not convinced this thing with her and Dylan is even real.'

'You're just cynical about relationships in general,' Amber said with a small scoff. 'Everyone knows they're perfect for each other.'

'Regardless,' Parker said. 'I'm not going to be in her wedding.'

Heart shifting lower in her chest, Amber curled her fingers in her hand, determined to change his mind by the end of the ride home.

No matter what it took.

THREE

———

'What is this?' Amber asked when the valet pulled up with Parker's car.

'This,' Parker said, unable to hold back his grin of affection, 'is a 1967 Ford Mustang Fastback with a 390 cubic-inch, V-8 engine.'

Face blank, she stared at him.

'She's fast and she's furious and she's as badass as me,' he said, knowing the response it would produce. And so what if he enjoyed the roll of Amber's eyes. He blamed the small slice of pleasure for the words that slid from his mouth next. 'It belonged to my father.'

A look of tenderness leaped into her eyes and his chest clenched hard, the black hole cinching tight around his heart.

Stretching out her arm, as if to take his hand, she said, 'I'm sorry—'

'Don't.'

He stepped back before he knew what he was doing. He wasn't sure where the harsh word had come from. But Parker also knew he couldn't bear to hear whatever she was going to say next.

And no way could he stand to have her touch him in comfort.

They settled into his car, and he was grateful for the distraction of merging with traffic. The misting rain turned into a steady drizzle and the *swish swish swish* of the windshield wipers filled the vehicle. Riding in silence, the awkward commute felt longer than it should have, and Parker was almost relieved when they drew closer to her turnoff and he had to ask her for directions.

Once he parked on her street and turned off the car, the rain began to come down a little harder. He slid off his jacket and turned to toss it onto the backseat, noticing her eyes on his chest. And the sharp stab of lust to his groin was unexpected.

'I'll walk you to the door,' he said, gearing up for a good-bye.

'No need,' she said. 'There's no sense in two of us getting wet.' She twisted in her seat to look at him. 'Parker, about the wedding—'

Stomach knotted with tension, he bolted out of the car and rounded to the passenger side, opening Amber's door. 'We're a block away,' he said. 'We should get moving.'

He closed the car door behind her with a forceful *thunk*, because the former stalker had lied to him. She was going to try to convince him to change his mind. And the last thing he needed were *two* females hounding him about an impossible task.

Amber frowned. 'It won't take long to get there, so we can—'

'We better hurry before the rain gets worse,' he said, taking her arm.

Leading her up the sidewalk, he glanced at the red-head from the corner of his eye. She had a nice figure.

Slim, but curvy enough in the right spots to capture a man's attention.

'Parker,' Amber said, sounding impatient. 'We need to—'

The skies opened up and began to release a load of rain as if it had grown too heavy to hold. Their mad dash to the awning wasn't fast enough, and, when they arrived, water dripped down their faces.

Parker turned to Amber, trying hard not to appreciate how good she looked wet.

'The last time I saw you that soaked you were trying to drown,' Parker said.

Sending him an overly tolerant look, she opened her mouth to speak again. But Parker had other ideas.

'There's something I gotta ask.' He narrowed his eyes at Amber with a curiosity that was genuine. 'Were you just pretending to be dead so I would do mouth to mouth?'

The shocked and offended expression on her face was instantaneous, and her mouth dropped open wider. 'I—'

She blinked and tried again. 'You—'

'Hey,' he said by way of protest. So far his choice of conversation had left her practically mute, which was exactly what he'd planned. 'You *followed* me around. I mean, come on, I couldn't seem to get rid of you.' A smile split his lips at the memory. 'I even caught you watching me make out with Susie Frances.'

Pink coloring bled up her cheeks. Parker would never forget the gaping look on Amber's face when he spied her peeking at them from behind the lifeguard house. He knew his gruff 'You got some kind of voyeur kink going on there, Ace?' had been totally out of line. But the expression on her face had been priceless. Poor kid didn't have a clue what he'd been talking about, but he remembered the look in her eyes.

From an awkward twelve-year-old it had been embarrassingly uncomfortable.

From a beautiful twenty-seven-year-old it made him embarrassingly uncomfortable in his jeans. Case in point, the way her eyes had skimmed over his chest in the car.

'I did not mean to spy on you while you were with Susie,' she said.

'Feel free to keep lying to yourself,' Parker went on. 'So...did you?'

She blinked. 'Did I what?'

'Pretend to be dead.'

'Yes,' she said with a huff of sarcasm that told him it wasn't true. 'And vomiting up seawater was part of my evil seduction plan, too.'

'Come on, you know you wanted to kiss me back then. It was hellaciously embarrassing, let me tell you,' Parker said.

The color climbed higher up her cheeks. 'Trust me, I didn't plan out almost drowning just so I could get your lips on mine,' she said. 'Which is a good thing, too, because it would have been a terrible disappointment.'

'You keep saying that.'

'Because it's true.'

'Awesome,' he said with a dry twist of his lips. 'My skills are being judged on a one-time incident of giving you mouth to mouth—' he paused, as if for emphasis '—while you were trying to, you know, *die.*'

'Sorry,' she said with a delicate lift of her shoulder. 'It's my only basis for comparison.'

In a fit of madness he wanted to wipe that look off her

face. 'Well,' he said as he stepped closer, hating how rough the word came out. 'There's an easy fix for that.'

Hands on her arms, he was vaguely aware goose bumps prickled her skin, and he wondered if it was from the chilling rain...or his touch.

No matter. He intended to be quick in his efforts, to dazzle her with his finesse. Get in; get out. Hopefully blow her mind. Or at least replace a stupid ten-second mouth-to-mouth moment with a kiss that was worthy of being judged. His pride was at stake here.

But when his lips touched hers, she let out a whimper that slayed him and canted her head up, opening her mouth beneath his as if she'd been waiting all night to do exactly that. And if he took advantage of the offer to sweep his tongue against hers, and instantly followed through on the crushing need to repeat the act, well...he was as weak as the next guy when faced with a beautiful woman in his arms.

He might have arched against her.

His breath might have caught in his throat at the glorious feel of her soft body.

Before he knew what he was doing he was shifting closer, his hands in the silk of her hair, and angling her head to increase the contact. To maintain the seductive slide of tongue against tongue. She tasted like maple and smelled like the syrup that matched the color her eyes.

For a heart-stopping moment he pushed aside the fact that she was too sweet. That she was the sort of woman that would expect more than he could give.

That she was the one person who knew the truth about how weak he'd once been.

The mood-killing thought hit like a jolt of lightning, and he tried to pull away. But her soft hand on his neck didn't allow him to escape too far, now only an inch of space separating them. Her breath was sweet, warm and moist on his lips.

Heart thumping harder than it should have from a simple kiss, he stared into the golden-brown eyes.

And then she feathered her mouth across his in a way that was so soft, so barely there, that Parker didn't know what to do with the moment. As lips ghosted across his, he frowned, frozen, adjusting to the foreign feel of something *not* focused on the act of sexual gratification. The barely-there touch of skin on skin that managed to gut him so thoroughly. Affect him more than any other more carnal action could have.

And an odd, soft feeling was seeping into his chest. A feeling he didn't quite know what to do with.

But he did not do sweet. Not in his relationships, not in his work, not in his *life*. Yet, for some unknown reason, he couldn't pull away. He didn't respond, but he couldn't move, either. Like a stupid deer in the freight-train-lights moment.

When she finally leaned back, her throat was flushed the same shade as her face, her fingers stroking against the hair at the base of his neck. Sending goose bumps, freakin' *goose bumps*, down his back.

What the hell?

Rain pounded the pavement around them, gushing off the awning and cocooning them in a rushing wall of water.

'So,' Parker finally said. He cleared his throat. 'I'd say that puts the kiss issue to rest.'

But, man, did it ever create a whole new set of problems.

Because he was staring at her face, still wet from the rain. A drop dripped from her hair and slid down her cheek, slipping past the corner of her mouth, and Parker was struck by the gut-wrenching urge to lick the trail. The slender body in the dress that now clung to curves he hadn't *truly* appreciated without the addition of water. And, as if the *want* wasn't bad enough, the strand of hair that clung to her temple added an air of vulnerability that was far worse than the feeling of lust.

From this proximity he could reach out and brush the lock from her forehead. Not that he planned on following through, or that he longed to. At all.

Damn it.

'You seem awfully confident,' she said softly.

'I am.'

'Shouldn't I have a say?'

Lifting a brow, he waited.

'It definitely puts the issue to rest,' she said.

And the smile on her face left him wanting to kiss her again, and he fisted his hand.

He worked in a world of bitterness and darkness and death and she dealt with joy and lightness and happily ever after. He couldn't bear the thought of being the one to snuff out those good feelings. And he would, too. Every woman he'd left behind him had been just a little more jaded, a little less innocent. Had believed a little less.

He didn't want to...

No, he *wouldn't* do that to Amber.

'Take care, Ace,' he said as he set her back.

And then he headed out into the night and the rain, before she could say something they'd both regret.

Focusfocus*focus*

Amber clutched her purse as she trotted up the steps leading to Rosie's Bar, hoping Parker was here. Three days after she'd set out to get him to change his mind and gotten so deliciously sidetracked, she'd finally recovered enough from his devastating kiss to face him again. It had been all she'd imagined and more.

And after years of fantasies, that was a supersize order beyond belief.

The beautiful lips had been softer than she remembered, the slide of his tongue electrifying. The smell of the leather jacket clung to his T-shirt in its absence. Hands hard on her head, he'd held her still as the kiss had quickly shifted from a teasing joke to something more, until he was nearly mauling her mouth with an intensity that had sapped the air from her lungs.

She pushed aside the swirl of heat in her stomach. No more getting distracted by her memories or the way he made her feel. She'd followed Parker into the elevator that night with every intention of convincing him to agree to be in Reese's wedding. But once she'd climbed into the car and been enclosed in the small space, his enticing smell, those captivating eyes and that finely honed body had derailed her plans.

And of course, then there'd been the leftover strain in the air from the mention of his father....

No, that wasn't right. The tension had come when she'd tried to show him how sorry she was for his loss. All she'd wanted was to offer a bit of sympathy. She might have been small when her father had died, but she still felt the loss acutely. And she'd been overwhelmed with the need for a simple squeeze of her fingers to communicate that she knew how he felt.

But Parker...Parker wouldn't allow even that small comfort.

The vision of him averting Reese's hug swam before her eyes, and Amber's lips twisted in disappointment and concern. He hadn't always been so distant. In fact, as a kid he'd been open and easy and fairly demonstrative. But that had changed as he'd grown into an adolescent. Amber had witnessed the slow transformation under his mother's treatment, and it was disheartening to realize that it remained a permanent fixture of his personality.

Bracing herself for another Parker encounter, she opened the door and entered the chaos of the noisy sports bar. She weaved her way through the throng of people, scanning the crowd.

And then her gaze caught on the back of ruffled brown hair with streaks of gold, spying Parker at a small table. He wore well-worn jeans, a long-sleeved T-shirt and the brown leather jacket. A black-haired man in slacks, a navy peacoat and no tie shared the table.

As she approached, Parker's green eyes collided with hers. 'What are you doing here?'

The words were delivered with more surprise than annoyance, but the pause that followed was uncomfortable, filled with Parker's heated gaze, chatter and the sound of clinking glasses.

The man sitting beside him sent Parker a curious look before sticking out his hand. 'Rob Winston,' he said with a smile and an accent that sounded southern. Texan, maybe. 'Ignore my partner here.' She returned his shake as he tipped his head in Parker's direction. 'His momma didn't hug him enough as a child.'

The words sent a shock through Amber's system. There wasn't a flicker of emotion in Parker's expression, the muscles in his face rigid. By the nonchalant way Rob had delivered the words, Amber knew that Parker's partner had no idea how close to the marrow his words had drilled.

It was written in the way Parker was studiously avoiding her gaze.

Because she remembered…

'Don't get your ovaries in a wad, Robin,' Parker huffed, though there was no real annoyance there, either.

'Don't be such a dirtbag, Parker,' Rob said good-naturedly.

Amber had the distinct impression that these words were uttered on a daily basis.

'So—' eyes on Amber, Rob indicated for her to take a seat, but she hesitated '—how do you know my dumbass of a partner here?'

'We grew up together,' she said.

This seemed to prick Rob's interest. He sat up higher in his seat and folded his arms on the table, leaning in with a light in his gaze that was unmistakable.

'I bet you have some good stories about my friend here,' Rob said. 'Please—' he waved at the chair beside him again in invitation '—join us and share.'

Ignoring Parker's gaze, Amber bit back the smile as she sat down. It was hard not to respond to the open friendliness in Rob's face, the amusing curiosity in his eyes. Which made it easier to bear Parker's disconcerting attention.

'You're right, Rob.' Her eyes slid to meet Parker's, who was staring at her with a heat that burned her to the core, making her words just a little too husky. 'I do have some doozies to tell.'

The responding flash in Parker's gaze sent a thrill tripping through her limbs.

'Was he always an obstinate SOB?' Rob said.

Amber smiled at the memories. 'Definitely.'

'He's relentless,' Rob said with an acknowledging nod

of his head. 'He once chased a suspect ten blocks before tackling him in the alleyway of a pawnshop. And that was *after* the guy had dumped a pail of rose-colored paint over Parker's head.'

Amber laughed at the image of Parker in pink sprinting up the street.

'He spent one whole summer teaching me how to hold a crab,' she said. Remembering her yells and Parker's patient laughs, she twisted her lips wryly. 'I kept shrieking and drawing my hands away. But he kept insisting I try again, no matter how loud I screamed.'

He'd paddled like a madman to rescue her from drowning.

He hadn't given up then, either.

Tilting his head, Rob went on. 'You should see him in the interrogation room,' he said. 'Of course, my hell-on-wheels partner here is the reason we have the highest closure rate in the department.'

That Parker was the best at his job didn't come as a surprise.

Chuckling, Rob glanced around. 'We should have the waitress bring you a drink,' he said to Amber. 'So we can swap war stories. Was he a shameless flirt back then, too?'

'The summer he was seventeen he dated three girls—' eyes fixed on Rob, she leaned in conspiratorially, ignoring Parker's frown '—at the *same time.*'

'I don't remember that,' Parker said.

Gazing at Rob as if Parker hadn't spoken, Amber went on. 'Leslie Campbell, Sharon Howell and Susie Frances.' She hoped no one would comment on why she remembered the girls' names when Parker didn't. 'Once I even caught him—'

'Hey.' Clearly unhappy with the turn in the conversation, Parker waved a hand in the air between his table-mates' gazes. 'I'm sitting right here, people.' He tossed a loaded look at his partner. 'Why don't you make yourself useful and go find the waitress.'

Rob chuckled again. 'But I'm—' his curious gaze slid to his partner, where he must have seen something interesting, because Rob cleared his throat and stood '—just going to find the waitress.' He sent Amber a quick nod. 'Nice to meet you.'

After an answering smile, Amber watched the man walk away to join a boisterous bunch at the end of the bar. Her gaze lingered more from a nervousness about looking at Parker again then from any real interest in his good-looking partner.

'Why are you here, Amber?' Parker asked, his voice wary.

Feeling the need for a sense of power, she shifted higher in her seat. And from his laid-back position, legs stretched in front of him, they were almost eye to eye. Her foot brushed his, and a flash of awareness lit his gaze, an awareness that reminded her that she had been well and thoroughly kissed by Parker.

'You know why I'm here,' she said.

'We're not finishing what we started.'

Was he talking about their make-out session or the conversation where she insisted he be in the wedding?

And why was the former more disappointing than the latter?

Amber lost track of the thought when he shrugged out of his jacket to loop it behind his chair, the muscles in his chest flexing from the move. The long-sleeved T-shirt stretched across his gorgeous form nicely, the pectorals and biceps filling it in a way that made coherent thought briefly impossible.

'You need to come get measured for your tux,' Amber said.

Parker let out a grunt. 'I'm not going to be in the wedding.'

'You have to.'

His gaze pierced her. 'I don't have to do anything.'

'Please, Parker,' Amber said, all teasing long gone. 'I know it means nothing to you. But it's really important to Reese.'

At the mention of his sister, Parker's gaze slid off into the distance and Amber could see the conflict on his face. He wanted to, but he didn't. And suddenly, it seemed imperative that Parker accept this little bit of his family's affections. Or, more accurately, his *sister's* affections. Somehow Amber just knew that if he didn't follow through with this he would remain distant, not only to his family, but to, well...*life*.

'I'm busy, Amber,' he said. 'I'm here with my friends.'

'And as soon as you agree to the simple deed that will make your sister happy,' she said easily, leaning back to get comfortable, 'I'll get out of your hair.'

The twist of his lips betrayed his displeasure. But this was too important. And much bigger than just one wedding.

When he didn't relent, Amber crossed her arms and pulled the same stunt she'd pulled after he'd saved her from drowning. 'If you don't agree to be in Reese's wedding,' she went on with an expression so innocent she knew Parker could see through it, 'I'll agree to that drink with Rob.'

Parker's gaze barreled back into hers. 'You wouldn't.'

'I would.' She sent him a small smile. They both knew she had enough stories to embarrass him from now until forever. 'I bet Rob would *love* to know you listened to 'N Sync.'

'When I was twelve,' he barked, eyebrows scrunched in horrified protest.

'You were seventeen when you let Susie Frances paint your toenails.'

'That was *joke*.' He glanced around nervously, as if suddenly realizing the potential risk to his reputation. 'And besides—' the sexy smirk edged up his face '—she made the humiliation totally worth my while.'

And Amber *really* didn't want to hear how.

'Okay,' she said. Time to go big or go home. She leaned closer, and this time her smile was brilliant. 'I'll tell Rob about the time I walked in on you in the bathroom and caught you—'

'Stop.' His hand landed on the table with a *thump,* and he eyed her as if half tempted to muzzle her mouth. His voice gruff, he muttered, 'Holy mother of—'

The curse—a creative one, no doubt—died as he plowed a hand through his gold-tipped hair, leaving it more tousled than usual.

'I'll do it, okay?' he said.

The boyishly ruffled hair, his obvious embarrassment and his agreement sent a twist of affection to her heart, and she leaned in close enough to smell the leather of his jacket.

'Thank you,' she said sincerely as she reached out, overwhelmed with the need to touch his hand in simple appreciation.

He must have misread her intentions, because his gaze grew dark as he drew back out of reach. 'You've had your kiss,' he said dryly. 'And that's all you get. As a matter of fact,' he went on, lifting his brow as if in challenge. 'Hands to yourself from here on out.'

Amber was surprised the surge of heat didn't leave her in a puddle in her chair. Her nerves pulled into a knot, partly from the mention of their kiss and partly in annoyance at the reminder she wasn't his 'type.' Which apparently included everyone *but* her. She inhaled a soothing breath. Parker Robinson seemed to avoid anything he didn't want to talk about—emotions, thoughts, feelings, his *past*—by burying it in sexual innuendo.

She remember Parker arching against her body, the catch of his breath against her mouth...and the pulse of pure, unadulterated pleasure knowing that she had caused both.

Clearly, he'd enjoyed kissing her. No one could fake that kind of response. And he was still attracted, she could sense it in his gaze, in his very posture. Except he kept insisting he'd never touch her again. Any other guy and she wouldn't care.

For some reason, Parker's attitude was starting to tick her off.

'I'm measuring you for your tuxedo,' she said, amazed she managed to sound so calm. 'Touching kind of goes along with the activity.'

She forced her eyes to remain steady on his as an impressive whirlwind of emotion swept across his face. Annoyance. Resentment. And a whole lot of lust.

Lust.

Chest slowly squeezing the air from her lungs, she desperately reminded herself that she didn't do casual hookups, no matter how attracted she was. More important, she'd never, ever, seduce a guy. And she wouldn't *dream* of chasing a fellow who was throwing up caution signs all over the place. Especially like the man seated across from her, a man who was less like a stop sign and more like a road-totally-closed-ahead kind of guy.

But…but she'd wanted Parker her whole life and the desire was so strong she was seriously considering making him an exception.

'Fine,' he said gruffly. 'But I work long hours, so it will be late before I can stop by your shop.'

Visions of him in her store swam before her eyes. At night. The two of them alone. All she could hear in her head was Reese's 'You should be more proactive.'

And if anyone was worth taking the initiative to seduce, it was Parker Robinson.

Decision made, anticipation coursed through her veins, and Amber swallowed so hard it hurt.

She cleared her throat. 'I make special, after-hours appointments fairly regularly,' she said. 'Just tell me when you can be there.'

Parker heaved out a breath and grabbed his beer bottle. 'Nine-thirty tomorrow night,' he said, taking a sip as he shot her a loaded look. 'Just a quick couple of measurements and then I'm gone.'

The set of those beautiful lips and the tone of his voice made it abundantly clear he was done. But Amber…

Well, as far as she was concerned, she was just getting started.

FOUR

————

At nine-thirty the next night Parker
pulled the door open to Amber's Bridals. The bell tinkled
way too merrily for a frustrating day that had started
with a dead end on the Miller case, expanding the black,
vast void in his chest. Which meant he'd spent the rest of
today numbly going through the motions. Or maybe the
numbness had been a problem for months.

Perhaps *years*.

Rolling his shoulders uneasily, he glanced around. He
had to hand it to the kid, she had one helluva store. Classy
to the core, the shop contained sleek hardwood floors and
an abundance of white dresses lining the walls, veils, fake
bouquets and pictures of models in wedding getup. And
bowls of...what were those? Rose petals?

Parker couldn't help himself. He let out a shudder.

'Don't worry.' Amber's voice came from behind. 'No
one has to know you were here.'

He let out a barking laugh. 'I'm losing every masculine
mark I ever earned just by passing through these doors—'

Turning, he was hit with a vision of Amber that
knocked him on his virtual ass. How had the geeky pre-

teen grown into such a vision? Red hair flowed past her shoulders. She was dressed in dressy jeans and a sheer top that clung to her breasts, the long-sleeve blouse flaring at the waist and sleeves. She managed to look young and sweet and incredibly sexy.

And with the current case he was working on, he felt old and hardened and done with humanity.

Amber crossed to lock the door and then turned to face him, remaining silent. The staring contest grew uncomfortable as Parker realized he was alone in a shop with a beautiful woman who had, at the age of twelve, looked at him as if he hung the moon, the stars and the bloody sun to boot. Unfortunately, the appreciation in her face now held the weight of experience. Not to mention the lady was a walking, talking advertisement for Happily Ever After and Parker was quite convinced that Content for Now was beyond his capabilities. Toss in the fact that they were surrounded by swarms of puffy white dresses—and, holy mother, were those fake *tiaras*?—and the situation was less amusing than downright *concerning*.

She hiked a brow that didn't ease the tension. 'You ready?'

What was that supposed to mean?

'Of course,' he said.

He wasn't an amateur. He refused to be intimated by the little slip of a thing that he'd taught how to capture crabs on the beach.

As he followed her down the hall, he made a point of ignoring the gentle, seductive sway of her slight hips and the fluid walk. Fortunately, the view was easier to ignore when she stepped into a large room containing two couches, an armchair and a coffee table mimicking an elegant living room, the furniture facing a small space surrounded on three sides by floor-length mirrors. And while he was sure broad daylight and the addition of people encouraged the appropriate air for viewing a dress, somehow the whole setup hinted at something...almost erotic. Especially with just the two of them. Alone.

Damn, what had he agreed to?

'Take off your jacket and shoes,' Amber said, waving in the direction of the furniture.

Parker shrugged out of his leather jacket and tossed it on a couch, toeing off his shoes.

'Uh—' her eyes dropped to his shoulder holster containing his weapon and handcuffs '—the gun, too.'

For some reason he hesitated.

'What?' she said, hand on her hip. 'You don't mind taking off the jacket and shoes, but you draw a line at the weapon?'

'Maybe it brings me a sense of security,' he said with a small grin. When she waited for him to go on, the oft-repeated joke tripped off of his tongue. 'Most people respect the badge,' he said. 'But everyone respects Smith & Wesson.'

'Is that why you do what you do?' she said, gesturing for him to step forward to the space in front of the mirror. 'For respect?'

Black void expanding exponentially in his chest, he frowned. Shoot. He'd been teasing and she'd jumped straight to the serious talk.

'How long is this going to take?' he said as he crossed to the designated spot.

She pulled out a small, flexible tape measure and moved closer, pulling his gut a touch tighter. 'I need to measure you for a shirt, jacket and pants,' she said.

Which was really no answer at all.

And suddenly she was right in front of him, bringing her scent and the clear skin of her beautiful face close to his. He leaned back and looked down at her dubiously, his frown drawing his brows down until they tried to merge with his eyes.

'Relax,' she said. But something in her tone made the suggestion impossible. 'This isn't going to hurt.'

He elected to ignore the twitch of her luscious lips and hoped to hell she was talking about being measured for the tux. Innocent expression clashing with the knowing light in her eyes, she looped the tape measure—and consequently, *her arms*—around his neck, setting his heart tapping harder in his chest.

The slight smile on her face made him nervous. 'There's something I've been meaning to discuss with you,' she said as she took the measurement, her fingers whispering against him just beneath his Adam's apple.

The simple brush of skin on skin sent a line of goose bumps streaking up his back. And how was that possible when she was only touching his stupid neck?

'Are you going to your mother's dinner party in two weeks?' she went on.

Fortunately it was a question he could answer without thought, because thinking was difficult with her so close. 'No.'

The word came out a little harsher than he'd intended, but the feel of her fingers was sending an uncomfortable thrum through his body. And how long did it take to get an accurate measurement? She wasn't launching a nuclear warhead here. An approximation would do just fine, thank you.

'Why not?' she said as she dropped her hands and stepped over to the laptop on the coffee table.

Free of her disturbing touch, Parker let out a breath of relief.

'Because I don't have anything to say to my mother,' he said. 'And if I show up I'll have to talk to her.'

A small frown tugged on her lips as she entered the measurement into her laptop. 'When was the last time you two had a conversation?'

The gaping pit around his heart seemed to expand twofold, and Parker worked hard at *not* frowning at the memory.

'She called my cell the day my father died,' he said, remembering the feeling of desolation, the sense of aloneness. 'I didn't answer.'

She turned and stepped closer again, studying him silently for a moment. The assessing gaze, the topic of conversation and her skin that looked as if it tasted of cream made the situation wholly uncomfortable.

Without a word, she came to his side, and he stared at her profile in the mirror.

'You should talk to her,' she said.

'I've got nothing to say.'

The pause was slight, but he sensed she had more to share. The words that followed were not what he'd been expecting.

'I'm going to measure your sleeve length,' she said.

With more care than he thought necessary, she measured from the spine at his neck, to his shoulder, and then drew the tape down his arm to his wrist. His T-shirt offered no protection from the slow slide of her fingers against his bare arm, and he ignored the shimmer of awareness that came with the move.

The simple brush of skin on skin on his arm shouldn't be so arousing, either.

'You did that on purpose,' he said.

Despite the unfortunate husky tone of his voice, she said, 'I have no idea what you're talking about.' She sent him a sedate look. 'Now raise your arms.'

He shifted on his feet, uneasy. 'Why?'

She rolled her eyes. 'No need to be so suspicious,' she said. 'I just need to measure your chest.'

Something in the set of her posture and the light in her eyes told him he needed to proceed with caution. To be on guard—and not because of the conversation about his family. The mood was electric. Heck, the air was so heavily charged he was surprised they both didn't glow. And he could see in her eyes that she knew it, too.

'Arms,' she said as she stepped in front of him again.

Sending a sharp look down at her too-close-for-comfort face, Parker complied, raising his hands as if surrendering. Which he wasn't, blast it all.

Amber looped her arms around his back, and, for a moment, the world came to a grinding halt....

He couldn't think.

Couldn't breathe.

If he leaned just a fraction of an inch closer, he would be able to feel the soft press of her breasts against the harder planes of his chest. She was looking up at him with those wide, beautiful eyes, and her face almost glowed. As though she was lit from within. A light that just might be able to absorb the blackness that churned inside.

Where had that thought come from?

Looking dazed, Amber stared up at him with her arms around his torso, and the words that came from her mouth were a surprise. 'You took off your jacket.'

Her tone of voice suggested there was more to that less-than-brilliant bit of observation.

Parker's brows pulled together, the rest of him frozen. 'You told me to.'

She looked as stunned as he felt.

'No. Not that...' she said, her voice stumbling a bit. 'I mean—you still smell like leather.'

A succession of emotions filed across her face, moving on from the shock and eventually ending with something that looked like anticipation. And...damn, there was no ignoring the vibe any longer because—

'But maybe that's just your signature scent,' she mused.

—it was written all over her face.

'Are you trying to seduce me, Amber?' he asked softly.

Sometimes it was best just to punch the elephant in the room in the face.

She blinked, as if clearing her vision, and then brought her hands back around to finish measuring his chest. 'Yes.'

Apparently she had no qualms about laying her cards on the table.

Tipping his head, he paused, feeling stronger now that they'd addressed the issue. He could handle this. He'd handled her starstruck adoration as a kid and he could handle her desire now. Feeling better, he watched her cross to enter the latest numbers and then return to stand in front of him again.

Everything would be fine, if he just didn't look at her face, or her mouth, or her chest....

Bracing himself, he held his breath as she measured around his waist, her fingers skimming just below the level of his belly button, too close to more...*sensitive* parts of his body. And his abdominal muscles clenched as if punched, despite the T-shirt between them.

'You should at least come to your mother's party to

see Reese,' she said as she bit the corner of her mouth in concentration.

Leaving Parker with the intense need to lick the damp spot from her lip. His head was spinning, and his shaft was thickening, and coherent thought took him a moment.

'Why?' he croaked.

See, he could form words. Sort of.

'Because she's family,' she said. 'And we all need family.'

Despite his discomfort, he let out a small huff of laughter. She thought she was going to seduce him *and* get him to talk to his family? Man, she really was a believer.

And then she knelt before him, and... *Oh, God.*

In the mirror, the vision of her on her knees in front of him sent his pulse bounding out a rhythm that threatened to burst from his body. She was joy and hope and light and the intense need to bury himself inside her, to take a little of that faith for himself, to sink into her *belief* was almost his undoing.

His mouth worked, struggling to function. 'Nothing about this scenario is going to work on me, Ace,' he said hoarsely, proud he could still form words.

'I'm just taking your measurements.'

A sarcastic scoff escaped his throat.

And then she measured from his waist to his heel, and Parker blew out a breath, relieved the act was fairly tolerable. Even being so stupid as to congratulate himself on his self-control as she entered the measurement into her computer.

'Next, your inseam.' She returned to kneel in front of him, and he braced himself. 'Spread your legs a bit.'

Sweat broke out along his lip at the erotic image her words produced. Parker was busy battling the flash of heat when Amber, with one end of the measuring tape, reached up between his thighs. His chest seized around his heart, preventing it from doing its job. And when her fingers brushed just to the left of his groin, pleasure pooled in his stomach.

Paralyzed, he used his gaze in a vain attempt to burn reason into her, his voice almost a growl. 'Does measuring my inseam include touching my junk?'

Eyes wide, she looked up at him. But beneath it all, he was sure he detected a note of false innocence. And a hint of nerves.

'Sorry,' she said as she drew the other end of the tape down to his heel.

With a wary scowl, he said, 'You don't look sorry.'

She swallowed and cleared her throat. 'Assume your normal posture, please.'

'I am.'

'You look like you're slumped over,' she said with a doubtful look.

That was because he was so hard now his body was protectively hunching around the sensitive area.

'And now I need to get the last measurement,' she said.

He should have known he was in trouble by the fine tremor in her voice. By the way she nervously licked her lips. But he was too mesmerized by the slide of pink tongue across her mouth to register what she was doing.

One hand holding the tape at his waist in back, she reached between his legs and pulled the measuring tape down his backside.

'You're measuring my ass?' he rasped.

'I need your crotch length,' she said.

Crotch length?

There was a joke in there somewhere, but, for the life

of him, he couldn't formulate the wisecrack. Especially when her hand slowly pulled the tape up between his thighs.

And Parker knew he was well and truly screwed.

Breathing a distant memory, a tiny speck in his review mirror, he couldn't move as her fingers flirted with touching his erection. She skirted too close for comfort as she continued up his crotch toward the front of his waist. Wringing his insides. Dragging his nerves through razor wire. And, just when it was almost over, she lightly brushed the tip of his shaft.

Desire burst like a supernova, jump-starting his flagging brain.

'Jesus, Amber,' he ground out, grabbing her wrist. Body throbbing, he narrowed his gaze. 'Is this measurement even necessary?'

She gazed up at him, looking stunned. 'You can never have too much information,' she murmured.

'Hell yeah, you can.' His grip grew firmer around her wrist.

Case in point: her skin was warm, her pulse bounded beneath his fingers and her expression was nothing but honest—pure, unadulterated want innocently on display. Along with something else. He should have pushed her wrist as far from him as possible, but he was transfixed by the light in her eyes. As if he deserved much more than just sex.

And the crushing need to capture a little of that hope for himself, to briefly fill the black hole that had been surrounding his heart for years, was too much.

'You win,' he muttered, and he hauled her up by her wrist, gaze intent on her mouth.

Amber didn't utter a word of protest as Parker pulled her body flush with his. Her wrist still clutched in his fingers, he tucked their arms behind his back until she was giving him a partial hug. But it wasn't a real embrace, because his other hand hung loosely at his side.

Green eyes holding hers, his voice gruff, he said, 'You know this is all you get, right?'

They were pressed together from chest to groin, and she was momentarily rendered speechless by his too-blunt words and the feel of his erection. The longing to be wrapped in his arms for real was intense. But he maintained his current posture, patiently waiting for a response, and he wasn't going to continue until he was sure he'd made his point.

She'd never chased a man before, had never actively pursued what she wanted. And she *wanted* this.

With an intensity that was too great to be denied.

'I understand,' she said.

The tension radiating from him since she'd taken his measurement suddenly dissipated, and he lifted his free hand to her face, lowering his mouth to hers.

God, it wasn't fair.

He was strong and sure and oozed a confident sensuality as his lips slid over hers, as if trying to absorb something more than a simple kiss. Meanwhile she was quaking, literally *quaking* at the knees. She was a grown woman with plenty of experience under her belt. She'd been around several blocks along the way but, for some reason, this time the trip felt different.

Amber supposed it was only natural, as she'd waited for this moment since she was a preteen. Before she really even knew what, exactly, her body longed for....

She remembered the heat from innocent brushes of skin on skin as she'd accepted the crab he'd gently placed in her hand. She remembered her heart pounding from dreams too vague to recall, only that they'd contained *Parker*.

And she remembered the mesmerizing mouth that had always triggered an anxious flutter in her stomach. Parker's lips were now slicking across hers, wet and warm and working her mouth so deliciously she had to clutch his T-shirt, dizzy.

With a small movement, his tongue tested her bottom lip, and a needy catch escaped her throat as she opened her mouth wide. He finally relented and gave her what she wanted, his tongue against hers. The taste, the soft strokes that went on and on, sent her senses soaring. Twisting his T-shirt tighter, she fought to have her other arm freed from his grip.

'Slow down, Ace,' he murmured against her mouth.

Pleasure flared higher. As a kid, the nickname had always made her feel special in Parker's eyes. She hadn't been, she knew. But it was the way he said it, as if she were the only one on the planet that was important. And right now he was licking, kissing and nipping his way down her neck, leaving her feeling the same way.

Against the bounding pulse at her neck, he said, 'There's no hurry.'

Oh, but holy heaven, *there was*.

Summers of innocent longing. *Years* of fantasies.

The mother lode of mental foreplay.

'Please,' she said, pulling against the fingers wrapped around her wrist.

He released her.

Instantly her fingers gripped the edge of his T-shirt and shoved, unceremoniously, up his torso. When he didn't lift his arms fast enough, she abandoned her plan to take it off and dropped her mouth to his naked chest. He tasted of salt and smelled of leather, as if the essence of his jacket had fused with his skin. She pressed open-mouthed kisses across his muscles, with the ridiculous thought that she could inhale this moment and keep it forever. Parker mumbled something she couldn't understand, something about taking their time, but Amber ignored him. She nosed a nipple and then licked the nub until it was raised enough to scrape her teeth across.

He sucked in a breath. 'Okay, okay.'

All thought came to a halt when his hands dropped to the T-shirt bunched just beneath his arms. Stunned, she watched the shifting of pectorals and bone and sinew as he shrugged out of the garment and tossed it aside. The strength in his shoulders, the easy play of muscle a beautiful, breathtaking sight.

Without hesitation, she spread her hands across the gorgeous display and pushed him back against the mirrored wall.

'Jesus, Amber,' he hissed.

Ignoring him, she stared at the light dusting of hair on his flat abdomen as she fumbled with his belt and the fastening of his jeans, finally pushing everything to the floor. The vision of lean hips, well-muscled thighs and a full erection left her breathless. Unable to continue.

And Parker finally seemed to grasp the urgency of their situation.

Hands and lips and teeth seemingly everywhere at once, he divested her of her clothing efficiently. When gone, she pressed her body to his, refusing to blush at the groan that ripped from her chest at the glorious feeling of, *finally*, skin on skin.

Parker swept a hand up her back and buried his fingers in her hair, his kiss raw. Mouth realigning this way and that as if to consume her from every angle. She lost track of time until the fingers in his other hand found their way between her thighs.

The visceral hit to her system left her pulling back from the kiss, gasping for air.

Lips parted, he breathed through his mouth—open hunger on his face as the fingers between her legs turned bolder. Until the desire grew so great tears pricked the backs of her lids.

Closing her eyes, she whispered, 'Parker.'

Which came out more like a strangled sound of pleasure than an actual word.

As if inspired, Parker's lips crashed back to hers. He pressed his hard shaft against the skin of her belly, as if seeking friction. The overpowering sensations were full of need. And want. And *need*. Amber could barely coordinate herself to return his kiss properly. Parker didn't seem to care, rocking his hips and nipping and pulling at her mouth for all it was worth. When he withdrew his hands, her body clenched in disappointment. Until he bent to pull a condom from the wallet in his jeans, sheathing himself.

Amber's mouth lost all moisture as she watched, transfixed, half terrified this was a dream and she'd wake up too soon.

Bracing his back against the mirror, Parker reached

for Amber and lifted her up. Surprised, limbs clumsy, she didn't follow the logic until he spoke.

'Wrap your legs around my waist,' he said.

Oh, *God,* yes.

Praying her muscles would cooperate, she complied, yet all she could manage was to hold on as he buried himself inside. Eyes wide, she froze, adjusting to the pleasurable pressure that threatened to send her flying apart. A threat that escalated when he gripped her hips and began to move in earnest, each time taking her a little deeper.

Heat swamped her senses, until she was no longer frozen. She wrapped her arms more firmly around his neck. Tightened her legs around his hips.

And threw herself into a carnal kiss, scraping her teeth lightly across his tongue.

The swearword that shot from Parker's mouth into hers was explicit. He clutched her close, buried himself to the base of his shaft and then paused.

It felt *incredible.*

Chests pressed together, heart thundering against his, Amber whimpered greedily and rolled her hips, seeking more friction.

'Amber,' he groaned as he slowly slid down the mirror until she was seated in his lap, his back against the wall.

Hands on her shoulders, blunt fingernails clutching her skin, he began to rock up into her. Friction, wonderful, glorious friction again. His movements slow and sure and hard.

'I need…' he mumbled, eyes closed.

His head drifted to hers.

Each hot press of his mouth was interspersed with a flick of his tongue against her lips, all in rhythm with his hips. As if he needed every part of her, everything, all at once. The pace didn't increase, but the intensity did. Until starved, naked, needy noises began to spill from his mouth.

Nothing had ever been this ridiculously, spine-tingling delicious. The feeling of wholehearted—and, heaven help her—*reciprocated* want.

Digging her nails into his sweat-damp shoulders earned her a garbled reply.

'I can't—' he slurred.

Greedy, Amber arched her back, fitting their hips closer together, taking more.

Wringing an incoherent response from Parker. 'Ah, 'mgonna.'

With the garbled word of warning his movements grew too needy for finesse, hips bucking as if seeking fusion with every thrust. Too far gone for a coordinated kiss, their mouths pressed close, damp and hot as they breathed each other in. The feel of him slicking between her thighs, beneath her, *in* her, tightened the cord of pleasure, pulling harder. Until she was so taut she feared being stranded on the edge of this precipice forever.

Afraid she'd never take that beautiful fall.

But then he gripped her shoulders, arched and thrust hard, groaning as he shattered.

And the sound of her name on his lips as he came pushed her off the ledge. A fiery electric pleasure shot through her veins, and her orgasm burst, painting colorful fireworks behind closed lids.

With a mumbled 'Parker,' she collapsed against him, and let herself be swept away by the aftershocks.

The smell of leather and sex filled Amber's nose as her breathing finally slowed enough for her to think straight.

Bit by bit she became aware of the hard chest under her cheek, Parker's pounding heart gradually recovering beneath. They'd managed to shuffle their way to the thick rug in front of the wrought-iron coffee table. Now, sweat-slick bodies cooling in the aftermath, she was draped across Parker, her palms resting on his shoulders.

His hands, however, were resting by his sides.

Parker gripped her arms, gently shifting her off, and her chest cinched tight at the movement. 'I should find my clothes,' he said, his voice rough from exertion.

She briefly pressed her lids tight, knowing he was doing more than pulling away physically. He was pulling away mentally, too, and the memory of his words punched the breath from her throat.

You know this is all you get, right?

Pushing up on her elbows, she stared at Parker. The sex had been fantastic, and now his soft hair was spiked in all directions, delectably mussed by her fingers. His cheeks were flushed from the energy he'd expended. And he'd exerted a good deal of energy.

After they'd finished the first round, while Amber was still limp and essentially incapable of thought or movement, he had rolled them over onto the rug, pinning Amber beneath him. And started in on her again.

No one had ever made her feel so sensual.

No one had ever pulled so much pleasure from her body.

But he didn't want more.

She watched him rub a hand down his face with a faint frown on his mouth, and a memory rose, unbidden, in her mind.

That last fateful summer she'd caught Susie and Parker making out, and while it was clear he knew exactly what he was doing, there was no emotion behind the act. As if he could have replaced Susie with either of the other two girls he was dating and been just as happy. And while, yes, horny teens were pretty much a given, from what Reese had said Parker hadn't changed his ways much.

Random women, random relationships and nothing that lasted longer than a few months.

Amber's gaze landed on his holster draped across the arm of the couch, an idea forming in her head. He wouldn't like it. Heck, he might even wind up *hating* her for it. But getting the stubborn man to let someone in, even if it was his sister and not Amber, suddenly overwhelmed everything else—even her intense need to flee the presence of the man she'd so shamelessly seduced.

The one who seemed incapable of wanting more.

Chest tight, nerves taut, she reached for his holster, and when he reached for his pants...

She snapped the handcuffs around his wrist.

FIVE

————

The click of the cuff around his wrist snagged Parker's immediate attention.

Rolling onto his back again, he stared up at Amber. Her hair was mussed, her lips bruisingly red from his kisses, and guilt pierced his chest. So, yeah, things had gotten a little rough there toward the end. But he was only so strong, and Amber's frantic words and feverish hands had hacked away at his control until he really shouldn't be held responsible for what came after.

The guilt stabbed harder, anyway.

'Okay,' he said, his voice like gravel as he dangled the handcuffs in the air, his body twitching with interest. 'I'm assuming you want another round.'

The edgy smile, the blush that crept up her face and the way she shifted her eyes to the left had him chuckling.

'For the record, Ace—' he stretched out his leg, resting on his elbows '—any woman who goes for the handcuffs has no business being nervous.'

She stared at him a moment more and it was as if she was looking everywhere but at his groin. Which wasn't the *only* part of his body that wholeheartedly approved of the addition of restraints, but it was the only part that could communicate its consent.

And then Amber reached for his boxers.

Frowning, Parker simply watched as she hooked the underwear on his feet, sliding them up his calves.

He lifted a brow. 'FYI,' he said, 'the addition of hand-cuffs usually means you're taking the clothes off, not putting them back on.'

Ignoring him, she slid the boxers higher.

Now he was *really* curious.

'Okay, I'll bite,' he rumbled. She met his gaze as he lifted his hips to allow her to pull his underwear into place, and he sent her a smile. 'You got a clothes-on fetish, right?' The thought sent a thrill working its way down his back, wrapping around his growing erection. 'I can work with that.'

Now that he was covered, she scooted until she was resting against the coffee table.

'No fetish that I know of,' she said. 'I just can't concentrate when you're so naked.'

She reached for the loose end of the handcuffs, looping it through the ornate leg of the wrought-iron coffee table before clipping it around his other wrist.

Totally intrigued now, he grinned at his helpless position—which was really kinda *hot*.

'That's one of the advantages of being naked,' he said. 'The inability to focus on anything else.'

Gaze admiring all the creamy skin before him, he took in the curve of her breasts and hips.

He shouldn't encourage her. He shouldn't be so weak. He shouldn't crave absorbing that mesmerizing light radiating from her expression. From her eyes. Seemingly from her very skin.

But he needed just a little bit more.

Desire licked at his limbs and his voice reflected his thoughts.

'You just need additional practice,' he said. 'And I'm—'

She reached for her blouse and slid it back over her head, and Parker stared, stunned. And while she had been rendered mute by the sight of him naked, he had a similar problem with the vision of her putting her clothes *on*.

When she picked up her underwear and pulled them into place, he finally found his words.

'What the hell are you doing?' he asked.

She studied him for a moment, and Parker was briefly grateful that the long expanse of her legs was available for admiring.

Amber said, 'You clearly aren't a man who likes to cuddle.'

The statement slammed into him. 'Cuddle?'

So what if the word spit from his mouth with a vengeance. He didn't like the turn in the conversation.

'And if there is anything that Parker Robinson needs,' she went on, eyeing him steadily, 'it's a good cuddle.'

Heart thumping in agitation, he was sure he made a ridiculous sight, what with being handcuffed to a table leg and his mouth opening and closing like a fish.

When he finally found his voice again, it was rough. 'Amber—'

'We're going to talk, Parker.'

The swearword that echoed through his mind wasn't fit to be uttered out loud.

Scooting over to sit by his side, Amber's eyes settled on his. 'Why didn't you answer the phone when your mother called the day your father died?'

The one-two punch to his chest had his jaw falling open

wider, and then he slapped his lips shut, his mouth growing grim.

'Damn it, Amber,' he said, struggling to prop up on one elbow, despite the restraints. 'We're not high school sweethearts.' Frustrated he couldn't even plow a hand through his hair, he went on. 'Let me up.' Anxiety pressed in on his chest, leaving it difficult to draw in a breath. 'I don't want—'

She gently cupped his cheek, her thumb landing at the corner of his mouth, and he froze, unable to do anything but blink like an idiot.

Looking up at her, he wanted to curse and rant and rail against the understanding in her eyes and the bloody confinement of the cuffs. He finally managed to pull off a sparse rattling of the chain between his wrists.

Which, unfortunately, earned him a gentle swipe of her fingertip along his lower lip. It was just a simple stroke, barely noticeable, but the tenderness curled like a knot in his belly.

'Why?' she asked again.

He lobbed a hard look in her direction and didn't spare the truth. Sweet little Amber wanted to know, so sweet little Amber was going to hear.

'You were following me that day,' he said. 'You heard what she said.'

Amber didn't pretend she had no idea what he was talking about.

Her gaze warm on his, she said, 'I heard some of what your mother said, yes.'

Unsure of which parts she'd missed, he gave her the full version. 'Marrying my father was a mistake.' His next words came out louder than he'd intended. '*I* was a mistake.'

Letting the words echo in the room, he forgot to breathe for a moment.

'I was just a symbol of everything my mother had done wrong,' he said. 'Of everything she regretted.'

None of it mattered.

The mantra had served him well in the past. He'd learned as a kid it was best to exist on the surface and ignore or bury or compartmentalize the rest. Because it was the rest that bit you in the ass.

Be polite to your mother, but don't try to get her to show you she cared. Hugs weren't necessary, but an occasional expression of some sort of affection would have been nice. He'd given up looking around the age of ten.

None of it mattered.

Or at least, that's what he'd told himself.

Until the summer he was seventeen and he'd tried again. But the years of being the rowdy boy who only got noticed when he got into trouble had taken a toll. Maybe by then his mother couldn't have cared, even if she'd wanted to.

'She hated my father's job,' he said. 'Looked down on what he did for a living.'

And Parker had *despised* her for being such a snob.

'Which was exactly why you followed in his footsteps,' Amber said as, still cradling his cheek, she stroked his lip again.

His mouth twisted beneath her finger. Man, she always was such an observant little thing. Even as a too-sweet, freaky stalker of a kid.

'Maybe in the beginning,' he said, though he knew she was absolutely right. Growing weary of his awkward posture, he laid down on his side. 'But now...'

Well, not *right* now. Cuz right now everything was dull and flat and he got little enjoyment out of much of anything. But there was a time when helping victims' families find justice had been incredibly satisfying.

'You've always been good at taking care of people,' she said.

Barking out a laugh of disbelief, he tilted his head as he stared up at her, amazed she was still cradling his face. Strangely, he was starting to like the comforting feel of her palm.

'Who did I take care of?' he said.

'Reese,' she said. 'When we were kids, anyway.'

She gazed down at him, like she had as a kid. The same light in her eyes. He just didn't get it. What did she see in him then? What did she see in him now?

And then she went on. 'And you took care of me....'

He couldn't talk about how he'd felt that summer he left his mother's home and never went back. As a seventeen-year-old he'd been too cool to admit he'd missed Reese's and Amber's company. As an adult it seemed too late to confess the truth.

With a huff of humor, he said, 'You're just saying that because I saved you from drowning.'

Finally dropping her hand from his face, she sent him a small smile. And he didn't miss her touch. Not at all. Damn it.

'Your father loved you,' she said, and he swallowed back the groan.

Apparently, nothing in his history was sacred.

His dad hadn't been the type to hug or tell you he cared with his words. But he'd shown him in other ways.

'But then he died,' Parker said, and he hated the way the words came out so harsh. So bitter. He tried to ease the mood with a small smile, failing by a mile. ''Cuz life is mostly just a nasty little bitch who's looking to collect.'

Amber's expression shifted into one of sadness and he hated that he put that look on her face. The urge to take it back, to put a smile on her mouth, was overwhelming. And then suddenly she was crawling over him and sliding onto her side to lie next to him. Shocked, he didn't move as she wiggled her way up between his cuffed arms, settling against him as she embraced his chest.

Staggered by the comforting contact, the press of b odies from torso to toes, he took a moment to respond.

'You know,' he said dryly, 'I don't do the morning-after thing.'

'I'm not asking you to.'

'And hugs don't count if they're not freely given.'

'I know,' she said as she gave him a gentle squeeze. 'That's why I'm freely giving this one to you.'

Paralyzed, he didn't know what to do with himself. Silence stretched between them as they lazed on the floor, wrapped in each other's arms. His by force. Hers by choice

And it was really intimate in a way that sex usually wasn't, and wasn't that just the kicker?

Something in Parker shifted. Just a little, but enough to voice the thought he'd been having for weeks. 'Plenty of people have it worse than me,' he said quietly.

He didn't know why he needed to say the words. Other than the fact that they were the brutal truth. And if there was anything he was comfortable with, it was the brutal truth. Maybe it was the comfort of her arms that seduced the words from his mouth.

'Who?' she asked. 'Who has it worse?'

He didn't want to look into her eyes, so he stared up at the chandelier on the ceiling. 'I'm working on this case,' he said. The dark cloud encasing his heart grew thicker, denser. Something he hadn't thought possible since the day his dad had died.

An acid rain just waiting to break.

'Our current suspect is just a stupid seventeen-year-old,' he said. 'And his parents...'

He didn't want to repeat the words they'd said about their son.

'You know,' he said instead, his voice hoarse. 'Family should stick by you, no matter what.'

Man, now the woman had both hands on his cheeks.

Turning his head to face hers, her gaze clear, she said, 'Yes, they should.'

Staring into her amber eyes, he clenched his jaw.

The case had been eating at him for a while, draining what little color remained in his already-mucked-up life. He refused to lean into the warmth of Amber's palms, but the urge was there. He remembered the stricken look on her face when she'd overheard his mom that day, and the comforting hand Amber lay on his shoulder later.

Not that he'd wanted her sympathy. No, he'd hated the caring in her touch, the gesture of concern from a twelve-year-old when he couldn't even get that kind of emotion from his own mother.

Something in him had died that day, something vital that he'd lost. And damned if he knew how to get it back. He was pretty sure he didn't even *want* it back.

Blocking Amber's beautiful gaze, Parker closed his eyes and concentrated on keeping his breathing even. She held his face, and her sweet scent surrounded him, the silky legs entwined with his. But it was the warmth of her body that captivated him the most. Surprisingly, he wasn't really thinking of her skin in a sexual sense, but more of the gentle give-and-take of shared heat. It was refreshingly simple. And kind of nice.

Like a handful of summer sun on a dark winter's day.

But the unfamiliar feeling of comfort, of contentment—of...*happiness?*—scared the bejesus out of him.

Parker didn't know how much time passed as he grappled with the dueling urges to push her away or pull her closer. Maybe he should do something more productive, like bang his head against the nearest wall.

'You're right, family should stick by you,' she said, and he lifted his lids. 'No matter what.' Amber raised her chin to look up into his face, her eyes warming him in ways he'd never imagined. 'Which is why you should come to your mother's dinner party,' she went on, and Parker didn't bother suppressing the groan.

Christamighty, not this again.

'To support Reese,' she went on.

Without warning, she slid down from between his arms, and he instantly missed the feeling of warmth.

That tiny bit of...security, for lack of a better word.

'You should go to the party, Parker,' she said again.

After sitting up, she slipped on her jeans. Her shoes came next, and he absolutely did not panic that she was dressing to leave. Because that would be a stupid thing to do.

'Why?' he asked.

'Because your sister loves you,' Amber said as she stood to look down on him.

Something inside him rejected the notion, and not just because Reese had never said so in as many words.

'And if you can't do it for Reese,' she went on. Her voice dropped an octave, creating an ominous pressure in his lungs. 'Then do it for me.'

This time the word came out harsher. 'Why?'

* * *

Reese stared down at Parker, her heart pumping wildly in her chest.

'Do it for the kid who saw you as worthy of adoration all those years ago,' she said.

The rest was on the tip of her tongue as she hesitated. But her insecurities suddenly seemed so insignificant compared to all that Parker had been through. He deserved the truth. He needed to *hear* the truth.

So she went on. 'And do it for the woman who's falling for you now.'

Denial, exasperation and a massive dose of confusion flared in his eyes just before he slammed his lids shut, muttering, 'Damn.'

She hadn't started out intending to share so much. But suddenly her choice to tell Parker the words that were so simple and complex, the words she was pretty sure he'd never heard in his life, was important—not just for Parker, but for herself. An extension of her decision to finally *fight* for what she wanted. And she wanted this man in her life.

Not the boy she'd obsessed about in the past, but the *man* of today.

Ironic, given it might be too late for Parker to ever truly let himself love anybody.

When he finally opened his eyes, a blank look on his face, she simply picked up the holster containing his keys and gently dropped it by his foot. Going on, she looked at him and spoke the words she knew he needed to hear.

'I'm falling in love with you,' she said. 'And you deserve to be loved, Parker Robinson.'

SIX

———

Whywhy*why*?

Two weeks later Amber was dealing with her last cus-
tomers of the day and preparing to leave for the Michaels'
dinner party, still unsure she'd made the right decision to
abandon Parker with his keys to free himself. Which he
had, of course. She'd checked, just to be certain. Part of
her thought she'd been making a statement by walking
out, taking the first step in seizing control of her romantic life by seducing the man she'd dreamed of for ages,
sharing the truth of how she felt about him and then ex-
iting with her head high. The other part knew the truth.

Coward*cowardcoward*.

Because she didn't have the strength to stick around
and *really* deal with the repercussions of her confession.

Fabulous, Amber.

Staring at the couple deciding on the style of the tuxedo
for their wedding, she smiled, a tiny bit envious. When
the groom-to-be leaned over and kissed the top of his fiancée's head, Amber's lips twisted. Such a simple gesture,
shared and accepted so freely. As if the act was a given.

For some people displays of affection came easily.

Amber's cell phone rang and, grateful for the distraction, she turned her back on the couple and answered.

'Amber,' Reese said. 'You'll be there tonight, right?'

'Of course.' Without thinking, she went on. 'Have you heard from Parker?'

My. God.

Would she always sound like that twelve-year-old little girl who loved Parker Robinson?

'No,' her friend said with a sigh. 'But at least he agreed to be in the wedding, so thanks for that.'

Amber murmured a 'No problem.' And how did she tell Parker's sister that the only reason he'd agreed to be in the wedding was because her friend threatened to tell embarrassing stories to his partner? Maybe Parker really was that shallow. Deep in her heart she knew he wasn't.

But if *Parker* believed it, then the truth didn't really matter.

Clutching her phone, Amber forced herself to focus. 'Your dress is due to arrive next week,' she said to Reese. 'I'll set up a time for the first fitting.'

Reese's enthusiastic 'Good' was heartwarming. She knew Parker had his doubts about his sister's marriage, but Amber envied Reese and Dylan because their relationship always looked so comfortable and easy. Just as Amber always thought love should be. Of course, Parker's very DNA made acknowledging the possibility of forever near impossible.

Behind her, the tinkle of the bell over the door signaled another customer. Signing off the phone, she slipped it in her pocket as she turned...and spied Parker just inside the entranceway.

Her head spun, her gut tensed and her heart hurt too much to function. Unfortunately the overly dramatic angst of her teen years didn't compare to the real, grown-up pain of a woman. Falling for him again was turning out to be easy. Doing something about it would be hard.

Now that she'd adjusted to his presence, her eyes roved lovingly over him. He wore jeans and his leather jacket, as usual. The only difference was the button-down shirt that he wore.

No matter, Amber was sure it smelled of leather. She'd spent enough time in his arms, kissing every inch of his skin to know his scent inside and out.

When the couple called out their goodbyes, Amber waved, working hard not to feel a sliver of jealousy as they held hands on the way out. Uneasy, she glanced at Parker, who was watching them leave. The slow barrel roll her belly was attempting wasn't helping her nerves, and she swiped a damp palm down her dress pants.

'Tuxedo rental,' she managed to say lamely, nodding at the retreating couple.

His brow furrowed in humor. 'Did you measure his crotch, too?'

'It wasn't necessary.' Despite everything, she had to bite back the smile. 'Only for you.'

His mouth quirked. 'I figured as much.'

Five heartbeats pounded in her chest before the awkward silence was broken.

'So...' Parker leaned a shoulder against the wall, crossing his arms with that earthy easiness that was so seductive. And how could such a simple movement be so sexy? 'What kind of woman leads a guy on by handcuffing him to a table and then up and leaves?'

'I put the holster with the key in reach of your foot,' she said. 'I knew with a little bit of time and effort you'd eventually escape.'

Parker let out a cocky *hunh*. 'I was free and out the door in two minutes.'

Clearly he was proud of his skills.

Hiking an eyebrow at the expression on his face, she said, 'Ten.' She tipped her head. 'It was *ten* minutes.' And when he shot her a sharp look, she gave a small shrug. 'I was watching your car from the window.'

The pleased look on his face was comical. 'You worried I wasn't going to get free, Ace?'

And here he was, choosing the shallow route again. As if the amount of time it took him to retrieve his key from the holster and unlock the cuffs around his wrists—not an easy task, she was sure—was the most important thing they needed to discuss.

'I think we already established that I *do* care,' she said.

Parker closed his eyes, and the easy look on his face died, his voice low. 'Damn, Amber.' He rubbed his neck and met her gaze again. 'I got good news today, so I'm in a first-rate mood. And you were the one who convinced me to go to my mom's tonight.'

Her heart soared at the words, and she realized that also explained his button-down shirt.

Frowning, Parker went on. 'But I don't think I'm ready for...'

He dropped his arm to his side and looked at her. Shifting against the wall, his movements were now stiff. He looked as if he was braced for battle.

A million questions crashed through her mind like a ten-car pileup, but she decided to start out simple.

'What's the good news?' she asked.

'That teen I was telling you about? The suspect in my latest case?' he said. 'Turns out he's innocent. He's been cleared.' The small shrug was simple yet meaningful. 'I don't know if that will help him with his parents or not, but at least he's got a second chance.' The relief on his face was obvious.

And *this* was why she was falling for Parker all over again. He liked to pretend he was above those pesky things called emotions. To pretend he felt no fondness or affection or hope. To pretend he didn't care. But it wasn't that he had no heart. The problem was his heart was so big, had been through so much, the need to protect himself was automatic.

Today was an encouraging step, but there was a real risk this instinct might never be undone completely.

'I'm glad you're going,' she said. 'I know Reese will appreciate it.'

Thick dark lashes slowly blinked across a mesmerizing green gaze as he stared at her for several moments. 'I'm not going just for Reese.'

Her breathing stalled, and she barely managed to murmur, 'No?'

Two pounding heartbeats passed as she longed for him to clarify.

'No,' he said. 'I'm also going for me.'

And while she breathed out a sigh of relief that he'd finally decided that he wanted family in his life, a small part of her was crushed he wasn't going for *her*. She'd known all along the most she could hope for was to help him reconnect with Reese, and this was as good a start as any. In truth, it was a miracle he was going tonight. And while Amber was glad Reese's wish would come true, the truth was, having him here—having him near *her*—was hard.

Because a part of her would always long to be loved by Parker.

'Well,' she said, shifting closer to the exit. Distance.

She needed *distance*. Time to regroup. 'Your sister will be happy to see you.'

'Yeah, but I can't say I'm thrilled with the idea of making polite conversation with my mom and stepdad,' he said, his feet firmly planted in place. 'Cuz I know things won't have changed.' His expression grim, he went on. 'William Michael of the Park Avenue Michaels hates any reminder that he wasn't my mother's first husband. My mother is weak, petrified he'll leave her. And, way back when, Reese was too young to notice,' he said with a tiny shrug. 'I've accepted all that.'

By the look on his face she knew it was true. He cleared his throat, suddenly looking uncomfortable.

'I was hoping we could go together,' he said. 'Having you around might make things a little...smoother.'

A confusing mix of tenderness and disappointment flushed through her chest, and she picked up her purse, heading for the exit. 'Then let's go.'

Amber could feel him following.

'But the other reason I came was because I wanted to see you first,' he said.

Her feet stuck to the floor.

'About—about what you said,' he said from behind.

Clutching her purse harder, she turned to face him.

'You know...' He shrugged awkwardly. 'Before.'

I'm falling in love with you.

The lag time from one heartbeat to the next seemed to lengthen to uncomfortable levels. So much so Amber was amazed she didn't pass out.

'As a kid—' he puffed out a breath grimly '—it sucked not getting what I needed from my mom. And it's...' With a small scowl he plowed a hand through his hair before gesturing at Amber. 'You're...' He dropped his hand, frustration etched in his every word. 'You know everything I don't want *anyone* to know.'

The raw, naked look on his face lasted several seconds before he let out a scoff.

'Which makes you the last person on earth I should want to see,' he said.

My God, this wasn't getting any easier.

'After that night,' he went on. 'I spent the first few days thinking you had some sort of...*misguided* sense of hero worship because of the whole drowning incident.'

She could hear the hesitation in his voice.

'And then I spent the rest of the time hoping it was more than that,' he finished in a low voice.

Her voice resolute, she said, 'It is.'

Now the lag time between heartbeats was ridiculously short as she watched the emotions parade across his face. Relief. Followed by something that looked like content-ment before landing on that cocky smile she loved so much.

Parker stepped forward, all awkwardness gone. The easy stroll was back, carrying him right up into her per-sonal space, and her stomach swooped at the sight. The gorgeous green eyes. The ruffled hair. And that mouth, that beautiful, beautiful mouth that had first captured her attention oh so long ago. Little had she known then how good it would feel pressed against hers in a *real* kiss.

'But the rescue was an incredibly awesome move on my part,' he said with a grin.

She rolled her eyes, delighting at his responding bark of amusement. When he reached out to brush the hair from her cheek, her stomach swerved.

He paused, his voice uncharacteristically riddled with

self-doubt. 'Even the thought of trying for something that lasts past a few months scares the crap out of me.'

Inhaling slowly, Amber steadily held his gaze. She'd spent years pining after something that could never be hers. Parker, specifically. And as lame as the idea was, especially given she'd been just a ridiculous *preteen,* it was time to admit the years of unrequited feelings had had a profound influence on her choices in life. And the thought of putting herself in a vulnerable position again was almost incapacitating. But Parker had spent years hoping his mother would change, and was willing to venture back into her circle again with little likelihood that the relationship would improve.

'That's the thing about letting someone in,' she said softly. And if he was willing to put his heart on the line for his sister, for *himself*...well, then maybe she should take a risk, too. 'It's both a beautiful and a dangerous thing.'

His eyes searched hers. 'So why me?'

Drawing in a deep breath, she tried to put her thoughts into words.

'I think over time,' she said slowly, 'the closer you get to a person, and the closer you let them *get to you,* the more the light and the shadows inside become more vivid. Clearer. More sharply defined.'

Love wasn't easy. And sometimes, especially with a man like Parker Robinson, it would be especially difficult. But she loved the parts of him that were dark just as much, if not more, than she loved the lighter bits. Because they defined him the best.

And for a moment, she almost felt sorry for Reese and Dylan. A comfortable relationship would definitely take less work, but Amber wouldn't trade the conflict or passion she shared with Parker for all the ease in the world.

She reached up to cup his face, and nothing, *nothing* would ever be as wonderful as the slight tip of his head into her palm. The contact wasn't much. But enough.

Encouraging her to go on. 'And knowing all those bits about a person makes it both more difficult, and—just as important, I think—more imperative that you take that chance.'

The tiny, nervous lick of his lips was almost heart-breaking.

'So...' he said. 'You want to give this thing a whirl?'

'Do you think it will work?'

'Almost definitely maybe.' His mouth curled at the edges. 'We have several things in our favor.'

'Such as?'

'First, I'm adorable and you worship the ground I walk on.' She lifted her eyes heavenward with a 'whatever' look, and he let out a chuckle. Amber wasn't sure if his shallow reply was a coping mechanism or if he just liked to see her reaction. She suspected it was a bit of both. 'Second,' he went on. 'I *want* it to work. And third...'

Amber didn't miss how quickly he'd rushed through the second, almost as if embarrassed. She'd let it slide. For now.

'And third?' she asked.

The quirk in his lips was adorable. 'I'm just stubborn enough not to give up.'

Eyes stinging, she swallowed back the mushy words and sent him a smile.

'I'm not going to have to handcuff you for every hug I want, am I?' she said.

He reached out and took her hand. The gesture was hesitant, the fingers that squeezed hers gentle. But the light in his eyes?

Sizzling.

'Oh, you'll need the handcuffs, all right,' he said, his voice husky.

And then Parker Robinson drew the sexy smirk like a gun from a holster. 'Just not for a hug.'

* * * * *

COMING NEXT MONTH FROM

H **HARLEQUIN**

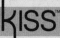

kiss™

Available June 18, 2013

#21 THE UNEXPECTED WEDDING GUEST
The Wedding Season • by Aimee Carson

Getting caught in her wedding dress by her ex-husband is Reese Michael's worst nightmare. Especially when her perfect-on-paper fiancé then cancels their wedding! But what's a girl to do when the man she could never forget is back, and as irresistible as ever? Mason might be her own personal brand of kryptonite, but surely life is meant to be lived a *little* dangerously...?

#22 ONCE IS NEVER ENOUGH by Mira Lyn Kelly

Nichole Daniels has had her share of heartbreak. But when a blue-eyed stranger offers her a taste of her every fantasy for three years, she's considering putting an end to her dry spell! Garrett Carter's reputation as a ladies' man...? Absolutely spot-on. The man for her...? Not on your life. But something tells her that, when it comes to Garrett, one night will never be enough....

#23 WHAT THE PAPARAZZI DIDN'T SEE
by Nicola Marsh

Liza Lithgow has her reasons for living in the spotlight. But now she's saved enough money to leave the red carpet behind, what better way to celebrate than with a martini and a man? The only problem is, the man in question turns out to be a publisher wanting her kiss-and-tell autobiography! What will Wade see—the glossy facade or maybe, at last, the *real* Liza?

#24 MY BOYFRIEND AND OTHER ENEMIES
by Nikki Logan

The moment Tash Sinclair sets eyes on outrageously attractive family rival Aiden Moore, she knows she's in trouble. They clash immediately, but as the fireworks fly will Tash and Aiden spontaneously combust—or will Tash do the unthinkable and fall for her own worst enemy? After all, you should keep your friends close, but maybe your enemies the closest of all...!

———

REQUEST YOUR FREE BOOKS!
2 FREE NOVELS PLUS 2 FREE GIFTS!

HARLEQUIN® KISS™

She hadn't seen him in ten years and he chose
her wedding day to show up...

THE UNEXPECTED
WEDDING GUEST

"Surprised to see me, Park Avenue?" The familiar, sexy rumble
and the nickname added to the surreal nature of being trans-
ported back ten years in time when she had laughingly told
Mason her college roommates' nickname for her, Park Avenue
Princess. And then he'd made the name his own, dropping
the *princess* part. Which for some strange reason had pleased
her no end.

But she was not pleased to see Mason.

Days away from her *wedding*.

Reese gritted her teeth, struggling to retain her cool as the
anger finally built high enough to surpass every other emotion—
shock, doubt and dread, just to name a few. Why was he coming
to see her again? After ten years, why *now?* Right when all of
her dreams were finally about to come true.

She forced her voice to remain smooth. "And the last time
I saw you, you were dodging the dog tags I hurled at you."

"Your aim was good."

"I should have used your baseball bat."

"It still made a nice punctuation mark for your demand for
a divorce." The corners of his eyes crinkled. "Claimed irrecon-
cilable differences, if I remember right."

She tipped her chin higher. "Temporary insanity was more like it."

"A *lust*-induced state of insanity." Heat flushed through her like a flash fire, though he steadily held her gaze. His expression more reflective than affected, he murmured, "A drug, that."

Her chest pinched, making breathing more difficult. Bad enough he had to still look good, now the unwanted memories invaded. Memories of Mason making love to her. The incredibly intense state of happiness they'd achieved, right before it had all been blown to hell. Correction, right before *Mason* had blown it all to hell.

Remember, Reese. Never again.

Never *again.*

"The sex wasn't a drug," she said, though at the time, she'd thought the same thing. But God knows she'd learned her lesson the hard way. She was no longer susceptible to the whims of her hormones. "It was quicksand."

And just as deadly to her peace of mind. Her sanity.

He hiked a brow and studied her a moment more. "Maybe," he said softly, his lips curling at the edges. "But what a way to go."

**Pick up THE UNEXPECTED WEDDING GUEST
by Aimee Carson, on sale June 18,
wherever Harlequin books are sold.**

Four friends. Three weddings.
Two explosive secrets.
One unforgettable
summer!

THE WEDDING SEASON

Reese, Cassie, Gina and Marnie were best friends.
Until *that* night.

They haven't seen each other in years, but now Reese is
getting married and she wants everyone there.

It will be a reunion to remember—and the wedding of
the year! But what these feisty women hadn't planned
on are the sizzling, scandalous and *very* surprising
consequences....

**Look for this fabulous quartet from these talented
Harlequin KISS authors—Aimee Carson,
Amy Andrews, Heidi Rice and Kimberly Lang.**

Starting June 18 with
THE UNEXPECTED WEDDING GUEST
by Aimee Carson

www.Harlequin.com

HKCONT0613